Among the Missing

10/27/23

Anne,
 I very glad that I got to meet you Gary on the trip to the UK. Good memories for all of us.
 I hope you enjoy the book.
  Barbara

BARBARA LAMACCHIA

Double J Press

Berlin, Massachusetts

Copyright © Barbara Lamacchia

All rights reserved. No part of this book may be reproduced or transmitted in any form or by any means, electronic, or mechanized, including photocopying, recording, or by any information storage and retrieval system without the written permission of the publisher and/or author, except as provided by U.S. Copyright Law.

Among the Missing is a work of fiction and all characters are fictitious. Any resemblance to a person living or dead is totally coincidental.

IBSN 978-1-7353479-7-4 (paperback)

IBSN 978-1-7353479-8-1 (ebook)

Library of Congress Control Number: 2023903037

For David

"When he shall die
Take him and cut him out in little stars,
And he will make the face of heaven so fine
That all the world will be in love with night
And pay no worship to the garish sun."

Wm. Shakespeare
Romeo and Juliet

Contents

Chapter 1...1
Chapter 2...24
Chapter 3...40
Chapter 4...55
Chapter 5...71
Chapter 6...92
Chapter 7...112
Chapter 8...130
Chapter 9...150
Chapter 10.......................................163
Chapter 11.......................................191
Chapter 12.......................................203
Chapter 13.......................................213
Chapter 14.......................................233
Chapter 15.......................................248

CHAPTER 1

DAN KERR HAD JUST OPENED HIS EYES AFTER A short nap on the plane. It took him a minute to orient himself; he usually couldn't sleep on a plane, or a train or in a car. Now fully awake, he remembered why he was flying — to go home. The occasion was bittersweet. His parents were celebrating their forty-fifth wedding anniversary with a family party. All the Kerrs will be there, well, not all. Brother Dennis aka Champ is MIA in Vietnam. Champ was never far from Dan's thoughts. The uncertainty constantly gnawed at Dan's mind—could he be alive? Now those three words were seared into Dan's memory and his heart—Missing in Action.

How clearly Dan remembered what rivals he and Champ had been as boys. Dan considered his brother little more than a stupid jock; a naïve fool who thought a professional team would draft him and return home in a blaze of glory. A torn ACL ended Champ's dreams. If not for that injury, who knows where he could be today? Would he have gone to college? Probably not if he couldn't play sports. Champ was drafted and sent to Nam within the space of a year.

To take his mind off Champ, Dan took out the diary his mother sent him. She found it one day when she was cleaning. Now Dan can reflect on his own shattered dream. At eleven, all things are possible. All dreams, no matter how elusive, can be caught and lived. Dan would be a writer — nothing could stop him; it was his destiny, his calling. Now in his late twenties, Dan realized Champ wasn't the only idealistic fool. Dan was every bit as naïve as his brother.

Dan had written a lot in college. A regular contributor to the literary magazine, he wrote fiction, poetry, fantasy—whatever possessed him. His work was always published, not because of its brilliance, but because of the paucity of other submissions. He had guessed the truth, but his ego refused to believe or accept any other explanation.

He was a writer, but still not as he imagined he would be. Like so many would be authors, he hammered away at the great American novel at night. By day, he was a reporter for a small newspaper in Ohio. Dan loathed reporting on fires and petty crime, but it paid the bills. He daydreamed about returning to Massachusetts. But in reality, a return home would mean he would have to rely on the largess of his parents since he had virtually no money and only a small bank account that became much smaller after he purchased his airline ticket.

Then Dan remembered the real reason he was flying home. The party was only an excuse to gather the family before his father's cancer worsened, yet Dan's paternal grandmother was in her nineties and still feisty. Aunt Julia, a brassy octogenarian, was still in her own home. Dan smiled at the memory of these two ladies—Gram with her no-nonsense approach to life; Aunt Julia with her hats and love of Jack Daniels. These ladies were sisters-in-law and still vying to out- do each other in the sweepstakes of life.

To take his mind off his family troubles, Dan ordered a glass of wine and just sat back, looking at the cloud banks, cottony canyons that slowly drifted by the plane. Dan's thoughts returned to his family. He hadn't seen most of his siblings in a long time. Will this be as pleasant a reunion as possible or will old animosities bubble to the surface? The absence of Champ will be like a gathering cloud of sadness that will hang over everyone and everything. How do families go on when one member is missing; no one knows where? Dan put aside thoughts of Champ, even though he knew to forget was futile.

Boston was very close now. The pilot was speaking, the signs on. Prepare for landing. Dan wished it was night. The city was beautiful from 3,000 feet with its lights aglow. The plane landed flawlessly, with a dull thump of landing gear. Dan's brother-in-law, Ncil, will meet him. No one else was available to do the honors. If not for Neil, Dan would have had to spring for an expensive cab ride.

The terminal was mobbed and there was no sign of Neil. Dan bought a coffee and parked himself to wait. The writer in him imagined the lives of the people in the terminal. Why were they traveling? Business, vacation? bereavement? Dan loved to watch people. Before him, he saw people of all ages, races, shapes, and sizes. All were just going about their business. There were no arguments or shouting matches; people held doors. There was no elbowing for a better place in line. Total strangers exchanged pleasantries and smiled at each other. This airport was a microcosm of the world, yet unlike the world.

Dan was so wrapped up in his reverie that he didn't see Neil until he was standing right in front of him.

"Hey, bro," said Neil, as he extended his hand to Dan. As they shook hands, Dan took the measure of Neil, a solid guy with a firm handshake and twinkling blue eyes. Neil seemed so content with his life. Dan liked him. As they strolled to the car, Neil chatted amiably. As he listened, Dan was remembering Neil and Mimi's wedding and how they looked as they exchanged vows. Dan smiled inwardly as he remembered how resentful he was that he was not in the wedding party. He was an altar boy, but he wanted the white tux like Pup and Champ. Champ again. Why does he haunt me?

Dan grew increasingly nervous as they neared Coltonwood. An unfamiliar flutter of the heart scared Dan as he happily awaited yet dreaded seeing his parents. How would they be? How will his father look? What could he say to a sick man? Should he ask Neil for his opinion? Dan tried to appear happy, but intrusive thoughts kept hammering away at his attention.

Coltonwood looked the same, but different. As Neil drove up Main St. Dan looked for his father's business, Bert's TV. A card store now occupied that space. The thoughts were relentless now that Dan was back in familiar territory. This trip was a mistake; he even thought of asking Neil to turn around and return him to the airport. How could he face his ailing father and constantly grieving mother? What could he possibly say to them?

The neighborhood had hardly changed. Here, 1980 looked the same as 1960. There was his maternal grandparents' house. They no sooner moved to a modern house than his grandmother died suddenly, leaving his grandfather a lonely, broken man who followed his wife in death not a year later. There was his paternal grandmother's house where she still lived. There was the window of the room that Dan shared with Champ and Pup. On closer inspection, Dan could see how the house had deteriorated. It almost seemed to sag, reminiscent of the house in the Poe story that symbolized the end of a family.

Mr. and Mrs. Kerr were at the door as Dan and Neil climbed the steps. There was no mistaking the grief in his mother's eyes, even though she did her best to effect a welcoming cheer. His father's handshake was still strong, but his face betrayed the corded look of age and illness. The quietness of the house did nothing to ease Dan's fears. This house was never quiet when the family was here. There was noise from morning to night, doors slamming, radios playing, the tv on endlessly. Now the place more closely resembled a tomb than a house.

Dan had hoped that Neil would stay and ease some of the tension, but he soon left to go home to his own family. Now the parents and the son danced an evasive troika around each other until Dan announced he was going to bed, exhausted from his long day and plane ride. The tension in the kitchen was nothing compared to the suffocating silence of his old bedroom. His bed looked the same as the day he last slept in it. Only a few feet away, Champ's bed stood as silent as a sentry at the Tomb of the Unknown Soldier. Dan had a wild thought he might like to sleep in Champ's bed but soon dismissed the thought as weird, if not depraved. Travel weariness soon overcame Dan as he stretched out on his bed. Sleep came fitfully and the shadows that danced on the walls seemed to mock him and remind him that there was a time when he and Champ fought like devils over silly things. He remembered with profound regret his feeling that Champ was just a dumb jock who would never amount to anything, his head as full of air as his basketball. Dan now ached to tell Champ that he was sorry.

The next morning brought sparkling sun and strange voices as Dan struggled to orient himself. The bed linen was draped over the side of the bed. He must have tossed all night long. What time was it? After a quick shower, Dan headed for the kitchen, the source of the strange voices. Seated at the table were his parents and a woman he didn't immediately recognize. After a confused minute, Dan realized the woman was Biddy, the youngest of the Kerr clan. He brushed her cheek with a kiss that she did not return. How is it possible that Biddy was twenty-three? She was just beginning her teens when Dan left for college. She, too, seemed a stranger to him.

"Chip, would you like some coffee? Breakfast will be ready soon."

Dan smiled. So many things had changed, but his mother still cooked breakfast, a good sign. Of what he did not know.

"So, Biddy. What are you doing with yourself these days?"

Biddy gave him a shy, wistful smile. "I'm a waitress at Stony's."

"Stony's?" Dan replied blankly.

Mr. Kerr supplied the details. "It's a new place downtown."

"It's not all that new," amended Biddy. "It's been there for at least three years."

"So it has, but three years to me is nothing. At my age, a year seems like just a few months."

"Chip, do you still like your eggs over easy?" asked his mom as she stood, spatula in hand, ready to fry some eggs.

Dan usually never ate eggs, but this was a special occasion. "That will be fine, Mom."

As he ate, Dan watched Biddy. He marveled at how much she resembled Mimi. The oldest and the youngest. At least Mimi was happy. Biddy evidently missed that memo. The baby of the family ate delicately, as though conscious of each bite. He noticed her lovely, tapered hands, and the perfectly manicured nails; there was a hidden vivacity about Biddy just waiting to be unleashed. When she finished her eggs, Biddy sat with both feet on the chair, coffee cup lifted delicately to her lips. When Dan saw her full face, he had to catch his breath. His little sister had become a beautiful woman. He would have to find some time to talk to her today or some time before he left.

Dan and his parents would go later that day to Mimi and Neil's home for a barbecue. Before then, Dan intended to talk to Biddy to get her take on what the situation was like in the house. How would he get her to talk? He couldn't broach the topic with his parents within earshot. He need not have worried because right after breakfast, Biddy asked Dan in a confidential tone what he was getting their parents for their anniversary. In the whirlwind of emotions surrounding his visit, Dan had never given a thought to a present for his parents. He thought about money because he didn't bring a lot of cash. He would have to use the plastic. His card wasn't maxed out, but it was close.

"Are you working today, Biddy?" asked Dan.

"Not until tonight. Why?"

"How about we go shopping this afternoon, just you and me? You can show me around town. It looks like a lot has changed since I've been gone."

With a handy excuse of showing Dan around, he and Biddy could leave the house, arousing no suspicion in their parents. Biddy drove downtown and showed Dan the lay of the land. Some stores had changed, but others had taken their place. Banks seemed to proliferate Main Street, prompting Dan to wonder if the economic climate of Coltonwood had changed that much. When he was growing up, the town was working class. Two banks met the needs of the population. There were only a few people in town who had money, one a doctor, another a lawyer. Everyone else lived from paycheck to paycheck.

"I'll show you the new mall. We can probably pick up something there for Mom and Dad."

"Yeah, I'd like to see it. The town where I live only has one large mall, but a lot of strip malls. It looks really honky tonk. I hope Coltonwood doesn't become like that. Most of the small businesspeople can't make a go of it because these large chains are moving into these malls. The downtown is disappearing."

"It's the same way here. Large chains are opening and destroying the downtown. In a few years, most of Main Street will be just banks and insurance companies."

Abruptly, Dan asked Biddy, "What are Mom and Dad like when there are no visitors to occupy their time?"

Biddy looked pensive and paused a beat or two longer than necessary. "Well, some days are good; some days are not. On a bad day, Mom will take a walk with her rosary in hand and wander around until she gets tired. On a good day, she might bake or go out to lunch with Dad or a friend."

"Are there more good days than bad?"

"It depends on the season. As you know, she's a mess around the holidays and for most of the winter. She's pretty good in the spring and summer, except on the anniversary of the day the telegram arrived."

"And Dad?"

"He's much better than Mom. He goes out with his friends a lot. They meet for coffee and stay for a couple of hours. That helps him a lot. He will putter around the house and work outside in good weather. Dad is so used to working long hours that he can't find enough chores to keep himself occupied for very long. He's ok."

The mall was enormous. The problem was what store to pick for a suitable present. Dan did not know what to get for his parents. Dan's dilemma was solved when he saw the restaurant where Biddy worked. He would get his parents a gift card.

The small party at Mimi and Neil's house began at six. Mr. Kerr did the honors and drove everyone. Dan could sit back and relax, and marvel at how much his hometown had changed. Plenty of building going on; open space lost, old buildings torn down to accommodate more modern structures.

Mimi and Neil's family had grown in more ways than one since Dan had seen them last. Patrick, the oldest, was now seventeen. He was followed by Fiona, fifteen, Maeve, twelve , Liam, ten, and Brendan, seven. Mimi was pregnant with her sixth child, due in the fall. All of these Mullaneys lived in a sprawling house with an oversized yard loaded with toys and other paraphernalia of childhood. There was a deck behind the house and a pool in the side yard. The grill was fired up, and the table set on the deck. Everything was perfect. Stepping into Mimi and Neil's house was like being surrounded by a warm blanket. Dan felt comfortable and safe within the confines of his sister's house.

Mimi re-introduced each of the children to Dan. The only one he really remembered was Patrick who was at work. Fiona was somewhat familiar, but the younger ones were new to Dan. One of the little ones, Brendan, immediately accosted Dan with a question: "Is your name Dan or Chip"? Brendan's uncle was amused by the query and the innocence that prompted it.

"You can call me either, as long as it's preceded by uncle," replied Dan.

"Ok, Uncle Chip. I'll call you Chip. Ok?"

"Chip it is."

Dinner was a cookout on the back deck. Neil was busy with the grill while Mimi gave Dan a quick tour of the house. It was not as large as Pup's spread, but spacious nonetheless. "I won't take you upstairs," Mimi said. "The kids' bedrooms are a mess. I have all I can do to keep the downstairs looking decent."

"Why don't you ask Mom? She had a big house and a lot of kids in it. But, of course, it was usually a bit of a mess."

"Now I don't wonder why."

Dan's parents settled themselves on deck chairs and surrounded themselves with grandchildren. Dan wondered if Neil and Mimi had them over often. They seemed much more relaxed. Even their voices seemed different.

True to form, Cissy and her family arrived late. Pup and his family were not there since Pup had a Rotary Club meeting. After everyone was settled, Dan sat back and surveyed the family. It amused him to remember the nicknames he had for his two older sisters—the drama queens. He marveled at how each had evolved into women. Both were good wives and mothers. He was even more amazed at the good job his parents had done raising so many children. Dan wondered if there was some secret formula entrusted to certain parents regarding raising children. Mimi and Neil seemed to possess that instinct, as his parents had.

Dinner featured Neil's special chicken barbecue sauce. Fiona and Maeve helped their mother serve the food. Dan tried to engage Fiona in conversation, but she was shy and didn't converse easily. Mimi volunteered that Fiona was an excellent student who was recently inducted into the National Honor Society. She was eyeing medical school. Maeve, on the other hand, had no qualms talking about herself. She was also a good student. Unlike her sister, however, Maeve would rather listen to Michael Jackson than do school work, but, according to herself, she had found the right balance between fun and school. Oh, and she also had a boyfriend.

Patrick, the oldest, arrived near the end of the meal with his girlfriend, Michaela, in tow. Dan stared in disbelief at his nephew, who was as tall as his father, and the image of Neil. The feel-good ambience of the party was disrupted when Patrick asked if he could have a beer like the other men. Mimi wasted no time informing him that the answer was no.

As darkness fell, Dan left the gathering, ostensibly to take a walk to see the yard. He wanted some time to himself to absorb the atmosphere of the evening, like a breath of fresh early morning air. It was hard to tell where the Mullaneys' property ended, and the woods began, but he walked until huge bushes loaded with briers arrested his forward progress. The Frost poem kept running through his head, "The woods are lovely, dark and deep but I have promises to keep and miles to go before I sleep."

As Dan stared into the woods, the image of Champ arose before his eyes, a ghostly figure emerging from the darkness, the ubiquitous specter that won't stop haunting Dan. It was then that he realized he hadn't thought about Champ the entire evening.

All the euphoria of the evening at Mimi's evaporated when Dan slid between the sheets of his boyhood bed. The same shadows of the night before danced around the room. Troubling dreams of no actual substance haunted Dan's sleep until dawn found him drenched with sweat. In the morning, he put on shorts and a tee shirt and slipped out of the house before anyone else was awake. His wandering took him along Main St. and up the hill to his church, the towering edifice that brooded over the city. He tried the door of the lower church and it yielded to a slight push. The smell and silence were the same as ever. How often had Dan stepped into this place of peace? The vigil candles flickered in their rows of iron in front of the statue of the Blessed Virgin.

Dan's plan had been to sit awhile then leave, but an unseen force drove him to take the back staircase to the upper church. Slowly and carefully, Dan ascended the staircase into the sanctuary, a place where he had spent many happy hours as an altar server. The huge stained-glass window along the east wall blazed up in the deepening sunlight. Dan saw dust floating in the sun's rays. He opened drawers and doors, and the contents thereof were the same as he remembered. He wandered to the altar, fingered the gold cross he had carried so many times. The huge windows behind the altar looked even bigger from this vantage point. Slowly, he walked down the center aisle and climbed the stairs to the choir loft. How different everything looked from here. He touched the keyboard of the organ and the note reverberated through the empty church, scaring him a little. Arms akimbo, he stared down at the pews and smiled as he thought of the time as a kid he had looked down and noticed how many people were half sitting, half kneeling.

Dan's reverie was interrupted when a door slammed. How could he explain what he was doing in the choir loft? He had to get out of the church quickly and quietly. The front door was not an option- surely it would have an alarm. The only way out was the way he had come in. Dan dipped low in the choir loft, fearing at any moment a priest would confront him. Then revelation dawned. The priest was getting ready to say the early Mass. Dan would have to wait where he was until Mass was over. Luckily for him, the early Mass was brief, a half hour or so. The outside door closing told Dan the priest had left, and he could leave as well. Even so, he looked furtively about as he slowly descended the stairs. No one was in sight.

Never had it occurred to Dan to feel self-conscious around his family, but that feeling overwhelmed him as he entered Pup's palatial home. He had the opposite feeling last night at Mimi's home, which felt like home. Dan could hardly keep from laughing when he saw his oldest brother regaled in lime green pants and white patent leather shoes. His shirt was burnt orange with a pattern of coiled snakes. Evidently, Pup was so busy making money he didn't realize the seventies had ended.

But Dan could not discount Pup's success. He had built this house with his own hands. It was a shrine to the early eighties version of the American Dream. No doubt Dan would be subjected to the grand tour of the house as soon as the host could tear himself away from the guests. Seeing the homes of two of his older siblings made Dan feel like the weak sister, the family failure who didn't own anything, who bought everything on credit, as little as that might be. The last thing he wanted was to have his older brother's success flung in his face. Pup had barely made it through high school, yet he owned this palace and all the land while Dan lived in a shabby apartment working for a fly-by-night newspaper where he wrote stories about fires and accidents in a one horse town in Ohio. He hadn't even written the book he had promised the family he would write. Luckily, no one except Aunt Julia remembered.

Pup's wife, Elaine, gave Dan a polite peck on the cheek. She was handling the situation well, but she didn't even know most of the Kerr family all that well. Pup met her when he was in the service, and they had married quietly in her hometown. None of the Kerrs attended the wedding. If she was out of her element living in Pup's hometown, she didn't show it. A born hostess, she received each guest and guided them to the snacks and drinks. Dan headed for the living room and spotted his sister Gabby, his favorite.

"Gabby, I'm so happy to see you," Dan gushed before he could stop himself. They embraced, but Dan felt a chilliness he didn't expect. Gabby was wooden and distant.

"Chip, I'd like you to meet Stanley, my boyfriend. Stanley, this is my brother Chip."

The hand that Stanley extended to Dan was moist and flaccid. Dan shook it briefly. Pup interrupted to ask Dan if he would like a beer. At this moment, a beer would be just right.

Dan returned his attention to Gabby, who was in rapt conversation with Stanley, oblivious to the rest of the guests. She looked at him with undisguised admiration. Hating to break up this love fest, but wanting to talk to Gabby, Dan casually asked, "So, Gabby, how's life treating you?"

This innocent question engendered a blistering response. "My name is Sheila. Please call me Sheila." Taken aback, Dan was momentarily speechless.

"But you've always been Gabby in the family. I wouldn't even think to call you Sheila."

"Well, you better start thinking because I no longer wish to be called Gabby. I'm really mad at whoever started calling me by that name. I'm quiet by nature and calling me Gabby was insensitive and mocking to my natural self. Family nicknames are stupid anyway. Do the people you work with call you Chip?"

"Of course not, but this is a family occasion. No one here is at work."

"I don't care. You will call me Sheila or nothing at all. Your choice."

Dan immediately knew that Stanley must have fed this garbage to Gabby. She would never act like this on her own volition. And, as if on cue, Stanley hissed, "I'm always telling Sheila how important it is to be one's genuine self. No masks, no pretending. Be a straight shooter. She has taken a significant step by ridding herself of the ridiculous nickname. Her true identity is asserting itself."

Dan seethed as he listened to this nonsense. And he had all he could do to speak civilly to this pompous jellyfish and not punch him.

"So, Chip, Sheila tells me you're a writer."

"I work for a small weekly in the Midwest. Are you a psychology professor or something?"

Stanley threw back his head and laughed. "Hell, no. I work for the New York Railway System. What made you think I was a psychology prof?"

"You talk like one."

Gabby had had enough of Dan's needling. She took Stanley's arm and guided him away. "Stanley, I'd like you to meet some of the other guests." Gabby gave her brother an over the shoulder sneer and a smile that was not pleasant.

To keep himself from smashing his beer bottle over Stanley's head, Dan went to chat with his two favorite ladies—his grandmother Margaret and his Aunt Julia. These ladies were sisters-in-law, but not friends. They tended to gravitate to each other because no one else in the room remembered flappers or model Ts. Margaret was feisty yet proper to the point of being prim. Julia was feisty and irreverent and overly fond of her paramour, Jack Daniels.

"Chippy," squealed Aunt Julia. "I'm so happy to see you. Have you finished writing the next great American novel? I want to be the first to read it. Do you still have that Thesaurus I gave you?"

Not to be outdone, Margaret interjected, "When are you going to get a real job, Daniel? You look like you're starving like most writers. You're such a bright boy. You could land a good-paying job in a New York minute."

Before Dan could answer either lady, Pup grabbed his arm and steered him toward the dining room, or so Dan thought. "C'mon down and see the hot tub," commanded Pup. "I remodeled the room just for that." Dan and Pup descended the stairs to Pup's newest display of craftsmanship. A hot tub lay sunk into the floor and dominated the room. The walls were festooned with pictures of football and baseball teams. The room screamed, "I used to be a jock!" Pup swept his arm in a semi-circle to make sure Chip took it all in.

"You really built all of this yourself? You've come a long way since you and Grampy made that room in the cellar. The one you occupied for all of three months."

Pup turned serious. "Do you think Mom and Dad are having a good time?"

"Why wouldn't they? You and Elaine went to a lot of trouble getting this party together. They seem like they're having fun. For them, any distraction is welcome."

After a tiny pause, Chip asked, "Pup, do you think Champ is still alive?"

Pup took a long drink of his beer. "No, I don't. He's probably floating in some rice paddy in Nam. Even if his body is found, how would anyone be able to identify him? Human bones all look the same."

"I think Mom expects him to come home. I don't know about Dad."

"You're right about Mom. She really thinks he'll walk through the door like he just had a long case of amnesia. Dad's been to war. He knows better. Of course, occasionally you see on the news a story about some farmer in France discovering remains from World War II but that's rare. Once a guy is MIA, the chances that he's still alive are slim to none."

"I agree, but will Mom ever understand that?"

"Probably not. She clings to hope. That's all she's got. Well, we better get back before we're missed."

The party was getting louder. More people had crowded into the living room. To Dan's astonishment, Stanley was talking to Aunt Julia. Dan eavesdropped on this conversation. He sidled into a corner, supposedly studying some pictures on the wall. He heard Aunt Julia bark, "Young man, you will address me as Mrs. Astor, not as ma'am."

Mrs. Astor? Where did that come from? Dan eased in a little closer. Stanley said something he didn't catch.

Aunt Julia again, "What is your opinion of women who keep their maiden names after marriage?"

Stanley gulped. "I, um, well. I don't approve of it."

"And why not? I heard what you said to Chippy about how a name asserts a person's true identity, the genuine self. So why do you have an issue with a woman's choice of name after marriage?"

"Well, Ma'am."

"Mrs. Astor," hissed Aunt Julia.

"Well, Mrs. Astor, you put things in a different light."

"Oh? How so?"

"Well, I, um…"

Aunt Julia looked unusually stern. "Young man, I have had four husbands, and I have dated numerous other men. I've seen the liars, the cheaters, the insolent, and the abusive. If you plan to propose to my niece, I will urge her in the strongest possible terms to reject your suit. You are a combination of all the above. I wouldn't let you walk my dog."

With that, Aunt Julia refreshed her glass and threw a wicked wink in Dan's direction. The wink meant mission accomplished.

"Ok, everybody, come into the dining room. Mom and Dad are going to cut the cake," yelled Pup. "Plenty of coffee and cake for everyone."

As people converged in the dining room, Dan looked around for Stanley—no sign of him. Gabby poked her head into the room, obviously looking for her boyfriend. Her eyes darted about the room. She seemed close to panic. She ran to Dan. "Have you seen Stanley?"

"No. And I don't want to. Don't worry. He won't drive back to New York without you."

Gabby shot him a disgusted look and hurried into the living room.

Coffee and cake were passed around, and soon people drifted towards the door. The party was ending. Dan spotted Mrs. Salina, the Kerr's neighbor and friend, who pulled him close to her by the hair. "AAAYYY, why you not talk to me? You better visit before you leave. You hear me? Stunada."

Dan gave her a kiss on the cheek and a promise to visit the next day.

Mr. and Mrs. Kerr thanked all their guests, at least the ones who remained. The couple looked flushed and happy as they hugged and kissed family and friends. The anniversary party was history.

Mrs. Kerr retired early that night. That was fine with Dan; he wanted some time to talk to his father man to man.

"That was a great party, Dad."

"Yeah. I didn't see the need for it, but now I'm glad that we had it." Dan addressed the elephant in the room head-on. "Dad, why doesn't anyone ever talk about Champ? Everybody acts as though he never existed."

Mr. Kerr looked suddenly weary; he rubbed his eyes, sighed, and said, "It's easier not to talk about him. Your mother pretends that he's still alive somewhere and I pretend with her. As long as there's no body there's hope. That's all your mother has to cling to."

"But do you believe he's alive?"

"No. I don't. Soldiers only return from war after many years in the movies. Champ is lost forever in some god damn swamp of a country no one ever heard of until we went to war. So many young lives lost, and for what? Are we any better because we fought that war? The hell we are."

Dan had never heard his father speak like this. Even mild expletives seldom escaped his father's lips except in situations of extreme provocation or dire circumstances. Champ's disappearance was the trigger that prompted Mr. Kerr to curse, however innocuously.

Dan waited as his father regained his usual calm equilibrium.

"You know, Chip. I've imagined the scene over and over again. Nothing that comes to my mind makes any sense. Was Champ captured and tortured and left for dead by the enemy? Very unlikely. Did he wander away from his troop and become disoriented and fall into some kind of natural hazard? Again, not likely. But what happened to him? I just can't fathom how a soldier goes missing, never to be seen again."

"Have you shared these thoughts with Mom?"

"No. I'm sure she probably has her own theories, but she doesn't speak of them, at least not to me. When she's having a good day, I just keep quiet. I keep extra quiet when she's having a bad day."

Dan was tempted to ask his father if it would be good to share his feelings, to talk. But Dan knew his parents were from a generation that didn't express personal sorrow. They sucked it up and carried on, no matter how heavy the burden. No psychiatrists for them. Chin up, grin and bear it.

The house had the same deafening silence as it did before the anniversary party, the same unspoken tension hanging in the air. Mr. and Mrs. Kerr and Biddy lived together under the same roof, but all lived separate lives.

The family, minus Biddy, attended church the next morning. Dan smiled to himself as remembered his escapade of the previous morning. During his boyhood, he knew everyone by sight, if not by name. Now, as he looked around, he didn't see any familiar faces. He marveled also at the half empty church. The place used to be packed on a Sunday morning.

After Mass, Mrs. Kerr offered to make a big breakfast for her husband and son, but Dan didn't want a huge meal. He had a date with his neighbor, the bombastic yet charming Francesca Salina. Besides his grandmother and Aunt Julia, Mrs. Salina was one of his top five favorite people. The other two had yet to be determined.

The Salinas had lived across the street from the Kerrs as far back as Dan could remember. Mrs. Salina's son, Bobby, had been Dan's best neighborhood friend. In his pre-teen years, Dan had been hopelessly in love with Angelina, Mrs. Salina's middle daughter. Memories crowded into Dan's head as he rang the doorbell. The door flew open and there stood herself, complete to the apron and sensible shoes.

"AAAYYY why you ring the bell? I thought you were a salesman. Next time, you walk right in. Hear me?"

"Yes, Mrs. Salina."

"AAAYYY, you a man now. Time to call me Francesca."

Dan was aghast. "I could never call you by your first name. Never. That would make us equals and I'll never be equal to you. Never."

Mrs. Salina narrowed her eyes at Dan but said nothing. The next hour passed rapidly as Dan sat in the kitchen as familiar as his own with Mrs. Salina. They dined on freshly baked biscotti and drank the strongest coffee on the planet. Dan knew he wouldn't sleep for days.

When Dan asked about the family, Mrs. Salina looked sad. With upraised arms, palms out, Mrs. Salina looked like a defeated general conceding the battle.

"I did my best, but those girls of mine have no sense. All divorced or just living with some man. I just get used to one man, then another one shows up. What did I do wrong?"

Not knowing how to answer, Dan said nothing.

Mrs. Salina regarded him with a wry smile. "You agree with me? You're sensible and smart. My girls have the sense of a coconut. All three stupid and useless. What can I do?"

"How's Bobby?"

"Bobby's good but he lives in Kansas. I never see him. If you see him some time, tell him to visit his mother."

Usually, talking to Mrs. Salina amused Dan, especially her fractured English. But this conversation depressed him. He had no consolation to offer, no words of advice. And he had a plane to catch in an hour. He kissed his favorite neighbor goodbye and took his leave.

Neil and Mimi drove him to the airport. How pleasant it was to be in their company. No conflicts, no complaints, just a family that loved each other's company. The chatter was light, mostly about the party. Dan didn't mention Champ. As they neared Boston, Mimi, bursting with child, turned, not without effort, to face Dan in the back seat.

Without preamble, Mimi said, "Chip, we'd like you to be the baby's godfather. What do you say?"

Dan, astounded, had to catch his breath. In a weekend full of surprises, this was the biggest and best of all.

All Dan managed was, "Yes, Mimi. Thank you."

He boarded his flight, a confused yet suddenly happy man, and winged his way back to Ohio.

CHAPTER 2

RETURNING TO OHIO WAS BITTERSWEET FOR Dan as conflicting emotions swirled in his head during the flight to the Midwest. Thoughts of Champ that had dominated his mind when he was home eased as he got closer to Akron. He smiled whenever he remembered Mimi's invitation to be the Godfather of her baby. Dan would have to check his account balance to see if there were enough funds for another trip to Massachusetts.

Monday morning meant a return to the office routine. Dan dragged himself to work wondering what boring event he would have to cover and then write a story to make said event sound like something not to be missed. In this small town, a town meeting was front page news, an accident a banner headline. The paper was staffed by a platoon of young cloyingly idealistic reporters who were convinced the next story would be Pulitzer material, which would mean a call from the *Times* or the *Washington Post*. These pipe dreams sustained the staff from week to week.

Although Dan covered the town and the surrounding environs, he didn't know many people. He and his fellow reporters would gather at a local bar, usually on a Friday night, to eat and drink, but Dan wasn't close to any of them. He was saved from complete loneliness by his landlady, Miriam, a hardworking middle-aged lady, the descendant of Alabama slaves. Dan rented a studio apartment in Miriam's basement. The rent was cheap, and Miriam's cooking was very good. Dan would often eat with Miriam and her family. At one such dinner, Dan told Miriam that he was to be a godfather, but he didn't know how he would pay for the plane fare. To his astonishment, Miriam proposed a solution to his dilemma.

"How would you like to watch my grandkids for three weeks in the afternoon and early evening? My daughter is taking a class. The course will end in three weeks, so it's not a long-term commitment. What do you say?"

Dan was surprised but pleased. He knew the kids, Marika and Kellen. They spent many Sundays with their grandmother, so their mother, Amelia, had time to study. Dan wanted to accept, but he knew that Amelia, a single parent, didn't have a lot of money, and he felt uncomfortable taking any money. Yet, he needed to pad his meager reserves, so the answer seemed obvious.

"What do you say?" Miriam repeated.

"Yeah. I'd like to do that. What can Amelia afford?"

"You can discuss that with her. I know she'd be pleased. It will be good practice for a godfather-to-be."

Dan and Amelia worked out the details, and Dan was to start the following Monday. Since he worked for a newspaper, he knew there would be times when he would have to work on the computer. But he knew that Marika and Kelllen were even-tempered kids not prone to fighting. Having grown up in the raucous Kerr household, Dan knew watching these kids would be a breeze. Dan looked forward to his time with Marika and Kellen, who were easy enough to reprimand should the need arise. One downside of being a "sitter" that he had never expected was the emptiness of the heart that he didn't have children of his own. Dan was closing in on his third decade and no marriage prospects had presented themselves. Whenever he felt this longing, Dan would hear Aunt Julia's voice. "I had four husbands, and they all died with smiles on their faces." Then she would laugh and take another sip of Jack Daniels.

Dan's time with Marika and Kellen was almost up when he went to work as usual, only to be invited to a staff meeting first thing in the morning. Odd, but not unheard of. The managing editor didn't mince words. The paper had been running a deficit for three years. The time had come to cease operations and today's edition would be the last. This announcement was met with silence from the staff, most of whom had constantly carped and complained about their now non-existent jobs.

When Dan's head stopped spinning, he knew what he would do. He would go home.

It was only when Dan awoke with a punishing headache the next day did reality hit- he was unemployed. He and some of his now former cohorts from the paper had consoled themselves at a local watering hole well into the night. Beer and nachos left Dan miserable and still unemployed. Now he would have to deal with the logistics of moving. He could fit his few belongings in this car—his clothes, his tv, his computer. All the furniture, even the bed linen, belonged to Miriam. He considered not having to sell anything a small blessing; the less he had to do, the better. Dan's biggest worry was his car. Would it make it back to Massachusetts intact? To that end, he went to his friendly mechanic for some routine maintenance that he had been neglecting, fully expecting that the mechanic would find a major issue that would cost upwards of several hundred dollars. Fortunately, that did not happen. The mechanic assured Dan the car would make it to Massachusetts.

Dan's part-time job ended, and the time came for him to say goodbye to Miriam and her family. They had dinner together for the last time, and Dan realized how close he had become to these people. Leaving them was hard, especially Marika and Kellen. The kids gave him homemade farewell cards that almost made Dan change his mind about leaving.

Dan had called his parents and informed them of his decision. His head kept reminding him he was an adult; he shouldn't be moving back into his parents' house. He was almost thirty and unemployed, unmarried with no possibility that either situation would change soon. His heart was torn. He longed to stay with Miriam, but he knew his parents needed him, even though they had never expressed any need or desire for help. Biddy was with them; they didn't need another adult in the house. Dan decided he would only stay until he found a new job.

With his car packed, Dan headed out of Ohio without glancing over his shoulder. He would drive for as many hours as possible, find a cheap motel, and resume the next day. The drive was tedious, made even more so by the ubiquitous country music pouring from the radio. As he drew closer to Massachusetts, the thoughts of Champ returned as much as he willed them away. With no real distractions, Dan couldn't clear his head. Champ is MIA ran like a mantra through his mind. Where is he? Is he alive? Could he be living somewhere, a victim of amnesia? As much as he tried to re-direct, the questions never let up. By the time he crossed the border into

Massachusetts, his mind was in such a frenzy of anxiety and uncertainty that he had to pull into a rest area on the Mass Pike and buy himself a coffee and a sandwich for something to do. Dan was tired in every fiber of his being, with most of the state of Massachusetts still ahead.

New questions assailed him—what would it be like to live at home again? Would his mother insist on doing his laundry? Was his father in need of care? Should he knock before entering the house? Where would he sleep—in his old room or elsewhere? "Stop this," he yelled. "Just drive."

Dan's pulse accelerated as he drove into his hometown. His sweaty palms kept slipping on the steering wheel. He should be happy to be back—what was it that was causing this new suffocating anxiety? He would have to see Aunt Julia as soon as possible. She would talk some sense into him. If she couldn't, Mrs. Salina would whack him with her rolling pin and tell him to stop being so stupid.

There was the house, the car in the driveway. The dilemma of whether to knock was resolved when his parents came out the front door to greet him. Had they been watching for him? If so, why? Together, they crossed the threshold, and Dan began the next chapter of his life.

*****

The first few days at home were a lark; all was congenial between Dan and his parents; his mother couldn't do enough for him. The only thing that marred this happy time was the issue of where Dan would sleep. On his first night home, Dan slept in his old bed. Travel weary as he was, he just needed to lay his head somewhere. The problem began when he announced he wanted to live in Pup's room in the cellar.

Mrs. Kerr's coffee cup stopped halfway to her mouth after Dan made this announcement. "But why, Chip? What's wrong with your bed in your room?"

Dan exhaled a long breath. "Mom, I'm an adult. I really appreciate that you and Dad let me live here, but I've been on my own for quite some time. I need privacy. Besides, you and Dad need and deserve your privacy as well."

Dan knew by the clipped tone that his mother was angry. "How much privacy do you think your father and I had with eight kids in the house? This is a home, not a hotel. You belong here. Your father and I are glad to have you back."

"I appreciate that, Mom. But the fact remains that I'm almost thirty. I need my own space."

"To do what? Entertain women?"

Dan was taken aback by his mother's words and tone.

"Absolutely not. I wouldn't do that. You and Dad set the guidelines and I follow them. I'm really astounded that you would even mention such a thing to me."

Mrs. Kerr sipped her coffee a little too fast, her brows knitted together in a half-formed scowl.

"Look, Mom. I've always wanted a room of my own. Why do you think Pup made that room? He wanted some privacy, a place that was all his own. That's all I want too. When I lived in Ohio, my apartment was just a room in the basement. The only difference is that I had my own bathroom."

Until now, Mr. Kerr had been silently absorbing this conversation. "He's right, dear. Chip deserves his own space. I'll be glad if someone is using the room. You remember how hard your father and Pup worked to make that room? It should be occupied."

Mrs. Kerr had no choice but to surrender. "All right," she said, rising from her chair. "But don't expect me to clean it."

Dan smiled and winked at his father. "Come on, Mom. Can't you at least dust once a year? Is that too much to ask? I had a maid in Ohio who did that for me. I've come to expect it."

"Then go back to Ohio and your maid."

Dan moved his few belongings downstairs and settled into Coltonwood. He loved to walk about. He became a curiosity much as he had been in Ohio but for different reasons. Coltonwood may have grown, but the established residents remained the nucleus of the town, and most knew him or his parents. Understandably, people wondered why he had returned and openly speculated about his father's health: Dan, the good son, had returned to take care of his parents in their old age. Some were not so kind; tongues wagged to the effect that Dan had failed in the cold, cruel world and had to come home to find employment. If someone had said that to Dan's face, he would have had a hard time refuting it. He felt like a failure who had to come home to lick his wounds.

The atmosphere at home was tense at times, but all was forgotten when the clan rejoiced as they welcomed Shannon Julia Mullaney into the world. Mimi gave birth about a week after Dan's return home. As for Dan, he was ecstatic about becoming a godfather and Aunt Julia was elated that Mimi had given the baby her name. True to form, Aunt Julia promptly bought a new outfit, hat, and all, for the christening. She even offered to host the post baptism party. Mrs. Kerr, offended, quickly put out the word that the party would be at the Kerr residence and nowhere else.

Despite the excitement, or perhaps because of it, the thoughts of Champ once again began to trouble Dan. That was the real reason he wanted Pup's room. Sleeping in his old room with all the attendant memories was intolerable. Dan had to be careful not to tell his mother this. She couldn't even talk about Champ, so there was no point in broaching the subject.

But there remained a much more pressing matter for Dan to attend to. He had to find some sort of job. To that end, he made an appointment with the managing editor of the local daily. He thought he recognized the name as being the same as a guy he went to high school with, but maybe not. On the day of the interview, Dan realized, much to his chagrin, that all his clothes were old and out of style. He had no money to waste buying new clothes. Maybe an open shirt would do? Maybe a tie and no jacket? His father loaned Dan a tie, and he was ready for the interview.

The managing editor kept Dan waiting for fifteen minutes. But during that time, Dan got to observe the frenetic activity of the city desk. The pace of the work was quick and efficient. The newsroom in the paper in Ohio was quiet with no sense of urgency. That paper was a weekly; the local a daily. The reporters and editors had to hustle to make a deadline. When the managing editor appeared, Dan did vaguely recognize him, but he gave no hint that he recognized Dan. The handshake was brief and cold, the man's attitude condescending. He looked to be about ten years younger than Dan, but how could he the managing editor?

"How can I help you, Mr. Kerr?"

"I worked for a newspaper in Ohio, and I need a job," said Dan, getting right to the point.

"We don't have any openings. What did you do at the place in Ohio?"

"I was a general assignment reporter. Occasionally I would fill in at the editor's desk. It was a weekly with a small staff, so I got to pull double duty now and then."

Without preamble or explanation, the editor began pecking at an electric typewriter. The rudeness appalled Dan, but he was in no position to object. Dan had an urge to just walk out, but maybe this guy would offer him something.

"Why did you come back here?"

"How did you know I'm from around here?" This question was addressed to the back of the editor's head. When he turned around and when Dan saw him from a different angle, Dan remembered who he was.

"The paper went out of business, and I returned home to be closer to my parents. My father has cancer, so I thought I might make myself useful to him and my mother. Do you know me?"

"We went to high school together. You were two years ahead of me. We both wrote for the school paper."

Dan hoped that some familiarity might break the ice, but the guy was implacable.

"Like I said, we don't have any openings, and I don't anticipate any in the near future."

Dan eyed him a little closer. "Is your name Phil?"

"No. That's my brother. I'm Matt. I have a pretty good gig going on here, but this is just small-time stuff. I'm honing my skills, you might say. I've applied to the *Globe* and even the *Times*, so I expect that my time here will be limited. I'm also writing a novel that I expect will be published within the year, then sayonara, *Coltonwood Clarion*. I'm on to bigger and better things."

As Matt spoke, Dan had all he could do not to laugh. This guy has a bad case of delusions of grandeur. Matt rose from his seat, a clear signal that the interview was over. "If you'll excuse me, I have work to do."

"Of course. Glad to see you again, Matt."

"Likewise, I'm sure."

Dan left the *Clarion* humiliated and furious. Returning to his hometown was looking like a colossal mistake. He made a vow then and there. Never again would he grovel before anyone, especially someone younger than himself. He had to return home and tell his parents the interview was a failure. Now what? He had walked to the newspaper, and he took a longer route home to allow himself to think about his options, if any. What else could he do? He didn't want to work at a bank or an insurance office. He could be a technical writer, but he would need to learn how. He had no money or desire to return to school. Besides, if he had to eventually become his father's caregiver, he would need a job with flexible hours. He would have to check out the town some more and see what industries had sprung up since he last lived here. If he could do manual labor, he could work for Pup. Dan immediately dismissed that thought. Never would he work for his brother.

Every morning Dan read the Classifieds, but most jobs required some type of technical skill. Writing was his best attribute, and he knew how to use a word processor.

About a week after his disastrous interview, Matt called him.

"Hi, Dan. This is Matt Jansen."

"Hi, Matt." He waited for Matt to speak.

"How good of a photographer are you?"

"Fair. Why?"

"We can use another stringer. You know what that is, don't you?"

Dan wanted to slam the receiver down, but instead said, "Yeah. I know what that is."

"Good. Could you do an assignment this coming Thursday? It involves an interview with the director of Human Services. He just started a food pantry, and we want to do the story. Interested?"

"Yes, I am."

"Good. His name is John Murphy, and his office is in the basement of the City Hall. He will be expecting you at three o'clock. You can come here and write the story and turn over the film. We'll pay you fifty bucks for this. Do you have a camera? If not, we have plenty here."

"I have my own camera. I'll do the interview. Thanks."

"Don't mention it."

Dan replaced the receiver and thought, "Wonders never cease."

Dan went to Town Hall at the appointed time where he was met by a young, affable wheelchair bound man who extended a friendly hand to Dan. "John Murphy. A pleasure to meet you."

"Dan Kerr. Glad to make your acquaintance."

"Welcome to my cave. This used to be a broom closet, now it's my office," said the man, laughing. "Have a seat, and I'll tell you about the new food pantry."

With notebook in hand, Dan listened as John described why a food pantry was necessary in a place like Coltonwood. "Hunger is a hidden problem," he began. "Some churches had small pantries, but stocking them became a problem because people just didn't see the need. That's when I asked one of the people on the City Council if we could have a central location for a food pantry. People were reluctant to go to the churches, especially if they had no affiliation. Having a central location in the town open to anyone seemed a logical solution. Of course, the City Council wasn't crazy about the idea, since they didn't see the need either. I got some of the clergy to speak to the Council and finally they relented. Then the problem became logistical: where would they put the pantry? So, I tooled around Town Hall and some other buildings for appropriate space. I found this closet at the end of a seldom used corridor. After the donations of shelving, we were in business. If you want the higher-ups to approve something, just do the work for them and they'll say yes to anything."

Dan smiled. "Very true. It seems to me that most people in Coltonwood are working, so why the need for a food pantry?"

"They are indeed working. In fact, the unemployment rate is very low. Our clients are the working poor. They have jobs but not enough money to meet their needs. You probably know that a large technology company recently opened in town and many local people work there. Sounds good, huh? Unfortunately, most of the townspeople are in low-level entry jobs that offer low-level wages. Yes, they get benefits, but the more benefits, the lower the pay. Hence the need for the pantry."

John continued. "What we need now is publicity. People need to know we're here so they can avail themselves of our services or donate. We have to get the word out. That's why I called the paper and asked for someone to do a story. It took some convincing. The managing editor didn't see the need either. I had to keep calling until he finally said yes."

Dan said, "Do you mind if I take a few pictures?"

"Not at all."

"First, I'll take a few shots of the shelves."

"Good. People need to see how empty the shelves are. We are in constant need of donations."

"Thank you for your time, John. The story and pictures will be in Saturday's paper."

"Fantastic. It's good to see you back in town, Dan."

Dan looked pensively at John. "Do you know me?"

"Sure. You and most of the kids in town were terrified of me at one time."

Then it dawned on Dan. This is Johnny M, the self-proclaimed bully. The kid who was hit by a car on Main St.

"Did you really set a fire and then run away the day you got hit?"

"Yes, I did. I set some boxes on fire behind the hardware store. The last thing I remember is feeling the grill of a car in my left side. I woke up several weeks later in a hospital in Boston. Yeah, I was an angry young man then. My old man was a drunk, and I knew what hunger was. He took off after my accident and I haven't seen him since. I finished high school with the aid of a tutor and then went to a two-year college where I earned a degree in Human Services. Then my mother and I moved back here. People have been very kind to us, and I want to give something back."

Dan smiled. "I really was terrified of you. The last thing I wanted was to run into you. But you never did catch me."

"Maybe not, but I beat up your brother, Dennis. I was the terrified one after that because I thought he'd get your older brother to beat me up. He was a tough guy. What's Dennis doing now? I never see him around town."

Dan took a deep breath. "Dennis or Champ, as we call him in the family, is MIA in VietNam. He went missing in 1973 and we don't know if he's alive or dead. I want to find out what happened to him, but I don't know where to start."

"Wow. I'm sorry, man. The guy you need to talk to is Sam Patterson. He's the Veterans Agent in town. One thing he does is try to locate missing servicemen. He's located in this building on the second floor. I can give you his number if you'd like."

Dan took the information about Sam Patterson and took a hurried leave of John Murphy. He had to get back to the paper to write his story and turn in the film. As he drove, it all made sense now. Matt had called him because he didn't think the story was important enough to send a full-time reporter, so he sent the stringer. As angry as he was, Dan had to keep his emotions under control. The story he would write would make or break the food pantry and undermine everything John Murphy was doing.

A well-written piece could also mean more work and maybe a shot at becoming a full-fledged reporter.

The next day, Dan paid a visit to Sam Patterson. The veteran's agent was himself a disabled VietNam veteran. He had lost part of his left arm in the explosion of a grenade. Dan introduced himself and Sam Patterson, a pleasant, balding young man, extended his hand.

"What brings you here, Mr. Kerr?"

"My brother is MIA in VietNam and I want to find him, dead or alive."

"How long has he been missing?"

"He went missing in 1973 near Da Nang Province. That's all I know."

Sam looked thoughtful. "That's a long time to not know. The longer the time, the less the chance of finding out anything about the guy. However, there is some new technology that gives us more hope than we've had in the past. Trouble is, it's rudimentary and often not accurate, but the technology will get better and help us locate missing servicemen."

Dan felt his heart sink. "How far away are we from this technology?"

"Maybe three years, maybe five. Until now, we felt lucky if we found a guy's dog tags, if not the man himself. Once in a while bones are found and the new technology enables identification. The best way is to use dental records, but that's not always possible."

"What are the chances that my brother may be eventually found?"

"As of right now, slim to none unless some physical evidence is uncovered. I hate to discourage you, but that's the reality."

"I see. Should I just forget about him? Pretend he never lived? He haunts me, Mr. Patterson. I dream about him; I think I see him in crowds. My mother has never been the same since the day the telegram arrived. If we knew for sure that he was dead, we could grieve and move on. But we don't know that he's dead. I just have to know. That's all I want."

"I can sympathize with you and your family. Not knowing is hell. I don't mean to sound callous, but my job is to help the living, the guys who came back and are struggling to adjust to life post war. I do keep up with all developments dealing with guys who are MIA. Occasionally we get lucky, but not very often. I'm sorry, but I don't want to give you false hope."

"Thank you, Mr. Patterson. I appreciate your time."

As he walked to his car, Dan felt a searing, blistering anger. He wished he had never heard the name Sam Patterson. The realization that there was little to no chance of finding out what happened to Champ was a knife that killed what little hope he had nurtured all this time. Now Champ would haunt him forever. Dan had to find a way to erase his emotional agony. Dan now knew that was only one answer. He would have to do whatever it would take to learn Champ's fate.

Dan's black thoughts were suddenly interrupted by the image of one Shannon Julia Mullaney. He was to be a godfather this weekend. He had pressing business—he had to buy a christening gift for the newest member of the Kerr clan.

CHAPTER 3

THE DAY BEFORE THE CHRISTENING WAS hectic in the Kerr household. Each member of the family was expected to help out, and no one was excused. Hence, Dan had to fetch chairs from the funeral home that would ring the tables that Pup was to bring later in the day. In addition, Dan had to mow the lawn, trim the hedges, and sweep the driveway. While his mother was at the hairdressers putting on a face for the big day, Dan had to man the phone and the front door as his sibs arrived to drop off whatever contributions they had made."

Pup arrived mid-day with the tables and an enormous bowl of macaroni salad prepared by his wife. Dan, Pup and Pup's sons arranged the tables in the backyard. The day was hot and sultry so after the tables had been set up, the guys had to break for a beer. Mr. Kerr joined his sons. As usual, Pup steered the conversation to himself.

"Dad, I'm almost finished with the development over at Duck Harbor. That was a project and a half. I had to truck in tons of fill. I didn't know that place was such a swamp."

His father laughed. "That's why they call it Duck Harbor. I can remember skating there in the winter. There's a brook that runs behind where the Mart is now. Sometimes I'd skate all the way to the city line. Didn't you guys skate there too?"

Dan remembered, "Yeah, I used to skate there with Bobby. The frozen brook was usually too bumpy to skate on for very long. Bridy skated most of the way one time. For a kid who spent most of her time on the floor coloring, she became a fantastic skater. Is she coming to the christening?"

"Yes, she's coming tomorrow, at least for the party."

"Alone?"

"As far as I know."

Then Dan asked the million-dollar question: "Is Gabby coming?"

"Yes, she is."

"Alone or with her sugar daddy?"

"Stanley is coming with her. She hinted on the phone that they had a big announcement to make."

"God help us. Is she really going to marry that jerk? I can't believe she's so taken in by his phony pronouncements. He'll be a family member and I'll have to pretend that I like him. He's an actor and a bad one at that."

Pup interrupted, "Dad, I just heard the doorbell. I'll see who it is."

The visitor was Cissy's husband, with a bowl of potato salad and several bags of chips, homemade dip, and several bottles of wine. Carl put everything in the refrigerator and joined the other men in the backyard. Dan had never felt really comfortable around Carl, but he couldn't figure out why. The guy was nice enough, if a little quiet. Perhaps a man of few words didn't fit well into the boisterous Kerr clan, but maybe Carl felt out of place amidst all the chaos of the family gatherings. He seemed to spend more time with the kids than with the adults. This, Dan thought, would be a good time to get to know Carl better.

"Hey, Carl. What's new?"

Carl smiled. "Not much. Are you all set for your big day tomorrow?"

"I guess. My wardrobe, or lack of, will reveal me as the tightwad I had to be as a newspaper reporter. The only jacket I have is from the Seventies with wide lapels. I had to borrow a tie from my dad when I had an interview last week. That's pretty bad when your father is more with it than you are."

Mr. Kerr, listening, said, "When you were small, I had one suit that I wore on Sundays. I had three pairs of pants that I had to rotate so I wouldn't wear the same ones twice. I had five shirts and five ties. I didn't really have any extra money to spend on clothes. I owned that suit for fifteen to twenty years. It's only recently that I've had a more varied wardrobe."

Carl said, "Dan, you're about my size. I can loan you a suit coat to wear for the christening. I can bring it to church with me tomorrow morning. What color pants and shirt are you planning to wear?"

"Khakis and a light blue shirt. What color is the jacket?"

"I have a dark blue blazer that would be perfect."

Dan, puzzled but pleased by the offer, said, "Thanks, Carl. I'll make sure the baby doesn't spit up on your jacket."

Carl laughed. "It wouldn't be the first time."

Dan and his parents attended morning Mass. Upon their return home, Dan attempted to cook breakfast for his parents. He managed to fry some eggs and put some toast into the toaster. It wasn't much, but his mother was thrilled. At this point in the morning, Champ's absence was irrelevant.

The christening was at two o'clock. Dan drove his parents, and they picked up his grandmother and Aunt Julia. Luckily, Mrs. Kerr was between the two adversaries and the short trip to the church was free of sniping and squabbling between the two older women. Most of the family was there when they arrived. Kerrs were not renowned for early arrivals at anything, so Dan wondered why he and his party were the last to arrive. A quick scan of the pews revealed Pup and family, Cissy and family, Bridy, Mimi and Neil and family with Neil's immediate family. Where was Biddy? Where was Gabby?

The ceremony only took about ten minutes. The officiating priest was introduced only as a Father Tony. Dan wondered at Father Tony's accent; he wasn't American. When Dan was a kid, the priests were all Americans. As Father Tony poured the water on Shannon's head, she screamed like a banshee, drawing chuckles from the assembly. Her godmother, Neil's sister-in-law, Carol, placed what looked like a white bib on her. Then it was Dan's turn. Father Tony nodded, and Dan reached to light the candle. The Paschal Candle was tall, and Dan had to stand on tiptoes to reach the flame, which flickered and danced courtesy of a nearby fan. Dan placed his hand in front of the flame, and it settled. He looked sheepishly at the people in the pews and in that quick moment he spied Gabby and her ever-present Stanley.

Dan groaned inwardly at the thought of having to converse with Stanley. Another furtive look almost made him drop the candle. "Champ. It can't be. My eyes are playing tricks." The Champ vision was, in reality, Dan's favorite cousin, Bart. This was odd, since only the immediate family had been invited to the ceremony. So distracted was Dan that he didn't hear Father Tony whisper to him to blow out the candle. Dan reddened and did as he was told. For a few seconds, his heart seemed to stop. Dan never realized how much alike Champ and Bart looked.

After the handshakes and congratulations, Dan made a beeline for Bart. The two cousins hugged and shook hands. Dan still couldn't believe it.

"Bart. What are you doing here?"

"I can't come to a family christening?"

"Of course you can, but this was just immediate family. How did you know?"

"Actually, Mimi invited me. We correspond and I have business in Boston next week, so I came a few days early."

Dan wanted to tell Bart about his Champ resemblance, but his mother took his elbow and moved him in the direction of the door. Mrs. Kerr kissed Bart and turned to Dan. "How do you like Mimi's surprise?"

"So you were in on it, too?"

"Of course. I'm in on everything in this family."

The christening party got off to a rollicking start when most people changed into shorts and tee shirts, given that the temperature was north of ninety. The beer and wine flowed freely, and the Kerr-Mullaney clan celebrated. Dan saw Aunt Julia and his grandmother on lawn chairs under the only shade in the backyard. He edged closer to listen to an animated conversation.

"… just let me have ten minutes with that girl. I'll straighten her right out," said Aunt Julia.

Gram retorted, "Sheila is free to marry whomever she chooses. She's old enough to make her own choices and decisions. Besides, why should she listen to you? Did you listen when people told you not to marry your first husband?"

"Of course not. Nobody could tell me anything. The difference is I always married for money. That lizard of Sheila's doesn't have a cent to his name. If a man doesn't have money, I can't think of anything else to recommend him. How do you like my new hat? I bought it just for this occasion."

"Women don't wear hats anymore, or had you not noticed?"

"I'd let you borrow it if women still wore hats."

"Go to hell."

Dan loved the repartee between these two women, and they didn't disappoint him. Bart was making the rounds of all the relatives, so Dan looked around for Gabby and Stanley. He didn't see either one. They must be in the house. Good. Let them stay there.

The day was oppressive; the heat seemed to shimmer and hang. It was certainly the hottest of the summer. Dan caught a fleeting glimpse of Stanley wearing a long sleeve white shirt and a dark tie. He had shed his suit coat but retained the rest of his wardrobe despite the blistering heat. At least he had dressed respectfully, even though Stanley's attire was more appropriate for a funeral than a christening. Yet, Stanley rose somewhat in Dan's estimation. Maybe, Dan thought, he would offer Stanley a pair of shorts as he did to Bart. But Dan figured Stanley would decline and create a scene. Best to leave well enough alone.

The two charcoal grills tended by Pup only added to the stifling heat, even though Pup was having difficulty getting the charcoal to burn. He created a momentary fireball with the addition of lighter fluid, but the flame died and the charcoal remained black. Pup entertained as though everyone was in his own backyard. Pup kissed and hugged, shook hands, slapped backs. He was a born politician.

Hunger and the heat soon took a double toll and even the kids who had been running around grew tired and cranky. Everyone wanted to eat and go home to their pools or air-conditioned living rooms. Cissy accosted Pup over the delay. Arms akimbo, Cissy demanded to know when the fire would be ready. "I spent most of the morning making hamburger patties and now you can't even get a decent fire going. What's wrong with you?"

Cissy and Pup had always been the most combative of the Kerr kids, especially with each other.

An enraged Pup waved a spatula in her face. "Would you care to stand here in this heat and try to get these fires going? La de dah, you spent all morning making patties. Aren't you special? If this was my house, I'd throw you out of it. Get back inside and whine to whoever is stupid enough to listen to you."

This exchange of pleasantries was interrupted when Mrs. Kerr leaned over the railing of the back porch.

"What's the problem, Pup? We need to get cooking. People are hungry."

An exasperated Pup said, "I'm doing the best I can, Mom. The charcoal isn't burning. The fires should be ready in about five minutes. Do you have anything that needs to be done in the kitchen? Julia Child here," indicating Cissy,"wants to put her culinary skill to good use. She knows how to make hamburger patties. Wow! What a prodigy."

Cissy, sputtering with rage, was about to swear when Mrs. Kerr interrupted. "Stop it, both of you. Don't spoil Shannon's day with silly fighting. Cissy, come on in. I do need you in the kitchen." Cissy turned on her heel and ran up the stairs, glaring at her brother. Mrs. Kerr probably didn't need Cissy in the kitchen, she was trying to prevent a family fight from erupting in front of the Mullaneys. She always wanted to project the image of the perfect family to others. Dan smirked at the thought; nothing could be further from the truth. But he did his mother an injustice. She knew the tenor of the family better than anyone else. Appearances do matter and she wanted to present a unified front to the outside world.

Mrs. Salina walked into the backyard with a large lasagna as Pup tried his best to get the fire hot enough for cooking. Dan immediately approached her and offered to take the lasagna. "Let me take that from you, Mrs. Salina."

"How many times do I have to tell you? Call me Francesca now. Where's your mother?"

"She's in the kitchen."

"Sorry I'm so late with this. Salina had too much homemade wine and he snore all night and I sleep too long this morning."

Dan never made it to the kitchen. The guests saw the lasagna, called for a spatula, and devoured Mrs. Salina's signature dish in record time. In the meantime, the burgers and dogs were grilling, but no one seemed interested. Cissy's patties were eaten by the people who had been in the house who didn't even know about the lasagna. Dan had some of both.

Sensing that the glory had departed with the devouring of food, Mrs. Kerr called everyone into the house for the cutting of the christening cake. It was too hot to take the cake outside, so Mimi and Neil, surrounded by their children, ceremoniously cut the huge sheet cake with a picture of newborn Shannon Julia on the top. Cissy quickly passed out pieces to people so they would stay longer. People were tired and hot; the kids were fussy. Most ate a little of the cake, then quietly thanked the hosts and left.

Bart drove Aunt Julia and his grandmother home. When he returned, the party was clearly over. Pup and Dan were folding the tables and loading the chairs into Pup's van. Bart joined them and all three guys settled under the tree where the older ladies had sat and enjoyed a beer. Dan didn't want to ignore Bart, but he had to tell Pup a story before he forgot. "I went to City Hall last week to interview the manager of the food pantry and guess who it is?"

Pup was uninterested. "Who?" he asked in a bored voice.

"John Murphy. Remember, he was Johnny M. back in the day. All the kids were afraid of him. All except you. Johnny was actually afraid of you."

"Yeah, I'd heard that John was working for the city. Is he in a wheelchair?"

"He is. He got hit by a car and was left paralyzed. I remember when that happened. It's true that he started a fire and was running away when he was hit."

"That was around the time that I went into the service. The old man was an alcoholic. He ran away after that happened. I haven't seen him since."

"Neither has John. Well, enough of that. I wanted to tell you before I forgot."

Pup gulped his beer and addressed Bart. "What do you do for work?"

"I work for the government in D.C."

Pup was impressed. "No kiddin'. What exactly do you do?"

"I work for the State Department. Most consider me a minor functionary or a paper pusher. I arrange the travel plans for the bigwigs who jet around the world at the behest of the president. I had some unused sick time, so when Mimi told me about the christening, I knew it was time that I showed my face again and caught up. This was a great party. Gram and Aunt Julia haven't changed. Just listening to them made the trip worthwhile. I doubt either one will ever die, at least not in this century."

The Kerr brothers laughed, then both turned serious. It was Dan who ventured to mention the unmentionable. "Champ has been missing in Nam for almost ten years. We have no idea if he's alive or dead. I've been trying to find out what happened to him, but I've gotten nowhere. Even the veterans agent pretty much told me to forget it and get on with my life. That's hard because I think of him all the time and I know everyone else does as well. I presume that he's dead, but I'd like to know. I won't have any peace until I know for sure."

Bart said, "Have you contacted your senator or state rep? That might be a good place to start."

Dan hadn't thought of that. "Thanks, Bart. I'll write to both. I have plenty of time on my hands these days."

Bart, ever the gentleman, stood when Gabby approached, but neither of her brothers did. "Hi, Sheila. It was a pleasure to meet your fiancé. Have you set a date yet?"

"No. Not yet. We still have a lot of things to talk about. Are you married, Bart?"

"Not anymore. My wife and I split up four years ago. It's not easy to stay married in Washington. Too much pressure and too many opportunities to go astray. I succumbed to both. I won't bore you with the details, but suffice to say I'm living alone these days."

Gabby smiled. "I'm sorry. It must have been hard for you."

"Nothing to be sorry about. The hardest thing is not being able to see my son. He lives with his mother in California. He visits during the summer for a couple of weeks. Make sure when you take the vow that you live up to it. I wish I had."

Dan interrupted. "Where is Sir Galahad? I didn't think he ever let you out of his sight. Or did he pass out from wearing a long-sleeved shirt and a tie in three-digit heat? He must have a remarkable constitution to be able to do that."

"Please, Chip. I don't understand why you don't like Stanley. He speaks very well of you."

Dan laughed. "I'll bet he does. He must have a theory about the dynamics of the Kerr family. He has an opinion about everything else, God knows. Do you have anything to say about his family? Are they a bunch of winners or what?"

"Stanley's family is very nice to me. We plan to live near them since his brother has an autoimmune disease and his mother has cancer. They need us."

"Oh, do they? How about your father, who also has cancer? How do you and Stanley plan to support him and the family as his illness progresses?"

Gabby stared at her brother. "You're so unfair, Chip. Our family is very large. Dad has plenty of support here. Why do I need to be here? Now you're here with Mimi, Pup, Cissy, and Biddy. I think that's plenty of support. I am entitled to lead my own life wherever I choose and with whomever I choose. If you'd all just accept the fact that Champ's dead, everyone would be better off. Stanley has helped me to get beyond the fact that Champ is MIA. I'll always be grateful to him for that."

Pup's temper had been close to combustion all afternoon, and he finally exploded. "Well, isn't that just fine and dandy? Do you know why I drink more than I should and why Cissy is a chain smoker, or why Biddy works ridiculous hours? We do it because we see Mom looking like a living ghost and if you think that's easy to witness, think again. She's been known to wander around with her rosary in hand, looking half alive. Not knowing if Champ is dead or alive is slowly killing her. Now she has to wonder how long Dad will live. That will be another huge loss when he goes. But, of course, you have your own life with Stanley and are insulated from all the issues we deal with on a daily basis. And to top it all off, you act as though everything is just peachy."

Gabby stamped her foot. "I don't have to take this abuse from you. How do you know what I feel? I think about Champ every day, but I can't give my whole life to wondering what happened to him. I had to move on, and I suggest the rest of you do the same."

"Ok, doctor. I'd like you to repeat that little speech to your mother and see what she thinks. Easy for you to say move on. You don't live with uncertainty every day. I can see Stanley has done a good job of brainwashing you."

With that, Pup stormed towards the house. All the yelling had brought Mrs. Kerr to the landing of the back porch. She leaned over the side of the porch and addressed Pup. "What's going on? Why all the yelling?"

"Ask Gabby. She has all the answers, anyway."

Pup's wife, Elaine, alarmed at the fury on her husband's face, asked, "John, what is it? What happened?"

"Let's go, Elaine. Where are the kids? I have to get away from my know-it-all sister before I say something I'll always regret. Are you ready?"

Pup kissed his mother and shook hands with his father and left with his family. Gabby came into the kitchen as they were leaving and glared at Pup. The look he returned was almost impassive; his eyes looked at his sister not with hate but with pity.

"Goodbye, Pup," Gabby sneered. Pup merely waved.

Minutes later, Gabby, with Stanley in tow, said goodbye. Gabby was civil, but obviously seething inside. When they were gone, Neil chuckled, "Sounds like there was a battle royal going on. Dan, were you lucky enough to have to referee?"

"Actually, no. I was too surprised to do much except watch the whole thing unfold. I was about to step in when Pup stomped off."

Mrs. Kerr said quietly, "Will you tell us what happened, Chip?"

"Pup and Gabby got into an argument."

"I gathered that. What was it about?"

Dan hesitated. He didn't want to lie or sugarcoat the incident since he knew his mother would know the whole story in a day or two.

"Pup is angry with Gabby because he thinks she is too wrapped up in her life with Stanley and she doesn't care about the family."

Mrs. Kerr frowned. "That's odd. Those two don't usually fight. There must be more to it than that. I'm just sorry they had to put a damper on Shannon's christening party. It seems someone in this family is always fighting with someone else. I thought I raised a civil brood."

Mimi interrupted, putting food into the refrigerator to smile at her mother. "Don't worry, Mom. Shannon doesn't know the difference. Every family has arguments. You should see my kids. Some days they fight from dawn to dusk. Someone is always getting punished for one reason or another. This will blow over in a day or two. I guess you've forgotten all the arguments and fighting among the eight of us. Dad probably remembers how many times he had to separate Champ and Chip when they fought. Remember all the fireworks when Anthony and Girard visited? At least none of us is as bad as those two. We didn't have to call the police."

The day had darkened, and thunder murmured in the distance. Mimi and Neil and family left to beat the storm and only Dan and Bart and Mr. and Mrs. Kerr remained. Dan was concerned that his mother looked suddenly exhausted. Mr. Kerr had slept for most of the afternoon and missed all the family drama. Dan and Bart finished the cleaning and then relaxed on the porch. Dan would finally have some quiet time to talk to his cousin.

"I'm really glad you came, Bart. What's your sister Aggie doing these days?"

Bart took a long gulp from his beer before he answered. "She's living somewhere in New York. No one knows exactly where. My parents have pretty much given up on her. We never see her or hear from her. She might be dead for all we know."

"Pretty sad. It sounds like our situation with Champ. Not knowing what's happened to him is the real reason there is always some kind of fight whenever the family gets together. I have to find out what's happened to him before this family is torn apart."

The thunder was more insistent and louder as the cousins sat and watched the storm. Lightning lit up the sky in all directions. The wind whipped the rain, and a fine spray penetrated the screens of the porch, sending a fine mist over Dan and Bart. When the storm finally cleared, Bart said goodbye. As the two men said farewell, they shook hands. Bart touched his cousin's shoulder. "Hang in there, cousin."

CHAPTER 4

A PUNISHING HEADACHE AND CAVERNOUS hunger reminded Dan that he had consumed too much beer and not enough food at yesterday's party. He lugged himself out of bed and upstairs to shower. In the kitchen, he saw his father behind the morning paper and Biddy across the table from him. Both greeted him perfunctorily as he dragged himself into the bathroom. Several minutes later, he emerged to find his father and sister exactly as they had been a half hour ago. Biddy poured Dan some coffee and offered him some cereal. He welcomed the coffee as if it were a life preserver, but the cereal was spurned in favor of toast, which he ate greedily. Dan smiled as he remembered his father's morning ritual of reading the Irish sports page and nothing short of a house fire could distract him. He reached for his coffee cup without looking and raised it to his mouth with practiced precision and replaced it again without spilling a drop.

Obits finished; Mr. Kerr was now ready for conversation. "Tough night, Chip?"

"No. Tough day. I drank way too much beer and I'm paying for it now."

Much amused, Dan's father said, "You should have seen the Kerr family gatherings when your mother and I were young. We would drink, play horseshoes, argue, and save the world all in one night. Then we all went to work the next day as though nothing had happened. Can't do that anymore."

Dan frowned. "Play horseshoes? You never mentioned anything about that."

"Well, it was a long time ago. Having eight kids pretty much makes you forget what you did before they came along."

"Did Mom and Aunt Julia participate in these gatherings?"

"Not really. It was mostly your uncles and great uncles, although Julia could keep up with the best of us in her time."

"She still can from what I can see."

After a small silence, Mr. Kerr said quietly, "You know there's going to be another addition to the family?"

Dan misunderstood and said, "Is Cissy pregnant?"

"No. I don't mean another baby. I'm talking about Stanley. He asked for Gabby's hand in marriage yesterday."

Dan almost choked. "I suppose you said yes?"

"Of course, why wouldn't I? He seems like a decent guy, and he took the trouble to ask permission to marry Gabby. How many men do that these days? That's good old-fashioned courtesy and I like that."

Dan was at a loss as to how to respond, and Biddy spent an inordinate amount of time buttering a piece of toast. So that explained the over-dressing despite the heat and the amount of time Stanley spent in the house. He was ingratiating himself to the Kerrs. The snake. He put on his best manners to make sure his future in-laws would see him as a good catch. Dan's headache returned with a vengeance when he thought of his favorite sister married to a psychopath.

Mr. Kerr addressed Dan. "I take it you don't like Stanley."

"No, I don't. I think he's an insincere phony. I'm concerned about Gabby's well-being. How will he treat her once they're married? He can talk a good game, but can he deliver in the clutch?"

"Chip, you have to remember that Gabby is over thirty and independent. She can marry anyone of her choice. I presume she knows enough about life to make a good choice in a marriage partner. She's not a teenager; she knows what's what."

"That's all true, Dad. But how much experience with men does Gabby have? She's always been shy and unsure of herself. Along comes this guy to flatter her, and she falls for his nonsense. I just have a bad feeling about Stanley."

"Well, Gabby is the one who has to live with her choice. Stanley has some redeeming qualities. He's not a felon, he works, he loves Gabby. I don't see that any of this is a problem."

"What does Mom think? Does she like him?"

"I guess so, but you'll have to ask your mother."

Now the thought struck Dan that it was odd that his mother wasn't up. Ordinarily, she would rise early and start getting breakfast. She never stayed abed this long.

"Is Mom sick? Why is she sleeping so long?"

"She's just tired from yesterday. She did a lot, you know. More than I did."

After breakfast, Dan retired to the back porch to think. The time since he had returned from Ohio had flown because he arrived just in time for Shannon's birth and subsequent christening. He had been busy helping to prepare for the party. He was amazed when he realized he had only been home for a fortnight; it seemed so much longer. Now he would have to settle into the everyday routine of being home. He would see how his parents lived and how they spent their days. But how would he spend his? Dan was pretty much unemployed. Should he look for another kind of work? How long would be a decent time to stay with his parents? They really didn't need his help, at least from what he'd seen so far. Even his father didn't seem as sick as he really was. He still hadn't written to Miriam. Do that today, he told himself.

Dan finished the letter to Miriam and decided to walk to the post office to mail it. A good walk always helped him to think. While he was downtown, Dan went to City Hall to see John Murphy. Dan was still incredulous whenever he remembered that John Murphy was the former Johnny M, the Coltonwood bully of his childhood. John was in his office and glad to see Dan.

"Dan, how are you doing, buddy?"

"I'm Ok, John, thanks. I was wondering if I could help out in some way with the food pantry. I have plenty of time on my hands and nothing much to do."

"Absolutely. You could go to the supermarkets in town and get the day old bread and produce. I've been doing it myself, but frankly, it's very hard for someone like me to do that kind of work. That would be a huge help."

"Excellent. When do I start?"

"How's tomorrow?"

Dan now felt as if he would finally start to do something productive. Helping out at the food pantry would give him a renewed sense of purpose and still give him time to do whatever work would come his way from the newspaper. He felt as excited as a teenager who's just landed his first job. When he arrived home, his mother was up and bustling about the kitchen.

"Where did you go, Chip?"

"I wrote a letter to Miriam and mailed it at the Post Office. Then I stopped in to see John Murphy at City Hall. I'm going to be helping him on Tuesdays and Fridays. I'll go pick up day-old bread and produce from the First National and the IGA. Finally, I'll be making myself useful." Mrs. Kerr received all this information doubtfully.

"Who is Miriam? Your girlfriend in Ohio?"

"No, Mom. I told you about Miriam. She was my landlady in Ohio."

"Oh, I thought your landlady had a different name for some reason. So, you'll be at the food pantry on Fridays?"

"Tuesdays and Fridays."

"What if the newspaper calls you to do some work?"

"No problem. One good thing about the news business is the flexible hours. I can easily do both things without interference. I'm going to visit Mrs. Salina; I'll be gone an hour or so."

"If you're going to visit Francesca, you'll be gone longer than an hour."

Dan crossed the street to the house that he knew as well

as his own. Now the old dilemma. Knock or walk in? Of course, he knocked, and the familiar voice screamed, "Come in!"

"AAAYYY, look who's here. Did you come to talk or eat?"

"Both."

Mrs. Salina wasted no time in placing a huge square of tiramisu in front of Dan, along with a mug of steaming coffee. His neighbor made the best coffee on the planet. No national chain could match it.

With her own coffee cup in hand, Mrs. Salina sat opposite Dan at the table.

Without preamble or warning, Mrs. Salina turned serious. "I'm really glad you came back. Your parents need you, especially your mother."

Dan felt his stomach lurch, his appetite suddenly gone. "My mother? I'm more worried about my father, even though he seems to be doing quite well for someone with stage two cancer."

"Your mother is having difficulty in the head. She's forgetting things she should never forget."

"I wish she could forget about Champ. Her life would be much better if she could move on from that."

Mrs. Salina sighed. "A mother's grief never ends. Don't expect that to happen. I'm not talking about that."

"Does she talk to you about Champ?"

"Not much. She used to, but not too much anymore."

"I'm talking about everyday things. We've been having

coffee together every Wednesday for forty years, but there are days when she doesn't come. I call her and she says she was busy with something, and it slipped her mind. I ask your father and he says she does very little in the house. She's not busy at all. You just got here, and the days were filled with the baby's birth and christening. When she is busy, she's much better. Now she's back to daily life. You won't have to watch too carefully to see a change in her. How long are you planning to stay? You need to think about yourself too. You have a lady friend?"

"I don't know how long I'll stay. No, I don't have the money for a girlfriend. When I was in Ohio, I didn't have time for a girlfriend. Besides, the only woman I would seriously like to marry is you."

"AAAYYY, what would Salina say? Probably you can have her."

"I used to be in love with Angelina."

"AAAYYY, that one. She's living with a loafer on disability. The only disability he has is laziness. She works three jobs, and he calls himself a house husband, whatever that is. She's the one who cooks, cleans, and looks after the kids. He does nothing."

"And Carmella and Sofia?"

"Carmella is single and living with someone. As soon as I learn the name, she has another one. Sofia is divorced. She had a nice guy with a good job. I guess he got sick of her big mouth and complaining. You see, I raised three stunadas. None of them even know how to make sauce. My Bobby has a good job, but he's still single. What can I do?"

"I'll keep an eye on my mother. Thank you for telling me

this. It's not something I want to hear, but it is something I need to know."

"I wish I didn't have to tell you this. But an awful thing is happening, and you need to watch her. She needs to see a doctor for the head. How do you call that?"

"A neurologist."

"She may not be too bad now, but that will change."

"Thanks, Mrs. Salina. You're a doll."

"And you're a big boy now. You call me Francesca. I'll watch your mother and I'll let you know so you can call the screwologist." Dan had to laugh, much to Mrs. Salina's bewilderment. "What's funny?"

"Nothing. See you later."

Dan's laughter quickly faded when he left for home. Never did he expect to encounter so many family problems once he returned from Ohio. In his preoccupation with Champ, he had obviously overlooked some other issues that needed his attention. While he had been visiting with his neighbor, Matt from the newspaper had called. Dan returned the call. "Dan, are you available to cover the school committee meeting tomorrow?" asked Matt.

"Yes, I can do that."

"Fantastic. The meeting is in the auditorium of the junior high school. It starts at seven,"

"Will I get a byline this time?"

"Absolutely. The only reason you didn't last time is because the story was a feature."

"Ok. I can do it. I presume the office will be open afterwards, so I don't have to go back in the morning to write the story."

"Yes, it will be open. The cleaning crew will be there. Just type the story and put it on my desk. I'll take care of the rest. It will run in tomorrow's paper."

That night, the Kerr family had dinner together, all four of them. It still seemed strange to Dan that the family had gotten so small. Biddy was home and could eat with the family. As they dined on lamb chops and party leftovers, Dan asked Biddy what she wanted to do after she finished college.

Biddy chewed for a few seconds and said, "I want to go into business, but not the restaurant business. I've had it with working long hours for measly money. I'm thinking I'd like to own my own business selling cosmetics, nail polish, things like that."

Mr. Kerr piped up, "Why didn't you tell me this a long time ago? I could have signed the business over to you."

Biddy smiled. "Thanks, but no thanks, Dad. Selling tvs and steroes is not my kind of fun. Besides, if I did want to take over the business, you and Mom wouldn't have such a comfortable retirement. I'd feel terrible if you had to go on food stamps."

Mrs. Kerr addressed Dan. "Chip, do you still want to work full- time at the newspaper? Oh, I forgot. Some man named Sam, or something called for you."

"You didn't forget. You told me, Mom. I have to cover the school committee meeting tomorrow night."

Now Dan could understand Mrs. Salina's concern.

Mrs. Kerr remained silent for a few minutes, then said, "Chip, why don't you talk to Pup? He belongs to the Rotary Club. He knows a lot of people in town. He could help you find a job."

"I appreciate your concern, Mom. But I'm a writer. I'm not interested in just any old job. Writing is in my DNA. It's something I have to do."

"Writing is in your what?"

"DNA. That means that writing is part of my genetic makeup. Just like building is part of Pup's genetic makeup."

"I know where Pup gets his talent for building from your grandfather. I don't know where you got your talent for writing. Certainly not from me."

The next morning, Dan drove to the First National to pick up bread and produce for the food pantry. He went to a door at the back of the store as directed by John. Dan was amazed at the amount of food that was piled into his car. His plan had been to stop at both stores, but he would have to make a delivery to the food pantry before he could go to the IGA. He and John arranged the food in bins in a room that was much too small for all that they had. John wouldn't open the food pantry until noon because an earlier opening could deplete the shelves in a few minutes.

Chip made his haul at the IGA and returned with another carload of bread and produce. He and John stacked the shelves, and the pantry opened for business. Dan had to flatten all the boxes and put them outside in the dumpster. By the time he was finished, Dan was tired.

"John," he asked, "did you do all this work yourself before me?"

"Yeah, I did. You're the first person to actually volunteer to help. If I didn't do it, it wouldn't get done."

After an hour-long nap and a quick supper, Dan made his way to the middle school to cover the meeting. Spectators were few; he counted nine other people besides himself. The meeting was notable for its tedium. It was almost as though the committee was meeting in secret. No one from the audience asked a question or volunteered an opinion. Dan raced to the front of the room to ask the chairman a question. The man gave Dan that steely eyed stare that was ingrained in most citizens of Coltonwood: that circle the wagons mentality born of a serious suspicion of strangers.

"Sir, could I ask you a question?"

The man cleared his throat. "Are you a parent of a student in the district?"

"No, I'm not. I'm a reporter from the *Clarion*."

The man frowned. "This is highly irregular. I've never been asked a question by a local reporter. Are you new around here?"

"No. I grew up here. I used to live in Ohio, but I recently relocated."

The local connection softened the man immediately. He smiled and said, "Fire away."

Dan asked the question, but the convoluted response had absolutely nothing to do with what he'd asked. The man strolled away, and Dan was struck by the similarity of people elected to serve the taxpayers. Covering meetings in Coltonwood was exactly the same as in Ohio. These people must have a notebook of canned responses for the rare occasions when they are asked to explain something.

The office was dark and quiet, and Dan wrote the story as quickly as possible. He searched his notes for a quote that sounded at least somewhat original. After three tries, he found one and incorporated it into the story. He arrived home just before midnight. Dan tried to read, but Champ kept interrupting his concentration. Dan had done very little to try to locate Champ, and now, in the dark of night, his conscience pricked him. "You have to find him." In the morning, he vowed to write to Senator Kennedy, for whatever it was worth. Images of Champ gave way to images of his mother slowly sinking into the abyss of dementia, of his father being ravaged from within by cancer, of Gabby becoming a victim of domestic violence. Sleep eluded him for most of the night. When he first returned home, he was free from troubling thoughts. Now they were back, determined to assail him at every turn.

The next morning, a groggy Dan picked up the phone. It was Matt. "Dan, I just got a call from Hank Goodwin, the chairman of the school committee. He says you asked him a question after the meeting."

"I did. Is that a crime in Coltonwood? That's what reporters do. They ask questions."

Matt actually laughed. "Technically, that's what we do, but the standard procedure is to introduce yourself before the meeting and tell the chair if there will be questions later."

An incredulous Dan sputtered, "Are you kidding me? Are these people so inarticulate they can't think on their feet? What's the point of covering the meeting?"

"No. It's just that you surprised him and didn't give your name."

"He didn't ask. I told him I was from the paper."

"No biggie. I'm sure he'll accommodate you from now on. You're a local guy, so you're golden."

"Good God," Dan thought as he hung up the phone. "What have I gotten myself into?"

In the days that followed, Dan was extra vigilant, watching both parents as closely as possible without being intrusive. When he wasn't at the food pantry, Dan felt a little lost, like someone exploring the same island, looking for something he hadn't seen on his previous trips. The ebb and flow of life with his parents was actually pretty boring, at least to him. His father was predictable; his mother was not. Every day his father would read the paper and attempt to eat breakfast. Once the obits had been finished, Mr. Kerr would pick at whatever was left of his food and finish his coffee. If it was a nice day, he would take a walk downtown, stopping to chat with everyone he knew. This could take the majority of the morning. Dan marveled that a man with stage two cancer would be able to stay on his feet for so long. Mr. Kerr would return home only to leave again at twelve-thirty to meet his buddies at MacDonald's for more coffee and a treat. During the afternoon, he would nap for an hour or two, but was refreshed in time for supper.

Mrs. Kerr was just the opposite. Many mornings she rose late, sometimes after ten. On those days, breakfast was cereal and toast. On other days, she would be in the kitchen cooking eggs before eight. Her routine was no routine. Sometimes she would do some light housework or just sit with the paper, frequently dozing. Other times, she would sit on the porch and listen to the radio playing from the kitchen. Dan didn't know if he should approach her or not. The woman had raised eight kids; she was entitled to some quiet time. Yet Mrs. Kerr was a sociable sort. She loved to talk in person and on the phone. Since Dan had returned home, the only times he saw his mother talk on the phone was to one of the kids about the christening party. The phone had been strangely silent since the party ended. He wondered if his mother would remember to have coffee with Mrs. Salina this week. Dan wondered how often his sibs visited or called. So far, no one had made any contact save for the party. Perhaps it was time for Dan to make the first move. He didn't want to carry this knowledge alone. He had to tell someone. Mimi had enough to do and enough worries with her brood of kids; she wouldn't be his first choice. Pup was the logical choice, especially since he had always been his mother's favorite. Even now, Mrs. Kerr was loath to criticize him, even when he clearly deserved it. Dan decided he would call Pup tomorrow and make arrangements to meet with him.

Pup was able to accommodate Dan the next day. They agreed to meet for a beer at a local pub. Pup was late, but that was nothing new. When he did arrive, it was like a head of state had just stepped off a plane. Several guys at the bar got up to shake Pup's hand. Of course, Pup had to talk to each one, leaving Dan to wait in the booth until he was good and ready to sit. Once he did and they ordered beer and wings, Pup's beeper kept going off and Pup would stop what he was saying and stare at the beeper.

"Who gave you that? Elaine?" asked Dan.

"No. This is my work beeper. My guys are always asking questions that need immediate answers, so I got myself one of these. Real high tech."

"Do you take that thing to the Rotary Club meetings so the other guys can see how indispensable you are to the company?"

"No way. That's my time away from work. If they have questions, they have to wait."

"Well, why not pretend you're at a Rotary meeting and put that thing away? I have to have a talk with you about Mom."

Pup bit into a wing and took a long swig of beer. "What now?"

"Mrs. Salina thinks Mom might be in an early stage of dementia. I think she's right. I've been watching Mom, and she does act differently than she used to."

"Francesca never knows when to mind her own business. She's had too much of Salina's homemade wine. I wouldn't put too much stock in anything she says."

Dan's anger flared. This was a side of Pup he couldn't stand; that cynical assumption that everyone had an agenda. "You need to remember, Pup, that Mrs. Salina is a family friend, especially to Mom. She's not some ridiculous crackpot who has nothing else to do but tell tales."

Pup said, "I don't mean to ride herd on Francesca; she is a nice lady, but do you know if she's mentioned this to Dad?"

"I don't know if she has or not."

"You can bet she hasn't because he'd demand proof and she wouldn't be able to produce any. You need to speak to Dad and ask if he's noticed anything. He does live with Mom, Francesca does not. He would be the logical person to ask."

Granted, Pup had a point. Dan would have to find an opportunity to speak to his father.

"Look, Pup. I didn't ask you here to start a fight. I'm concerned about what Mrs. Salina told me, and I thought you should know."

"Who's fighting? I don't want this to become the next in an unending line of Kerr family crises. We've had enough of those. Discuss this with Dad and see what he thinks, and we'll take it from there. By the way, I called Gabby and apologized for my behavior at the party. Not that I'm all that sorry, but Elaine gave me holy hell as we drove home, so I didn't really have a choice."

"How did Gabby sound?"

"Fine, I guess. I really do feel kind of bad for her. But she made her bed now she has to lie in it."

With that, Pup finished the wings and picked up the check.

"This one's on me.

CHAPTER 5

WHEN DAN AND CHAMP WERE KIDS, THEY would anxiously await the mailman in the days before Christmas. When he would arrive in the lowering late December light, they would run for the door with Bridy toddling behind. Together they would sift through the cards and see who sent greetings to the Kerr family. The same ritual was repeated after a fashion many years later when Dan was a high school senior, anxiously awaiting his acceptance letters. Every afternoon after school, Dan would comb through the mail hoping to see the envelope that pointed to his future. Now he had to be much more clandestine after he wrote to Senator Kennedy. He had rented a post office box so his parents wouldn't see the letter that might engender false hope. Dan would check the box every day during his walk, but so far, he had been disappointed. However, the day after his semi-disastrous meeting with Pup, there it was. Elbows on the tables provided at the post office, Dan carefully opened the letter. The contents surprised him so much; he had to read the letter three times.

Senator Kennedy informed him of an agency that had been formed for the sole purpose of finding the remains of missing servicemen from all previous wars. It was almost like an archaeological dig as men worked to unearth and identify remains. Dan's hands shook as he read the letter. Finally, he might have some hope of locating Champ. The letter had warned that the work was slow and tedious and nothing was guaranteed. Dan didn't care. That night he penned a letter to the person in charge of the project and calmly asked for the name of Pfc. Dennis F. Kerr be added to the list of missing servicemen.

When Dan went to work at the food pantry the next day, he couldn't wait to tell John Murphy. Between sips of coffee, Dan related to John the particulars of the Senator's letter. "What kills me," said Dan, "is that dumb ass Veterans' Agent didn't so much as mention this to me. He must know about it."

"Sorry, man. I really thought that Sam would be able to help you. I can't speak for him, but I think Sam sees his mission as geared for the living, not the dead. But it does seem strange that he wouldn't know anything about this agency or whatever it is."

"Well, I sent the letter back this morning. I'm willing to wait it out. You and my cousin Bart are the only people who know about this. My family has suddenly become so crazy, I don't dare tell anyone else."

John grinned. "Don't worry. Your secret's safe with me."

*****

"Mom, will you teach me how to cook?" Dan surprised his mother with this question one September morning at breakfast.

"Will I what?"

"Teach me to cook."

Mrs. Kerr looked pointedly at Dan. "Don't you like my cooking anymore? You couldn't get enough of it when you were a kid."

"No. I love your cooking. It's just that I want to learn; it's a skill I'd like to acquire."

"What did you do when you were in Ohio?"

"Miriam cooked for me. Whatever she made, she would share with me. Otherwise, I'd be subsisting on Ramen noodles and hot dogs. I do know how to boil noodles and hot dogs. That's the extent of my culinary expertise."

Mrs. Kerr's smile was sly. "If you'd get married, you wouldn't have to worry about cooking. Your wife would do it."

Dan sighed. He was tired of these not-so-subtle hints that he should be married. "Mom, correct me if I'm wrong, but I think you need to meet someone before you can get married. I haven't met anyone I want to marry."

"What about Maria in Ohio?"

"Her name is Miriam, and she's just a few years younger than you. Not a good match for me."

"You can watch me cook American chop suey tonight if you like."

"Super."

Later that day, Dan received a call from Matt. "Dan, you are now the official meeting correspondent. You will cover the City Council, the Planning Board, the School Committee, and the Conservation Commission. I'll mail you the schedule for the month. Also, the editorial board has added a new feature once a week, a cheesy article on city officials. Guess who will be doing the interviews?"

"I take it that would be me. Who's the first victim?"

"None other than His Honor himself. Before the end of the week, you can see his secretary and book a time for the interview."

That will be a pleasure, thought Dan. He had gotten to know the mayor's secretary, Rosalina, through the food pantry. She was one of the most dependable donors. Sometimes she would bring coffee to John and Dan and sit and talk. Dan liked her. She was smart, articulate, and funny. He'd thought about asking her out, but he was unsure of her status and too embarrassed to ask John. That information would come in time.

Dan was settling in nicely in his new/old home. His star was rising at the newspaper, which left him poised to fill any unexpected vacancies which happen often with small operations. The more he could show his face around town, the better. He got an unexpected boost that very afternoon when his father asked if he would like to go for coffee with him and his buddies. Dan accepted immediately. Mr. Kerr decided he wanted to drive, which to Dan was strange. Usually, he did the driving whenever he went somewhere with his parents. He felt like a teenager being driven by his father, but he rather liked it as well. This was the perfect time to talk to his father about his mother.

"Dad, have you noticed anything different about Mom?"

"How so?"

"I mean, does she seem forgetful or out of it sometimes?"

Mr. Kerr mulled this over. "Not that I can see. Everyone our age is forgetful to a certain extent. I wouldn't worry too much about it. Why do you ask?"

"It's just that Mrs. Salina told me she's worried about Mom, that she's getting forgetful."

"Francesca said that? Did she mention anything in particular?"

"Yes. She said that Mom has been missing their Wednesday coffee together, a ritual they've had for a lot of years."

"Francesca mentioned that now that I think about it. Well, here we are. Come and meet my buddies."

Dan wanted to continue the conversation, but his father was anxious to see his friends and drink his coffee. Three older men clustered around a table near the window facing the street. Mr. Kerr introduced them to Dan. All three looked somewhat familiar, but their names didn't ring any bells with Dan, who used this time to listen to what these men had to say, especially about life in Coltonwood. It almost felt like an assignment for the paper. They did not disappoint Dan. The men complained about the tax rate, the mayor, their ward councilors, trash pickup or lack of, traffic congestion, the price of gas. The string of complaints was endless. Part of Dan's mind wondered why anyone would sit and have coffee with people who did nothing but complain, but another part understood why. This was a chance for these men to get some things off their chests, to be with other people who thought the same as they did. Everything was fine until Mr. Kerr volunteered that Dan worked for the local paper.

The most vocal critic, a heavyset man named Dick, demanded to know why the paper was not more critical of the mayor, whom he described in such unflattering language that Dan was taken aback.

"I think the paper likes this bastard. They never write what he really does, like go on vacation for weeks at a time, leaving the city in the hands of the City Council, who are also a bunch of weasels."

Dan tried to explain that the editorial board of the paper set the tone for whatever stance the paper took on the mayor or the local issues. He suggested the man write a letter to the editor and demand an explanation of the paper's policy.

"Wouldn't do any good," Dick rasped. "Nobody in the government in this city listens to what the citizens and taxpayers have to say." Translation: this guy just likes to complain; he's too lazy to even write a letter.

On the way home, Mr. Kerr turned to Dan. "Did I tell you Gabby called the other day?"

"No. What did she want? Don't tell me she married Stanley on the sly."

"No, nothing like that. She wanted to know if she and Stanley could come for Thanksgiving. She said they want to talk about the wedding. They're looking at a date in the spring. Now that will make your mother happy."

Dan winced. The thought of sitting through Thanksgiving dinner with Stanley was painful. The thought that Gabby really intended to marry him was even more so. It was useless to argue. Stanley had bamboozled the Kerrs into thinking he was a good guy and a good match for Gabby. He knew that once the Kerrs embraced someone, that bond was for life. Since they had gotten lucky with Neil and Carl, their good guy sons-in-law, they assumed that Stanley would be good guy number three.

Mrs. Kerr allowed her son to watch her cook that night. When they were ready to start, Mrs. Kerr was fumbling through the junk drawer, obviously looking for something.

Dan, somewhat alarmed, said, "What are you looking for, Mom?"

Not looking up, Mrs. Kerr replied, "My recipe for chop suey."

"Why do you need a recipe? I can pretty much do this in my head. You never used a recipe when you made this when we were kids."

"Do you remember how I did it?"

"Of course. It was one of my favorites."

As Dan busied himself with preparations, he eyed his mother surreptitiously. He didn't like the look in her eyes, sort of a faraway, vacant stare. He knew then Mrs. Salina was right. His mother did have a problem that needed to be attended to as soon as possible.

Dan tried hard to make small talk as he cooked, but his mother would just use her mad tone: "umm," "yeah" to whatever he would say. He remembered that from childhood. These non-answers to questions usually meant she was angry about something but didn't want to say what. The trick was to get her to say what was bothering her, but that was like pulling teeth. Dan successfully cooked his first meal, much to the delight of his mother, who was very much herself as they sat to dinner.

That night Dan was jolted awake by a dream about Champ. In the dream, he and Champ were boys having one of their many fights. Champ was unusually violent, grabbing chairs, lamps, books, whatever he could get his hands on and flinging them at Dan. His face was that of a man, but his body and tone of voice were boyish. He kept shouting over and over, "Give it back to me! You stole it and hid it. I want it back. You have to find it." Finally, his fury spent, Champ collapsed on the bed and disappeared. Dan awoke covered in sweat, the bedclothes on the floor. His chest gasped and heaved. He looked at the room, but nothing had been disturbed. Sleep eluded him for the rest of the night.

Dan's skin was still crawling from the nightmare when he showered and ate the next day. Only one thought cheered him. Today was the day he would make the appointment to interview the mayor. That meant, of course, that he would see Rosalina, the mayor's secretary. Dan loved her name. It conjured images of haciendas and ladies in mantillas and swirling skirts whirling to sultry Latin rhythms. He would have to put on his reporter's hat to find out if she was married or not. Then the word married made him think of Gabby and his skin crawled again.

Dan wanted to arrive at the mayor's office early with the conscious intention of asking Rosalina to lunch. However, when he got there, she was just finishing her sandwich. He poked his head through the half-open door. "Good morning."

"Hi, Dan. Please excuse me. When the mayor's away, I like to eat at my desk and catch up on work. Come in. What can I do for you?"

"My paper wants me to interview the mayor for a new series on local government officials. He's the first one."

Rosalina smiled. "Well, I'm afraid you'll have to wait a week. The mayor is away and not expected back for at least another week. Do you want to make the appointment now or wait until he's here? I would advise you to wait since he frequently cancels appointments when he's just returned from vacation."

"The managing editor isn't going to like this. He was hoping to run the feature next week. But if you think I should wait, I will."

"I just don't want you to plan out your day and then have him cancel at the last minute. He's away a lot, so I frequently have to tell people to reschedule. Most people are not as nice as you're being. There are many people who would love to wring the mayor's neck."

"Are you one of them?"

"Actually, no. I like the mayor, but you need a lot of patience with him. Of course, I see a side of him that most other people don't."

Dan decided to take the plunge. "Would you like to go for coffee since your boss isn't here? He won't know if you take an hour off."

Rosalina smiled warmly at Dan. "Thank you for the offer, but everyone knows when the mayor's secretary isn't in her office. I will take a rain check for that coffee, but I have to stay here since many distinguished citizens love to stop by the office."

"For what if he's not here?"

The warm smile again. "To see me, I guess."

*****

With each passing day, fall was tightening its frigid fingers with dustings of frost, especially in the early mornings. Dan had always loved the fall and the football games that came with it. He never missed a game when he was in high school. Pup played for four years and Champ for three. Dan was always more of a spectator than a participant but having brothers on the team conferred a certain status, at least in his hometown. He loved Saturday afternoons when he would go to a home game with either his friend Bobby or school buddy, Saba, Ron Sabacinsky. Even if neither one could go, Dan went alone, confident he would find someone to sit with. He always walked to the game, even in the rain. His allowance would be burning a hole in his pocket, and he would buy a hot dog and a drink. The best days were early in the season, sunny lazy afternoons made exciting by the sound of the high school band and the cheerleaders spurring on the Colts of Coltonwood High. Even now, the memory of those days could quicken Dan's pulse.

But this was the beginning of a new decade and much had changed since the glory days of the sixties. Now the team played under the lights on Friday nights. The opponents were the same, but Dan didn't know any of the players. Still, the lure was there, and Dan attended the opening game of the 1980 season. The lights were as bright as day. The crowd was large and enthusiastic, but still Dan felt a little sad; it just wasn't the same. The biggest change was the cold. At least at afternoon games, the sun would be warm, but there wasn't a ghost of warmth at a night game. The bleachers were now metal, not wood, and very cold. He began to regret that he had not driven; it would be a cold walk home. Even more amazing was the price of a ticket. He figured a few bucks would get him past the gate. Instead, Dan had to break a ten, leaving him with just enough change to buy himself a coffee.

When he was a boy, Dan could count on seeing teachers selling tickets or working in the concession stand. He knew one of the science teachers was in the booth as the public address announcer. Several other teachers would prowl the sidelines as coaches. Dan felt a little lonely when he looked around, vainly hoping to see at least one familiar face. He saw none. With nowhere to sit, Dan had no choice but to walk around, hands in pockets, and try to watch the game. After fifteen minutes of doing so, he was cold and ready to leave. Dan decided to buy a coffee and then head for home. The line at the concession stand was so long that he almost left. The woman who handed him the coffee smiled at him from underneath a baseball cap. "Here you go, Dan. No charge." He took a second look. The woman was Rosalina. He hadn't recognized her. His heart did a somersault, and no words came. Feeling like a fumbling adolescent fool, Dan took a sip of coffee, almost spilling it. "Thanks, Rosalina. Is this your second job?"

She laughed. "I volunteer my time at the games. My son is on the team."

Dan felt his heart drop. She is married. She has a son. How unexpectedly he had found out Rosalina's status.

"You don't look old enough to have a son in high school," Dan spluttered to cover his disappointment and embarrassment.

"Oh, I am, but I can't talk now. See you later." Now Dan realized that a line of at least ten people had formed behind him, people not too happy to wait for their coffee while he babbled to Rosalina. Dan muttered a halfhearted apology and walked right out the main gate. The football game that he was so looking forward to ended up being nothing but an exercise in futility. He sipped his coffee as he stalked home. Disordered thoughts pinged in his brain as he slouched on his way. He regretted his decision to return from Ohio. It seemed that home meant nothing but problems, and he had become the point person to identify and solve them. Maybe it was time to move on and start afresh somewhere else. Dan knew that he couldn't leave now. He was much too embroiled in his family's lives to just bolt. He would have to accept the present as it was and plan for the future. Dan had hoped that the future included Rosalina, but that didn't seem to be the case now.

Once his brain fog cleared, Dan decided he had to have some kind of action plan for the next few months. Number one had to be his mother's health. Somehow, he had to get her evaluated so at least the family would know her status. Second, he would have to get some sort of medical briefing on his father's health, which continued to baffle him. Mr. Kerr didn't show any signs of serious illness. He was active and alert and busy. Could the doctors have made a mistake? Was his father in remission? For how long? He needed answers to these questions.

Despite all the problems, Dan was beginning to enjoy life in Coltonwood. His work at the food pantry was rewarding and fulfilling in a way he never could have imagined. Covering local meetings was dull work, but necessary if he ever wanted to rise in the ranks at the paper. Thanks to his daily walks, Dan was in the best shape he had been in since college. The walks had an added psychological advantage: he could clear his head and think without all the baggage interfering.

Dan knew that the chances of ever finding Champ's remains were slim, but he checked the post office box every day anyway. He groped to remember a poem by Emily Dickinson that he had read in college, something about hope and feathers. The poem was short but loaded with meaning. Aside from his walks and work at the food pantry and the paper, the thing that helped his morale more than anything was his growing skill as a cook. Dan loved to go to the store and buy whatever he would need to create dinner that night. He had relied on his mother's recipes, but now he was ready to venture into riskier territory and try some dishes his mother had never cooked. Best of all, his mother loved when he cooked and she loved the result. Dan was buoyed by the fact that Thanksgiving would be at the Kerr home this year. Gram Kerr would be spending the holiday in Poughkeepsie with Bart's family. Usually, she would host Thanksgiving as she had done every year of Dan's life. It was time to create some new traditions, especially since his grandmother was well into her nineties. This was Dan's chance to help the family move forward.

Dan was disconsolate after the fiasco of the football game and finding out that Rosalina was indeed married. He chastised himself for making an adolescent fantasy into something real. He had secretly deluded himself into thinking that he could have a future with Rosalina. Time to forget her and move on. Yet that was impossible since he saw her all the time at the food pantry and there was still the matter of his interview with the mayor. He would have to make the appointment with Rosalina, and there was no way to avoid that. Dan decided to take the path of least resistance and call for the appointment rather than make a personal appearance. His hands shook a little as he dialed the phone and, much to his relief, he got Rosalina's voice mail. He left the information and quickly hung up.

The next time he worked at the food pantry, John asked if he was all right. Dan assured him that he was just a little tired. He'd be fine once he started stacking shelves and greeting customers. He became so engrossed in his work that he didn't notice Rosalina when she stopped in with a bag of groceries. The sound of her voice actually startled him.

"Hi, Dan. Where would you like me to leave this bag?"

Dan reddened and tried to cover his embarrassment by moving boxes and bags to make room for Rosalina's donation.

Rosalina continued, "I got your message. You have an appointment with the mayor on Friday at one o'clock. Make sure you're on time. He's notorious for missing appointments, but he won't wait for someone who's even a minute late."

"Thanks. I'll make sure I'm early."

Dan was up late Thursday evening, he read all he could about the mayor and formulated questions that the mayor couldn't fudge. It had been a while since he had interviewed a public official at length, and he wanted to get it right. Dan was early and Rosalina was at her desk, looking lovely as always. They made small talk as Dan waited to be summoned to the inner sanctum. He noticed the furnishings and carpeting in Rosalina's office were all new and expensive. Her desk was enormous, and her chair effectively swallowed her small frame.

"Nice digs. Is all this new?"

"Yes. As soon as he was elected, the mayor ordered all new furniture and carpets for his office and mine. Wait until you see his office. It looks like a room in the White House."

With that, the massive door opened, and the mayor summoned Dan with a wave of his arm and hurried back to his chair behind a desk the size of a small ship. Dan extended his hand and introduced himself, but the mayor declined to extend his. This irritated Dan and he decided to make this interview one the mayor would never forget. He flipped open his pad and began.

"Mr. Mayor, how can you justify the fact that you gave yourself a five percent raise two weeks after you took office, yet the city's union employees had to settle for one percent and in some cases, zero?"

As Dan waited for the mayor's answer, he didn't know if he was more surprised by the mayor's youth or his arrogance. His Honor settled into his immense chair and looked at the ceiling as he began his reply.

"I justify it by saying that my job is more important and stressful than any job held by a union employee. You see, it's just me. I have to make the decisions, I have to take the flak, I have to make Coltonwood look good, I have to attract industry, I have to attend every opening of every business from hair salons to day cares. Other city workers work together. They're like bees in the hive or ants in the anthill. They work together for the life of the hive or the hill." The mayor smiled, obviously pleased by his alliterative response.

"Are you saying that your job is more dangerous than that of a firefighter or a cop? Or more challenging than that of a teacher?"

"Hell, most of the fires in this city are small-time stuff. Those guys spend more time playing cards at the station than they do fighting fires. Same thing with the cops. Most of them ride around in their cruisers all day and drink coffee. As for the teachers, they're seasonal employees. They have more time off than Congress. They don't deserve anything."

"I see." Before Dan could say anything else, the mayor expanded upon his answer. "I was elected because I promised the taxpayers that I would not raise taxes for any reason. I'm their watchdog and they expect me to be an attack dog if necessary. The unions were used to getting anything they wanted in the past. It was time to end that practice."

"But a lot of union people live in Coltonwood and pay taxes. How can you justify denying them raises they've earned after the service they've given to the city?"

"I get that, but fiscal restraint is job number one for me. We all have to tighten our belts to make Coltonwood run in the black rather than the red."

"Then how can you justify all the new furniture and carpeting in your office? This must have cost a lot of money. None of the other offices in City Hall have been done over, just yours."

"People expect the mayor's office to look good. I invite people from business and industry to this office and I want them to leave with a good impression. A dumpy office sends the wrong message."

The mayor glanced at his watch. "I have a meeting in ten minutes. Any other questions?"

"Tell me about your background."

The mayor settled back in his comfy chair, now not at all hurried. "I was born and raised in Coltonwood. I'm a graduate of Coltonwood High, Class of 1972. I graduated from Norwich University and then did a hitch in the Navy. After the service, I came back and went into my dad's business, Leaders Building Supply. I served on the City Council, the youngest ever elected and now as mayor, also as the youngest ever. I know your brother John very well. He's a great customer of the business. Great guy. He should run for mayor when my term is up. He could win in a landslide."

Dan stood, as did the mayor. This time he extended his hand to Dan along with his million-dollar pol's smile. "I'm happy to know you, Mr. Kerr. Call on me anytime."

"Thanks, Mr. Mayor."

"When will this piece be in the paper?"

"Next Wednesday."

Rosalina looked up as the door to the mayor's office opened. Her smile faded when she saw Dan.

"You look like you could use some coffee."

"I could use more than that."

Rosalina leaned in. "The mayor will be leaving soon. Meet me at Zippy's. We can have that coffee we both need."

Dan left in a daze. Had Rosalina just asked him for a date? Big deal. It meant nothing if she was married. Nevertheless, he settled himself into a booth at Zippy's and looked over his notes while he waited. This mayor was a major nut job. Dan was still astounded by what he saw as he was leaving the office. In one corner there was a poster of Kiss on an easel, in another a poster of Alice Cooper. He wondered what the captains of industry who visited the office, not to mention the taxpayers, thought of those posters. Dan was flummoxed by the whole experience with the mayor. He wondered how on earth he could write an unbiased profile of this wing nut.

Rosalina slid into the booth opposite Dan. She smiled. "I felt bad at the football game that we couldn't talk. I looked for you when I had a break, but evidently you had left."

"Yes, I left. I was cold, and I had to walk home. I know I'm showing my age, but I don't like football games on Friday nights. It was nothing like the games on Saturday afternoons in the sun and the parade after if the team won. That was the last game I'll go to. I was really disappointed." Rosalina had no way of knowing that Dan left because of her, not necessarily the cold.

"A traditionalist, obviously. My son is a freshman and plays sparingly, but I like to be at the games with the other parents. Coltonwood has a good booster club. We've raised a lot of money for sports."

"Does your husband go also?"

Rosalina sipped her coffee. "He might. We're divorced, so I don't know his schedule. He has the kids most weekends, but they don't say much when they come home. You might know him. He was the quarterback on the team that your brother Dennis played on. Bryant Wilson. Does the name ring a bell?"

Dan sat bolt upright. "Yes. Champ used to talk about him all the time."

"Champ?"

"Sorry. That's his family nickname. We all have family nicknames."

"What's yours?"

"Chip."

"That's perfect for you. I think I'll start calling you Chip instead of Dan."

Dan became serious. "Rosalina, I really need to talk to you about the mayor. I think the guy is deeply disturbed, but I don't think we should have this conversation here. What are you doing Saturday night?"

"Having dinner with you. I'll be ready at six."

*****

Dan and Rosalina cruised east on Route 9. Their destination was the restaurant where Dan's parents always celebrated their anniversary. During the ride, Dan told Rosalina about John Murphy's history as the most feared bully in Coltonwood.

Rosalina listened, clearly mystified by Dan's tale. "I can't believe the John Murphy I know was once a bully. He wouldn't hurt a fly."

Dan agreed. "Not now, but there was a time when John, known as Johnny M. could and usually beat up any kid he wanted to. Naturally, no self- respecting bully would beat up a girl. It just wasn't done. Johnny's special targets were the guys at St. Tom's. I'm sure he probably tuned up a lot of public-school guys, but he really had it in for St. Tom's. He was a scrawny kid, but quick on his feet and even quicker with his fists."

"I've never heard anything about him, and I have a brother around your age. He never mentioned him."

"Maybe not, but Johnny was a legend around the downtown area."

"Do you know how he was paralyzed? I never had the heart to ask him."

"Yes. I remember it well. Johnny had set fire to some boxes behind the hardware store downtown. He was running away when he ran into traffic and was hit immediately. Nobody expected him to live, but the docs sent him to Boston to some special hospital and he not only lived but changed his whole life around. His father was an alcoholic. Supposedly, he left town and hasn't been seen since Johnny's accident. Many years later, Johnny and his mother returned to Coltonwood."

Rosalina still didn't appear convinced. "It just seems strange that I never knew any of this. Coltonwood was a small place then. Usually everybody knew everything that happened."

Dan pulled into the parking lot and had a hard time finding a place to park. He said a silent prayer that he had made reservations. Dan and Rosalina were seated immediately and ordered a bottle of red wine.

Rosalina looked around. "I've never been here before. I know this place is known for its salad dressing. Good choice."

Dan smiled, then turned serious. "Rosalina, I have to speak to you about the mayor. I'm still appalled by his demeanor and lack of knowledge. It seems like Coltonwood elected the village idiot to lead the city. I've even thought of drafting an initiative petition to have him recalled."

Rosalina sipped her wine and swallowed a piece of bread. "I've known the mayor for a long time. His mother and my mother have been friends as far back as I can remember. He's a spoiled rich kid, for sure, but he's not dumb. I do believe he has the best interests of the people at heart. It's just that he's in over his head. One of the reasons he takes so much time off is he attends conferences and gatherings to try to woo business and industry to Coltonwood. His biggest problem is his age. Older people just don't take him seriously."

"There's more to it than that. What's up with the posters of Kiss and Alice Cooper in his office? It looks like the bedroom of a heavy metal moron. How could anyone really take someone like that seriously? He spends a ton of money on carpeting and furniture and then puts these posters in the room. It doesn't make any sense."

"I agree with you on that. It does seem incongruous. I've tried to gently suggest that he remove them, but he won't. Some members of the City Council have demanded that they be removed, but the mayor is just implacable. I think he derives comfort from seeing his favorite groups around him, but it is definitely adolescent. You're not the first to think seriously of recall. The City Council is just about ready to draft the petition you mentioned."

"Does the mayor know this?"

"Yes, he does, but he doesn't take it seriously. His father is a big shot in town and most of the members of the council are in his debt for one thing or another, so it's highly unlikely that he will be removed. The voters are going to have to vote him out."

Dan felt himself getting a little hot under the collar. He didn't invite Rosalina to dinner to have it turn into a political round table. Time to change the subject. Dan tried to remember the last time he had wined and dined a woman. Far too long ago. Rosalina was unique. She was intelligent and well spoken, but he didn't really know her, yet he would take as long as necessary to find out.

CHAPTER 6

DAN AND ROSALINA SAW EACH OTHER AT least once a week. Whenever she could, Rosalina would sneak out of her office and get coffee at Zippy's and she and Dan and John would take a break. John seemed amused by their relationship, but he never teased either of them. One afternoon after their impromptu coffee klatch, the mayor paid an unannounced visit to the food pantry. He stood for a moment in the doorway and then greeted both men. The mayor must have liked the piece Dan wrote about him, for he greeted Dan cordially, the polar opposite of their first meeting. His Honor asked John if he needed anything, and John didn't hesitate. "I need more space. November and December are the busiest months and there is just not enough room in here to store all the food that will come in. Even an old closet will do for storage. I need it as soon as possible."

The mayor seemed taken somewhat aback by John's bluntness, but he agreed to find some space. John asked if there was room in any other buildings downtown that could serve as a permanent home for the food pantry. The mayor said he would ask the various heads of agencies if they had any space to spare. John said, "The pantry has to remain as close to downtown as possible. A lot of the people who come here live near Main St. and some don't have transportation. People leave here with bundles of food and walk home. It's necessary that the pantry be accessible to these people. They're the ones who need it the most."

The mayor promised to get back to John as soon as he could. Dan thought it odd that the mayor had never mentioned the article Dan had written. But, then again, the mayor was rather odd. At least he took the time to make a personal appearance, and there wasn't even a crowd around.

The profile Dan would write for the month of November was that of John Murphy himself. Dan was pleased that Matt at the paper was using his head. There was no better time to highlight the director of the food pantry than in the month of Thanksgiving with Christmas hard on its heels. This would be an easy interview for Dan. He could easily write the profile himself, but he would interview John, who never failed to surprise him with little tidbits about himself. John Murphy was a most interesting guy.

"I'll agree to this on one condition," John admonished Dan. "This article has to be about the food pantry, not about me. Agreed?"

"Yes, sir. Don't worry. I won't mention all the times you wanted to beat me up."

"I still could. My arms are ten times stronger than they were then. You should mention my accident. People are always wondering why I'm in a wheelchair. Most think I was disabled in Viet Nam, and I want to correct that mistaken notion right now. I'm not a war hero, far from it. No need to go into a lot of detail, just the facts so people will understand."

"Got it. Anything else you particularly want to highlight?"

"Yeah. Please emphasize that the pantry operates year-round. Our donations are over the top in November and December, then fall to practically nothing in January. Hunger doesn't revolve around holidays. Not that I'm not grateful for people's generosity around the Holidays, I am, but it shouldn't end there."

"Ok. Anything else?"

"Yeah. We need more room. We also need more shelving and storage containers. But the greatest need is for space. As I told the mayor, the pantry needs a permanent home. There is a lot of hunger and need in this city, whether people acknowledge it or not. The food pantry should not be a place that people are ashamed to go. It should become a part of life here. People's circumstances can change in the blink of an eye, and this pantry should be accessible and available to anyone in need."

Dan had seldom heard John speak so forcefully. He was a passionate advocate for the disenfranchised and his voice needed to be heard through Dan. Almost everyone in Coltonwood read the paper every day, even though most lamented its lack of content. The word will get out, if only people would respond.

John actually interviewed Dan, much to the amusement of the scribe. The profile would be easy to write, much easier than the profile of the mayor. After he filed the story, Dan went home for some rest when his grandmother called. No rest for him now.

"Daniel, I loved the piece you wrote about the mayor, that putz."

"Thanks, Gram. I take it you don't like the mayor."

"You take it correctly. Why anyone would vote for someone like him is beyond me. People in this city are just plain stupid."

"Did you call to tell me that, Gram?"

Dan heard a chuckle. "No, I didn't. Do you know I won't be having Thanksgiving this year? I'm going to Poughkeepsie for a brief vacation. Ha."

"Yes, I knew. I'm hosting this year and I'm very sad that you won't be here. I always associate Thanksgiving with you. Now I have to rearrange my thought process. That's hard to do."

"Well, you'll have to try. Your aunt and uncle are coming to get me later this week. I know what they have up their sleeves. They think just because I'm over ninety, I must be non-compos mentis and unable to take care of myself. If I hear one word about a nursing home, I'm calling you to come and get me and take me home."

"Gram, I've never been to Poughkeepsie. I don't know how to get there."

"Nonsense. You're a smart boy. You can figure it out."

"Gram, why are you going if you don't want to?"

"I'm going because I'm still able to travel and I haven't been there since before your grandfather died. I don't want your uncle saying I never go to his place. It will be a nice change of scenery and probably the last trip I'll ever take. I also want to see how your aunt puts on Thanksgiving. I can give her some pointers if she needs them. As if she'd listen to me. Seriously, your uncle is my son, and his children are my grandchildren. I have one foot in the grave, so this will probably be the last time I'll see them. I feel good, so I'm going."

"You won't mind such a long car ride?"

"Don't be ridiculous. I wear Depends."

Same old Gram.

Aside from Thanksgiving, Dan had other matters to attend to, such as his father's appointment with the oncologist. His father's condition continued to puzzle Dan and he was anxious to meet and question the doctor. Dan drove his parents to the medical center where the doctor's office was located. The complex was enormous and Dan wondered how his father managed to find his way around. The walk from the parking garage to the hospital seemed unusually long, especially for an elderly person. The first stop was the lab for a blood draw, then on to the doctor's office. The waiting room was full when they arrived, and Dan anticipated a long wait. He wasn't disappointed. An hour later, Mr. Kerr was summoned to the inner sanctum. Dan wondered how people awaiting a diagnosis could stand such a long wait; it seemed cruel to expect such sick people to have to wait so long. Dan was of a mind to voice his complaints to the doctor but changed his mind when he saw her. He had been expecting an older person, a seasoned veteran accustomed to making people wait. Instead, the doctor was young and stunningly beautiful. Dan almost fell off his chair when she walked in.

The doctor held out her hand to Mr. Kerr. "Bert, I'm so happy to see you. And Theresa, how are you doing?" She looked at Dan. "Are you Mr. Kerr's son?" Dan, feeling like an awkward adolescent, merely muttered, "I'm Dan."

"I'm happy to meet you." She turned to her patient. "Bert, you look wonderful, and your labs are the best I've seen. You've been on a drug holiday, is that right?"

"Yes, I have, and I've never felt better. I walk every day and I haven't had so much as a cold. I'm strong and seldom tired. Of course, all of this is because you're my doctor. One look at you could cure me of anything."

The doctor smiled and glanced at Mrs. Kerr, who rolled her eyes. "The best thing to do now is another scan. I never expected to see you doing so well. I really can't explain it. Are you able to have the scan today or would you like to come back? I know you've had a long day."

Mr. Kerr looked at his wife and son. "We're here. Might as well do it now." Mrs. Kerr looked confused and exhausted, but she nodded. "Chip?"

"I'm good with whatever you decide."

The doctor consulted her notes. "Your last scan was a year ago. I'll call and see if the radiologist will be able to read it today. If he can't, I can schedule it within the next couple of days. I'll only be a moment."

Dan and his parents ate in the hospital cafeteria, and the scanning went swiftly and smoothly. Only after they were home did Dan notice how exhausted both parents looked. The conversation in the car had been animated and light. Now that they were back home, the silence and the tension returned. It was almost as if the walls and the floors exuded bleak emotions. Dan was ready to ask his mother if she would like him to cook when he was interrupted by a knock at the door. His father looked through the glass and said, "It's Francesca," as he opened the door.

Mrs. Salina swept in like a queen ahead of her retinue. "I made lasagna, and Salina made a new batch of wine. We need help finishing both. Who's coming? Six o'clock."

Dan noticed his mother relax in the glow of her good friend. "We'd love to help you dispose of food and wine. Did you think we'd say no?"

"You better not. Salina will be asleep at seven. Who else can I talk to? Not that he listens to me."

Dan knew that the invitation was not impromptu. Mrs. Salina knew that Mr. Kerr had to see the oncologist today and she wanted to help in the only way she could. Dan also knew he was not included nor did he want to be. This dinner was for four old friends to laugh and enjoy each other's company.

Much of the reason for the gloom that seemed to hang over the Kerr household was that Veterans Day was fast approaching. Dan had missed previous years, but he knew from conversations with his sibs that the holiday was particularly difficult given Champ's MIA status. In one sense, Champ was a veteran; he served, but he never returned. The war dead are honored on this day, but was Champ dead? There would be no honors for him, just the incessant wondering: where is he? Dan knew that the dreams would start again. His rest had been, for the most part, uninterrupted for several weeks. But with the approach of the holiday, they would darken his nights again. In addition, he had been assigned to cover the parade that morning with the instruction to interview as many veterans as he could.

Dan made breakfast for his parents and Biddy that morning. Omelets for everyone along with English muffins, home fries and bacon. Mr. Kerr and Biddy ate heartily, but Mrs. Kerr did not make an appearance early enough to enjoy the feast. Dan had to leave since the parade started at eleven. He felt the old heaviness around his heart, but he put it aside since he had work to do.

The parade had changed little since Dan's childhood. The high school band led the Scouts, who led the veterans from WWII, Korea, and VietNam. The older men rode in cars, the younger marched. The route was up Main St. to the Veterans Memorial. There the mayor would speak and lay a wreath. The best trumpeter in the band would play Taps, and the second best would answer with the echo. That was it. The band would march to the parking lot of an elementary school where they would disband. The whole thing was over shortly after noon.

Dan had to corral some of the veterans before they were driven away. He approached one older man and asked if he could speak with him. The man was tall and straight for his age with lively blue eyes and a well-healed scar just under his chin. Dan introduced himself and the man extended his hand and shook Dan's with a firm grip.

"Are you a World War II veteran, Sir?" Dan realized the foolishness of the question as soon as it was out of his mouth.

"I am. I served in Italy for fourteen months. I got shot in the jaw and came home to recuperate. Then I got sent to England for much easier duty for another year."

"What branch were you?"

"Army. I enlisted, thinking I'd have some easy duty, but that's not the way it turned out. But I was luckier than my brother. He enlisted in the Navy. He served on board a submarine that was torpedoed off the coast of North Africa. Needless to say, all the crew died. My mother never got over his death until the day she died."

Dan felt the heaviness again. "I'm sorry, Sir. My brother is MIA in VietNam. My mother is having a terrible time. I think she expects him to return home one of these days."

The man looked more carefully at Dan. "What did you say your name is?"

"Dan Kerr."

"Is Bert your old man?"

"Yes, sir."

"I bought my first tv from Bert. Good guy. Did your brother play football?"

"Both of my brothers played high school football. John played in the early sixties and then Dennis."

"Which is missing?"

"Dennis. He's been missing since 1973."

The old man shook his head. "Terrible thing. That's one war that never should have been fought. Too many lives lost for nothing. At least we fought to stop Hitler. No rhyme or reason for Nam."

"Thank you, Sir. I won't take any more of your time."

"It's been a pleasure to talk to you, Kerr. Tell your old man Clyde says hi."

"Yes, Sir. I will."

"I'm really sorry about your brother."

"Thank you, Sir."

Most of the marchers had dispersed and Main Street was open to traffic. Dan had only spoken to one veteran and didn't get much information. He had to find at least one more guy. He spied a young man with long hair, clothed mostly in leather. It was worth a shot.

Among the Missing

"Excuse me, Sir. Are you a veteran?"

The man turned. "Yeah. Who are you?"

"My name's Dan Kerr from the *Daily Clarion*. Would you mind if I asked you some questions?"

Dan could tell the man was mulling something over in his mind. "Kerr?

"Did you go to St. Tom's School?"

"Yes, I did."

"Shake hands with your old buddy, Mike Dello Russo."

"Mike! I never would have recognized you."

"Most people haven't since I got back from Nam. You write for the local rag?"

"I'm afraid so. My assignment was to cover the parade and interview some vets. Could I ask you a few questions?"

"I can't talk about Nam. If I did, you wouldn't be able to print what I said in a family newspaper."

"Could you tell me what branch of the service you were in and how long you were there?"

"Since you're an old buddy, yeah. I was in the Marines. I served for about a year when I got dinged by a landmine and lost part of my right foot. I got sent home and discharged. Now I'm a disabled vet living on a lousy government pension. I have a part-time job at Reuters Garage. Rick is another old buddy, and he lets me work at his place when I'm able. Sorry, man. That's all I can say."

"No problem, Mike. I'm really glad to see you," was all Dan was able to say. The sight of his old friend made him tongue tied and sad.

Mike laughed, sort of. "I'll make sure I buy the paper and read your story. See you later, Kerr."

Dan felt as though he had been kicked in the stomach. He slowly made his way back to his car, feeling totally unable to write the article about the parade. One part of him wanted to just throw away his notebook and resign from the paper. Another part of him knew he had a job to do, and it wasn't finished yet. The newsroom was bustling. He would write and submit his story and get out. Then he remembered. He had failed to ask the older man his name. How stupid could he be? What kind of reporter fails to ask a source's name? Dan felt he should have chosen some other profession, one that didn't deal with so many sad stories.

As he was typing the story, the man's first name came back: Clyde. All he had to do was make a phone call. "Hi, Dad. Dad, do you remember a guy named Clyde who bought a tv from you a long time ago?" Mr. Kerr didn't hesitate. "Clyde Himmer. That was a long time ago. Why do you ask?"

"I interviewed him after the parade, but I forgot to ask for his last name. He said he knows you."

"I haven't seen him in years. There's only one guy in town with that name, so it's got to be him."

"Thanks, Dad. How's Mom?"

"She's all right. You want to talk to her?"

"No. I'll see her at home. I have to get back to work."

Dan's journalistic instinct gave him the kick start he needed to write the story. After placing the article on Matt's desk, Dan left. He felt restless and groped for some understanding of what he was feeling, but his head couldn't interpret his heart. Champ, Mike, Clyde's brother. All lives lost or changed forever by war. Humans fighting other humans. Why? Dan drove aimlessly around town until he found himself at the cemetery where his grandparents were buried. He had to talk to his grandfathers, both veterans of WW I, the War to End All Wars. Both had survived and returned home to lead normal lives. Neither had even been wounded. Why some and not others? Why Champ?

The day had turned cold, and the wind tossed his hair and wound around his ankles. No words would come as Dan stood before the stone of his grandfather Kerr. When had he last visited the cemetery? He couldn't remember. What did it matter? The wind swirled and whistled. The jacket he wore was much too thin for this weather. Leaves crunched under his feet as he strolled to the gravesite of his maternal grandfather, where words failed him once again. Dan thought of his grandmother, who had died so suddenly shortly after Pup had left to join the Marines. He and Champ had served her Funeral Mass. He remembered with equal clarity what a broken man his grandfather had become, only to join his wife eight months later. He remembered his mother's deep grief after her mother's death. She had just begun to accept the loss when her father died, also very suddenly. People said he died of a broken heart.

The cold bit into Dan, but rather than feel depressed, he actually felt an unusual strength and the heaviness that had weighed him down lifted. Dan had experienced some sort of catharsis, but he couldn't name it. He only felt it.

Once Veterans Day was over, Dan could let himself get caught up in the preparations for the Thanksgiving dinner. He envisioned a huge celebration with family and perhaps even the Salinas all marveling at what a great cook and host he was. Much of Dan's unrealistic ideas were the result of being free of dreams about Champ. He had really expected that Veterans Day would spark a return to the dreams that had haunted his sleep for almost a decade. A lot of mornings he could recall dreams of his brother, but they had the same evanescent, fleeting feeling of ordinary dreams, lingering for a little while then disappearing with the dawn. Dan could only hope that the dreaded dreams of Champ had ended.

His mother brought him back to earth when he told her his plans for the holiday. "Chip," began Mrs. Kerr, "we can't fit all those people into the house. The dining room table only seats ten. Where are you going to put the other people? Besides, Pup and Mimi have other plans for the day. Who else were you planning to invite?"

"Maybe the Salinas. It's just that Gram always had so many people. That's the only way I've experienced Thanksgiving."

Mrs. Kerr said patiently, "Gram had the room for all those people, and she had the experience of feeding so many. You just learned to cook a couple of months ago."

"You could help me. We'd make a great team in the kitchen."

"My days of cooking for so many people are over. You forget that when everyone was home, I cooked for ten people every night. Enough is enough."

A deflated Dan had to admit his mother was right. "I guess I'm just too excited to think straight."

Mrs. Kerr smiled and took her son's hand. "Novice cooks are always excited by Thanksgiving, but you need to think realistically. Do you know how much food you would have to buy to feed all those people? Gram didn't do all the cooking. Everyone who came had to bring something. Otherwise, she never could have managed. The same is true for dessert. People who didn't bring a main dish brought dessert. Another person would be in charge of coffee; someone else would be in charge of cleanup. Gram made it look easy, but many people contributed to help her out."

Mrs. Kerr continued, "Ten people is still a lot. You need to think about how much food to buy, what size turkey, desserts, vegetables. You can't manage all that yourself. It's too much for anyone. Call Cissy and Bridy and Gabby and see what they can bring. Then you can start to plan."

That night Dan called Cissy. "Hi, Cissy. Just wondering what you're bringing for Thanksgiving."

"I already told Mom I'm bringing green beans and a pie."

"What kind of pie?"

"Apple. Why are you asking me this?"

"I'm doing the cooking for Thanksgiving, so I need to know who's bringing what."

"Why are you cooking? Is Mom sick?"

"No. Mom's fine. I'm learning to cook and Mom was glad to get someone to take her place. She said she's tired of cooking large meals."

"Well, if you're cooking, you better have the number of the poison control hotline handy."

"You're not funny, Cissy."

"I'm not trying to be funny."

"Any chance you could bake two pies?"

"Absolutely not. I did all the work for the christening party and most of the food wasn't even eaten thanks to Pup. I'm making one pie and that's it."

"All right. Sorry I asked. Dinner's at one. Give my best to Carl and the kids."

"Fine. Bye."

Once a drama queen, always a drama queen, thought Dan after this conversation. Poor Carl.

Next call to Gabby. "Hi Ga… er Sheila."

"Hi Chip. What's up?"

"Uh, could you make a pie for Thanksgiving?"

"No. I don't have time and I don't really know how to bake a pie. I'll bring an appetizer. That I can do."

"Ok. I'm cooking this year, so Mom said I have to find out who's bringing what."

Brief pause. "You're cooking instead of Mom? Why?"

"Because I'm learning to cook, and I want to give Mom a break. Don't worry. Mom will be assisting me."

"Thank God. You had me worried for a minute there."

"I appreciate your confidence in me. That comedienne, otherwise known as Cissy, suggested keeping the number of the poison control hotline handy."

Gabby laughed. "Are you sure she was kidding?"

"Would Stanley be willing to bake a pie? I understand he can do anything with the greatest of ease."

"Can't you ever say anything nice about Stanley? I'm sick of these constant put-downs."

"That wasn't a put-down; it was a compliment. You always misinterpret what I say about Stanley. He's told me many times about how multi-talented he is. Dinner will be at one on the big day."

Gabby, huffy now. "Ok. Is that it?"

"No. Give my love to Stanley."

Click.

Dan's next call was to his younger sister, Bridy. "Hey, Bridy."

"Hi Chip. I presume you're calling about Thanksgiving."

"That is correct. Could you bake a pie?"

"Me? You've got to be kidding. First off, I work too much to do any baking. Second, I haven't baked a pie in years and Thanksgiving is not the time to learn. I could bring some wine if that would be all right."

"That would be wonderful. Any kind will do. It's nice to know that all the Kerr women are not difficult. I just called Cissy and Gabby. Neither was particularly happy to hear from me."

"You know that Cissy is a superannuated teenager. Gabby is so infatuated with Simon. Or is it Sherman or Seymour? What is his name?"

"Stanley."

"I knew it was something with an S. Anyway, she doesn't know which end is up. Are they really getting married?"

"Apparently. They want to talk about the wedding while they're here."

"I will definitely bring wine. I think we can all use it."

"Fine. See you on the big day."

"You bet."

The week of Thanksgiving was beyond hectic at the food pantry. Since Dan's article had appeared in the paper, the pantry was inundated with donations from individuals as well as supermarkets and restaurants. There was so much food that some of it had to be stored in the halls and even in the mayor's office. Pup had built some shelves with casters which were invaluable now that everything had to be shifted around to make room for more donations. John and Dan worked tirelessly to sort through the mountain of food and to fill the boxes that were to be distributed by the Rotary Club to people in need. City Hall employees were allowed to help pack boxes. The mayor himself even pitched in to help.

The last of the boxes had been packed by Tuesday afternoon, but there was still so much food left John called churches and social service agencies to ask if they could use some. The pantry would be closed on Thursday and Friday, so John wanted to get rid of as much food as possible before the holiday. John even asked the people who worked at City Hall to take whatever they needed. Dan took two butternut squashes from the crate that a restaurant had donated. By the end of the day on Tuesday Dan was more tired than he could ever remember feeling.

While Dan was at work, his aunt and uncle, Alice and Ron, Bart's parents, had stopped by the house. They had come to pick up Gram and take her to Poughkeepsie for Thanksgiving. Over supper that night, Mr. Kerr mentioned to Dan that he and his brother Ron had discussed the possibility of putting Gram into a nursing home due to her advanced age. Dan chuckled inwardly as he remembered his phone conversation with his grandmother. No one could get Margaret Moriarty Kerr to do anything she didn't want to do. Then Dan grew seriously worried when he recalled that his grandmother had said that he would have to drive to Poughkeepsie if anyone so much as hinted that she belonged in a nursing home. Dan couldn't drive to the next town given his fatigue from working at the food pantry. Besides, he had to prepare to host his first Thanksgiving dinner.

Due to Dan's hectic schedule at the food pantry, he wasn't able to do much preparation for the dinner until Wednesday. His mother had explained the basics of pie baking and then promptly deserted him for her coffee date with Mrs. Salina. Dan's father was busy cleaning the house, so Dan was on his own. He combined the flour and shortening, feeling quite confident that this pie making business was a cinch. His mother had told him to cut in the shortening with two knives until the shortening resembled small peas. So, Dan cut and cut until the muscles between his shoulder blades began to ache. Cut, cut, cut. The pieces were still too big. Cut, cut. Still too big. Turn the bowl around. Cut, cut. Still too big. He switched hands with the knives, still too big. Finally, Dan had had enough. This would have to do.

Next step—add water. Simple enough. The ice water continued to chill in the refrigerator, so it was nice and cold. One tablespoon, stir, another tablespoon, stir. After Dan had added five tablespoons of ice water, the dough was still too flaky. One more should do it. Still too flaky. One more. Still too flaky. Now totally exasperated, Dan poured what was left of the water into the bowl. Stir, stir, keep stirring. It will come together. Some of the dough was sticking to the fork, and he had to keep stopping to remove it. Keep stirring. More dough on the fork. Keep stirring. Now the dough looked as though it would meld into a ball. His mother had warned him not to handle the dough any more than necessary. Dan gathered the now sticky mess into some semblance of a ball. The dough kept sticking to his hands. Now what? Flour. Of course, just dust some flour onto the ball and it won't be as sticky. After washing his hands for the umpteenth time, Dan showered the flour onto the ball, yet the dough still stuck to his hands. Time to chill this monster.

As the dough chilled, Dan washed the bowls and knives and spoons and prepared to roll out the ball. He took a carving knife and tried to cut the ball down the center. The knife stuck halfway, covered with dough and flour. He pulled the ball apart and tried to fashion two small balls from one large one. He took one of the smaller balls and flattened it on the board. As soon as he rolled the pin over the small bolus, it stuck to the pin like a malevolent tongue of Silly Putty and stayed there. Dan tried to pry the dough off the pin, but ended up with pieces of dough between his fingers and stuck to his palms. No amount of flour would coax the dough into flattening. Dan now knew why his sisters had refused to bake a pie. Yet he had seen his mother do this so effortlessly. Maybe that was why he thought he saw a slightly malicious smile on her face as she left the house. She knew Dan's first attempt to make a pie would be an abject failure.

Dan wondered what he would tell his mother. He felt like a fool. Then it struck him. What if the whole dinner turned out like this would-be pie? At least tomorrow his mother would be home to coach him when he needed it. He wished he had taken one of the pies from the food pantry. But, oh no. Dan

Kerr had to prove to himself and the womenfolk that he could bake with the best of them. He wished more than anything that Thanksgiving would be at his grandmother's house, as it always had been. Telling his mother about his baking disaster was not as bad as he had anticipated. When Mrs. Kerr came home from her neighbor's house, she immediately saw that the pie baking hadn't gone well. She smiled at Dan. "What happened?"

"The dough was too wet, and I couldn't get it to roll out," an abashed Dan admitted. "This isn't as easy as I thought it would be. I'll have to buy a pie."

"No, you don't. Mrs. Salina found some frozen pies she had forgotten about. She has more than she needs for tomorrow. Why don't you call her?"

"She'll never let me hear the end of this. How can I call her?"

"Easily. You pick up the phone and dial. Simple."

"AAAYYY. So, you failed to make a pie. If you fail once, you try again. Stunada. What kind you want?"

"Apple."

"Get yourself over here and take one."

Dan did, and he had a feeling that Mrs. Salina's overbaking was no accident.

CHAPTER 7

THE DAY DAWNED CLOUDY AND COLD. DAN WAS up before sunrise to put the turkey in the oven. He washed, dried, seasoned, and then slid the bird into the oven. That done, he went back to bed, but sleep eluded him. He was too worried about how the day would unfold. At least he had done well with the turkey, but that's pretty hard to mess up. As Dan watched the dawn creep slowly under his window shade, he marveled that he had been free from thoughts and dreams about Champ. He hadn't even gone to the post office to check his box. Could it be that finally he had shed the chains that had held him for so long? Next, he thought of his mother and how good she had been these last few weeks. Her memory was accurate and her demeanor much like her old self. Mrs. Kerr would see half of her children today, but half was better than none. She also believed that the Kerr family would be hosting another wedding in the spring. Dan cringed at that thought.

After a long, hot shower, Dan joined his parents and Biddy for breakfast. The turkey was cooking nicely and the succulent aroma permeated the house. Dan wolfed down some toast and coffee, surprised by his hunger. Mrs. Kerr put down her coffee cup and eyed him curiously. "Are you ready for your debut as a gourmet cook?"

Dan was nonplussed. He had decided to do his best and let the pieces fall where they may. "I am with your help."

"I'll do the stuffing and make the gravy. You will have to do the potatoes and the squash. That should be easy enough."

"I think I can handle that."

Biddy offered to set the table as Dan seated himself at the table with five pounds of potatoes waiting to be peeled. He remembered his mother's admonition to leave as much of the potato as possible, only take the skin. Biddy eventually joined him, and the two of them peeled away. Suddenly, Biddy looked up and around. "I just heard a car door. Someone's here."

Mrs. Kerr looked confused. "Already? It's much too early." Mr. Kerr looked out the kitchen window. "It's Bridy. She must have left pretty early."

In the next instant, Bridy stood in the doorway, a wine bottle in each hand. "Here I am."

After embracing each family member, Bridy gratefully accepted a cup of coffee. "I left early to beat the traffic, but there was no traffic to beat. I sailed here so easily it was almost spooky."

Her mother smiled. "Well, we're glad you're here, early or not. You didn't see Gabby on the road, did you?"

"No, I didn't. I presume she's coming with Sidney."

"Stanley. Yes, she's coming with Stanley."

Dan groaned. Bridy looked at him. "I can never remember that guy's name. I hope I don't call him by the wrong name. Are he and Gabby really getting married?"

Annoyed, Mrs. Kerr said, "They better be. I don't like living together before marriage. Gabby said they want to talk about the wedding, so I presume that means they're getting married."

Despite the topic of conversation, Dan loved the easy intimacy of the family seated around the kitchen table, just enjoying the calm before the storm. The tempest wasn't long in coming. Cissy and Carl, with their two boys, Michael and Matthew, arrived along with green beans and an apple pie.

Cissy spoke. "Carl, put those beans on the stove."

Carl did as he was commanded and immediately sought refuge in the living room. Cissy spoke again. "My pie came out really good, Mom. You'll be pleased."

Now Dan realized the first crisis of the day was looming. They didn't need two apple pies; he would have to return the pie to Mrs. Salina, hopefully without Cissy's knowledge. Too late. Cissy spotted the other pie on the counter.

"How did your pie come out, Chip? It looks really good, but it doesn't look like a blueberry pie."

Dan had no choice but to confess. "It isn't blueberry; it's apple. I tried to bake a pie, but it was a disaster, so Mrs. Salina gave me one of her pies."

Cissy erupted like a volcano. "I told you I was going to make an apple pie. Why did you take one of her apple pies? Are you trying to show me up? I can't bake like Mrs. Salina. Nobody around here appreciates all the work I do. The same thing happened at the christening party. I do all the work, but nobody wants to eat what I cook. That time it was Pup. Now it's you. That's it. Never again will I do anything for anyone."

This tirade was interrupted by Mrs. Kerr. "All right, Cissy. That's enough. Chip, bring back that pie and get another. Francesca has plenty."

Dan shrugged into his jacket to make the pie exchange and Matthew, his nephew, tugged at his sleeve. "Uncle Chip, can I go with you?"

"Of course. I'm only going across the street."

Had it been anyone besides Mrs. Salina that Dan had to see, he would have just kept the pie. She would make a fuss, but her fussing was always good natured, never malicious. Carmella, the oldest daughter, answered the door. "Chip, what a surprise. Come in." Eyeing Matthew, Carmella stooped to greet him. "And what's your name?"

"Matty."

"I'm happy to meet you, Matty. How old are you?"

"Six."

This attempt at small talk was interrupted by Mrs. Salina's signature greeting, "AAAYYY, why are you here? I thought you had to cook dinner. Was the pie no good? Why are you returning it?"

Dan laughed. "I'm sure the pie is excellent. The problem is that I forgot Cissy was making an apple pie when I took yours. She had a cow when she found out, so here I am exchanging the apple for another kind. This is Cissy's son Matthew. He just had to meet you since he loves celebrities."

"AAAYYY, fibber. Would you like a treat to take home, Matthew?"

Matthew's eyes lit up. "Yes!"

"Here's a cannoli, but don't eat it before dinner because your mother will get mad if you can't eat your dinner."

Matthew, well acquainted with his mother's temper, promised to wait.

"Here you go. You have brothers or sisters?"

"Yes. Michael."

"Here's one for Michael. Make sure you give it to him, otherwise your uncle might eat it. He loves my baking and cooking."

Dan and his happy nephew returned home. The kitchen was steamy with all the cooking and smelled like heaven. All the guests had arrived and Dan still had to mash the potatoes and the squash. His father was carving the turkey, and Dan had to steal a slice to taste. It was excellent. "Good turkey. You ought to try roasting a turkey, Dad. It could turn into a second career."

As he mashed, Dan strained to hear the conversation in the living room. He couldn't hear words but chatter and bursts of laughter. Once he heard Aunt Julia's unmistakable cackle. So far, so good. So on he worked, mashing potatoes and squash. Dan's mother had cautioned him to make sure all the guests were seated before taking food to the table. With that in mind, Dan peered into the dining room a few times and asked everyone to get to the table. Why would people hesitate when they knew a big meal awaited in the next room? He knew why. Some of the guests were well lubricated and only wanted to sit and talk; they didn't want to move.

It took the imperious voice of Aunt Julia to clear the living room. "Get in there and eat. Chippy didn't cook a big dinner for nothing." After this pronouncement, Aunt Julia motioned to Dan. "Chippy, would you escort me to the loo?"

"Of course, Aunt Julia. It would be my pleasure."

Dan was surprised at how tightly Aunt Julia held his arm as though she were drowning, and the arm was the only available life preserver. She swayed a little, and Dan had to tighten his arm to prevent her from falling. "Will you be all right, Aunt Julia? You seem a little unsteady."

"I'm always unsteady when I get up from a chair. You just wait for me. If I need help, I'll bang on the wall."

As they approached the bathroom, the door opened and Stanley exited. He gave them a wave and Aunt Julia gave a brief snort, but said nothing. Presently, the door opened, and Aunt Julia emerged much steadier than before. As she took Dan's arm, she sniffed. "That guy is not only a lizard, but also an oaf. He left the seat up."

When the food had been passed around and grace said Dan could finally sit and enjoy his meal. Best of all was the satisfaction that came with knowing he had orchestrated the dinner. Granted, his mother helped and he couldn't have done it without her, but he relished the warm feeling when he saw people savoring his cooking. Dan poured himself a generous glass of the excellent Cabernet that Bridy had brought and sat between Aunt Julia and Matty. Dan had noticed that Aunt Julia had been unusually quiet and not quite herself. She ate very little and finished her meal long before everyone else. Now that she wasn't eating, Aunt Julia suddenly became loquacious, but her question was directed to Stanley, not Dan. "Tell me, young man, what are your parents doing today?"

Stanley looked up and around, obviously surprised by Aunt Julia's gentle inquiry.

"Well, they always go to my aunt's house for Thanksgiving and Christmas. They never like to be home for the holidays since my oldest brother was killed in Viet Nam. He was a helicopter pilot, and his chopper was shot down. My mother never got over it."

A stunned silence gripped the table. Dan felt bile rise in his throat. Consumed with rage, he had to stop himself from reaching across the table to choke Stanley. Fists clenched, Dan looked instinctively at his mother, but he was unable to see her from his vantage point. The dinner had gone from festive to funereal in just a few seconds. Nobody spoke or ate. Matty, aware of the change, whispered to Dan, "Uncle Chip, why is everyone so quiet?"

Dan regained his equilibrium and whispered back, "People want to be with their own thoughts right now. It's ok."

"Can I eat?"

Dan couldn't resist smiling. "Of course. Eat all you want except the cannoli."

"The what?"

Mr. Kerr reached for a wine bottle and flourished it. "Anybody want more wine? There's plenty here."

No one responded. Gabby punctuated the silence with a pithy observation: "This family would be much healthier if we spoke about Champ and stopped acting like he never existed. We should acknowledge his life instead of pretending he didn't die."

Cissy suddenly pushed back her chair. "I need to have a cigarette. Excuse me."

Carl raised his glass to his father-in-law. "I'll have some more, Bert."

Then Bridy found her voice. "Stanley, I'm very sorry about your brother. Gabby, your remark was inappropriate and uncalled for, especially at Thanksgiving dinner. You owe everyone at this table an apology, especially Mom and Dad."

Another silence was broken when the phone in the kitchen rang. Dan scrambled out of his chair to answer it. Pup was calling from Texas. "Hey, Chip. Just calling to wish everybody a Happy Thanksgiving. It's eighty-five degrees here. We're going to the beach after dinner."

"I'm happy for you, Pup," Dan said acidly.

"Hey, what's the matter with you? Was your dinner a flop?"

"No. Sorry, but we're in the middle of yet another Kerr family debacle."

"A what?"

"I'll let you talk to Mom."

Dan summoned his mother from the dining room. She looked haggard, but composed. Talking to her favorite always calmed her, so Pup had unwittingly done a good thing by calling when he did. Dan gave his mother the phone and returned to the table. With the anchor of the family absent, the table was in an uproar. Gabby was screaming at Bridy. Mr. Kerr was doing his best to restore order. Aunt Julia calmly sipped her wine while Biddy screamed at Stanley, who looked bewildered and scared.

Dan yelled at the top of his lungs. "Everybody shut up. This is a family dinner, not Saturday night at the fights. All this is going to do is upset Mom, so everybody just shut the hell up."

Once again, Bridy rose to the occasion. "Now that dinner is over," she announced, "I'm going to play Gram so we can organize the cleanup. Mom, Dad, Aunt Julia, and Chip are exempt. Everyone else has to do something. Any volunteers to wash dishes?"

"I'll wash the dishes," said Biddy.

"Ok. Who's going to dry?"

Stanley's hand went up immediately. "I'll dry."

Michael, who previously had spoken fewer than five sentences the entire afternoon, offered, "I'll help Stanley."

"Fantastic. Now who will put the dishes away? Any takers?"

"Seeing none, I hereby appoint Cissy."

The appointee started to protest, but thought better of it. "And what are you doing, Bridy, besides playing Gram?"

"I'm going to wash the dessert dishes."

Thus all the players took their places with some towel slapping going on between Stanley and Michael. Dan decided he really needed some fresh air to clear his head and try to process what had happened at dinner. His anger had focused first on Stanley, but now Dan came to realize that Stanley was no more to blame for his answer than Aunt Julia was for asking the question. The person he was furious with was Gabby for her assessment of the family's mental health. And what of the parents? Most of these people would be going home in a few hours. It was Dan who would have to deal with the aftermath. At least Biddy and Bridy would be there, so he wouldn't have to go it alone.

Dan walked downtown despite the cold. He passed City Hall and thought of Rosalina. He was very glad that they had decided to celebrate the holiday with their respective families. Dan would not want Rosalina to get the wrong impression of his family. He thought of John Murphy and wondered how his day was going. Dan walked to St. Thomas Aquinas Church and as he did so, he thought of the Thanksgiving when he and Bart did the same thing and were scared by all the shadows in the empty church. Dan tried the door. Locked. He started for home via a different route.

Refreshed by his walk, Dan returned home to find most of the family engaged in their various tasks. He loved how his little sister had taken on such a leadership role. Bridy, the skinny kid who used to love to lie on the living room floor and color, had blossomed into a self-assured woman who was not imperious like Gram or Julia, but gentle with an understated sense of humor. Matty approached Dan before he could even remove his coat. "Uncle Chip, my job was to take the pies into the dining room. I didn't even drop one."

Dan loved this kid. "That's great, Matty. I knew you could do it."

Matty looked up at Dan. "Mommy's mad because you were supposed to make a blueberry pie, but you didn't."

Dan shook his head. How, he wondered, did Cissy manage to produce such a healthy, even-tempered kid since she's so ridiculously finicky and nervous? He glanced at his older sister, and she was indeed in a snit, grabbing dishes too quickly and slamming cabinet doors. Dan decided to ignore her.

He poured himself his second glass of wine and retired to the living room where an unregarded football game flickered on the tv. Carl snored quietly on the couch and Aunt Julia, head flung back, snored delicately in the recliner. Dan joined this raucous group and watched the game.

Clean-up finished; Bridy summoned everyone back to the dining room. Dan nudged Carl, who looked around sheepishly and stumbled into the dining room, and he gently massaged Aunt Julia's arm until she opened her eyes. "Aunt Julia, would you care for some pie?"

Instantly awake, Aunt Julia replied, "Lead me to it."

No sooner than everyone had been seated than Dan heard the familiar "AAAYYY," resonate from the kitchen. Seconds later, Salina, Francesca and Bobby walked into the dining room. Mrs. Salina carried yet another pie, and Salina had a bottle of homemade wine. Mrs. Kerr jumped up from her seat. "What a surprise. You're just in time for dessert if you can find some seats." Dan, Bobby, Biddy, and Carl repaired to the kitchen so Salina and Francesca could sit. Pies were sliced and passed around, coffee was poured and Mrs. Salina held forth, prompting gales of laughter from her audience. "AAAYYY, my daughters come, and they leave. I make a huge dinner but they eat like birds, so they won't get fat. They don't eat pie. Why do I bother? They like Salina's wine but not my cooking. Stunadas. They change men like clothes. Now they go to people they don't even know. What can I do?"

Dessert was much more jovial than dinner. In addition to the entertainment, Salina poured generous draughts of wine. Gabby was clearly miffed that Stanley was consuming too much. He ignored her protests and entered into an earnest conversation with Salina about wine. Evidently, Stanley was an expert on wine, another feather in his imaginary cap. Dan forgot his earlier anger and reminisced freely with his old neighborhood friend, Bobby. Carl also knew Bobby and the three of them forgot Biddy was with them as they laughed about old times. Biddy was not Cissy. She made the best of it and laughed even when she had no idea why.

Around eight o'clock someone suggested that turkey sandwiches would be in order. Dan removed what was left of the turkey. He didn't trust himself with the carving knife, so that task was delegated to Mr. Kerr whose hand was none too steady either. Bridy took bread from the freezer and placed each slice in the toaster and popped up the lever before the toasting was complete. After several times doing this, the toaster began to smoke much to the amusement of all present. Bridy slapped mayo onto the bread to a chorus of "I want ketchup. I want mustard." "I want grape jelly." Biddy reached for a sandwich, misjudged the distance, and tumbled to the floor, laughing so hard she was unable to get up. Bobby swooped an arm under her and placed her back on her chair.

At ten o'clock most of the guests were reluctant to leave. Aunt Julia was in no condition to go home and despite her protests, was helped into the master bedroom, leaving Mr. and Mrs. Kerr to find other accomodations for the night. Stanley was clearly unable to drive to New York, so he and Gabby were forced to stay as well. Mrs. Kerr was alternately furious at her family for overindulging and magnanimous in dispensing hugs and kisses. She placed her hands on Stanley's shoulders at one point and told him she loved him. He responded by enveloping her in a crushing bear hug. Dan, still in some possession of his faculties, wondered what the morning would bring.

After Francesca and her family left, Dan was unable to keep his eyes open. Whatever work remained to be done would have to wait until morning. Fortunately, no one had claimed his bed, and he gratefully crawled under the covers some time Thanksgiving night. As he dozed, Dan struggled to remember the quote from Shakespeare about sleep, something about a sleeve. What play had the line? He would have to look it up in the morning.

Dan's slumber of late had been undisturbed, but that ended. Champ appeared with Mike Dello Russo and both were chained to a statue on Coltonwood's Main Street. Champ yelled at Dan to free him while Mike tore furiously at the bonds that held them fast. Champ had the hollow-eyed look of a corpse while Mike bled copiously about the head. Dan cautiously approached and got close enough to hear Champ yelling. "Damn it, Chip. Help me. Don't just stand there. Get me out of these chains." Upon closer inspection, Dan saw that Champ's teeth were missing and his hair was waist length. His hands were chafed raw from pulling at the chains. His uniform was in tatters and the laces missing from his boots. "Help me, Chip. Do something. Get Dad. He was a soldier in a war. He'll help me." With that, Champ fell to the ground, exhausted from yelling, then he would start again. Dan forced his eyes open to rid himself of the image. He lay in bed soaked in sweat, heart pounding, gasping for breath. This had been the worst dream yet.

Eventually, Dan regained some semblance of control and made his way downstairs. The house was quiet and dark. He peered into the living room, where Stanley snored softly on the couch. Dan opened the refrigerator, looking for something to calm himself. He took out a gallon of milk and poured himself a glass. The kitchen clock read four ten. Just twenty-four hours ago, Dan had gotten up to put the turkey into the oven. Thanksgiving now seemed months ago. Instead of drinking the milk, Dan hastily dressed and headed across the street to the pond behind the Salinas' house. The morning was cold and the dawn yawned lazily over the horizon. The man-made pond had a skin of ice on top. In another month, it would be frozen solid.

Dan remembered all the good times on this pond that Salina had dug and filled for his own kids as well as the neighborhood kids. Every Christmas Eve the Salinas would host a skating party to be followed by the traditional Italian meal of seven fish. Most of the people in this tight-knit neighborhood would come. People would be everywhere in the house, on the stairs, in the cellar, even the bedrooms warming themselves with Mrs. Salina's food and Salina's homemade wine. Dan had spent most Christmas Eves of his life at the Salinas' party. But time had its way and now the Salinas just have snacks and wine after skating. Dan closed his eyes and he could see Champ, who was an excellent skater, threading his way around the not so good skaters. On many a winter's day, Champ would skate by himself, practicing his slap shot. Where is he now? Dan feared for his sanity if these dreams persisted. Should he seek professional help to rid himself of the dreams? How could he learn to control his subconscious? How could anyone else tell him how to do that?

Morning crept over Coltonwood and Dan knew he had to get back before everyone started getting up. He picked up a stick and flung it as far as he could beyond the Salinas' backyard. His soft curse was lost in the rush of the wind.

On his way across the street, Dan had seen the kitchen light, so someone was up. His father whirled in surprise as Dan walked through the door.

"Where have you been?"

"Over at Salinas."

"Are they up?"

"No. I was at the pond."

"Why?"

"I needed to clear my head. I had another dream about Champ last night. The worst one yet."

Mr. Kerr sank into a chair. "What happened in the dream?"

"It was awful. Champ was chained to the Veterans Memorial and Mike Dello Russo was with him, also chained. Champ kept asking me to free him. He looked like someone who had been dead for years. Mike was covered in blood. Champ asked me to get you. He said you could free him."

Mr. Kerr shook his head sadly. "I'm sorry you have these dreams, Chip. I wish I knew how to make them stop, but I don't. Well, I guess I'll start cooking breakfast. The gang will be up soon."

The first person to make an appearance was none other than Aunt Julia, pert and sassy as ever. She poked her head out of the master bedroom. "Is there anyone here who can help me dress?" Casting a wily grin at Mr. Kerr and Dan, she added, "I'd prefer a lady, if you two gents don't mind." Dan went off in search of one of his sisters as Mr. Kerr gallantly escorted Aunt Julia to the bathroom. Ablutions finished, Bridy and Biddy both assisted Aunt Julia and helped her to the breakfast table where she entertained the diners who ate hungrily of scrambled eggs, bacon, toast, and coffee. Between bites, Aunt Julia mused, "One of my husbands, I think my second, used to cook breakfast every morning before he went to work. I trained him well. None of the others had such consideration. A lady should be pampered by her husband, don't you think, young man?" This addressed to Stanley.

"Absolutely, Aunt Julia. A good wife is worth her weight in gold."

Aunt Julia visibly stiffened at the familiarity, but continued on. "Yes, most men fail to properly appreciate what they have. My husbands learned to appreciate me; I can tell you." Only Stanley laughed. "I bet they did."

Mrs. Kerr didn't arrive for breakfast until everyone else was just about finished. She looked pale and tired and cast a faint smile around the table. "Did I miss breakfast?" Her husband jumped up. "Absolutely not, dear. I'll cook some eggs for you, and I know you like your bacon wiggly. Coming right up."

Within the hour, the guests had departed, and Dan was left at the table with his parents and a sink full of dishes.

An exhausted Dan slept away most of the afternoon. He awoke feeling anxious. Tonight was the night he was to meet Rosalina's children. They had never been properly introduced because when Dan would pick Rosalina up for a date, the kids were never there since they spent every weekend with their father. Part of Thanksgiving had been spent with their father's side, so they wouldn't visit again until Sunday. Dan was puzzled by his apprehension; he got along well with his nieces and nephews, and he had had a fantastic relationship with Miriam's grandchildren. Of course, Rosalina spoke often of her kids, so Dan had a pretty good idea of what to expect. Rosalina was cooking dinner and Dan had promised to bring French bread and cheese to complement the pasta supper.

At the last minute, Dan bought flowers for Rosalina. He hoped this would help to start a conversation as soon as he walked in the door. The water was already boiling when Dan arrived. Rosalina's daughter Marla was seated at the kitchen table, reading. The boy, Bryant, was nowhere in sight. Dan politely shook Marla's hand, and he was surprised by the strength of her grip. Bryant was summoned from somewhere and he slouched unwillingly to the table. He took Dan's outstretched hand and shook it briefly. The hand was warm and flaccid. Before he could pull out a chair, Rosalina asked Dan to slice the bread. Dan immediately complied, as it gave him something to do besides sit and make phony conversation with the kids.

Although he had absolutely nothing in common with Marla, it was she who kept up most of the conversation. She was well spoken with a touch of understated humor which belied her age. Bryant, however, was taciturn and sullen during the meal. Dan tried to induce him to talk about football, but the boy would only give tepid responses to Dan's questions. Bryant paid more attention to his plate than he did to the humans around the table. Dan wondered if the boy was always this way or if this performance was for his benefit. He would ask Rosalina in private.

Post dinner, the kids dutifully cleared the table and placed the dishes in the dishwasher. Dessert plates and coffee cups for the adults were arranged around the table. Marla chattered constantly as she did her chores, oblivious to the sullen silence of her brother. Bryant reminded Dan of his cousin Agatha, Bart's sister. She too was pathologically quiet and would only speak if spoken to. Now no one in the family had any idea of her whereabouts. Dan hoped Rosalina wouldn't have a similar experience with her son.

Once the meal was over, the four repaired to the living room to watch a movie. Marla made her selection and Rosalina asked Bryant if he was satisfied with her choice. "Yeah, whatever." Those were the only words he uttered for the remainder of the evening. Dan left at ten feeling alternately happy and sad. He was happy that Rosalina had such a joyful child in Marla and sad that she had such a despondent child in Bryant. How on earth did she manage? Dan wondered.

CHAPTER 8

WITH THANKSGIVING OVER, THERE REMAINED a scant three weeks until Christmas. Dan had plenty of work at the paper covering events in town that presaged the holiday. The food pantry had to be re-stocked after Thanksgiving to be ready to meet the heavy demand at Christmas. Dan and John worked tirelessly to take care of the day-to-day inventory while trying to stockpile as much as possible ahead of the rush just before Christmas.

With Christmas so close, Dan had a private dilemma in regard to Rosalina. He would get her a nice present, but just how nice he didn't know. She would not get a ring; he hoped she was not expecting one. Dan just wasn't ready for the commitment a ring would suggest. And what of the kids? He just met them. He would have to get them something, but what? Joke presents, perhaps? The last thing Dan wanted to do was give the impression that he was ready to be their stepfather. There had been a shift in his relationship with Rosalina, one so subtle that Dan didn't know what exactly had happened. Dan had dated a lot in college, mostly brief flings, fun while they lasted. Yet his relationship with Rosalina was something new, and he was almost thirty. He decided to let time decide, for now.

Dan paid particular attention to his mother's demeanor and mood. He did see the post- holiday letdown, but that was to be expected. Yet there was something else, not depression or forgetfulness, but rather a sadness punctuated by deep sighs and almost imperceptible headshaking. Something was bothering Mrs. Kerr, but she, true to type, gave no indication as to what was troubling her. Mrs. Kerr was not the type to sit and discuss her feelings. Nor would she be forthcoming if asked directly. Dan would have to take a circuitous route to discover the issue. To further complicate matters, Dan's grandmother returned from Poughkeepsie unwell. Uncle Ron drove her to Dan's parents' house rather than to her own and helped her inside. He then announced flatly that his mother and Bert's belonged in a nursing home and that she was no longer capable of caring for herself. Gram shot her son a withering look and simply said, "I am not going to any nursing home. I will die in my own home in my own bed, thank you. Bert, could I lie down for an hour or so? I'm really tired from such a long ride." Mr. Kerr showed his mother to the master bedroom and helped her onto the bed. An hour later she was dead.

Dan's heart lurched when he saw the yellow memo on his desk. He knew it was not good when a phone message awaited him when he had just returned from an assignment. His heart lurched again when he saw that the message was from his father; he was to call as soon as he could. Two thoughts collided in his mind as he read the message; something had happened to his mother or Champ's remains had been found. As he dialed the phone with tremulous fingers, he desperately hoped it was the latter. His anxiety about his mother was immediately relieved when she answered the phone.

"Mom, I just got a message from Dad to call immediately. What happened?"

"It's your grandmother. Your uncle brought her here and she asked to lie down. When your father checked on her, she was dead."

Dan reeled at this unexpected news. Despite his grandmother's advanced age, he never thought her in any imminent danger of death. She seemed one of those indomitable people whom death would not dare approach, let alone take. He couldn't even recall that she had ever been sick, other than a cold now and then. Memories of his grandmother came so fast and furious, Dan had to grab the desk to steady himself. Once his head had cleared a little, Dan was confused. "What was Gram doing at the house?"

"I'm not sure myself. Your uncle just showed up with Gram and told your father, right in front of Gram, that she couldn't live alone anymore. Gram said she was tired, and she lay down on our bed where she died."

"Is her body still there?"

"Yes, we have to wait for the Medical Examiner to pronounce her dead before her body can be moved to the funeral home. Can you come home now, Chip?"

"Not just yet, Mom. I have to write an article first, then I'll be right home."

Dan's disordered thoughts had to be calmed before he

could even make sense of his notes. He poured himself a cup of coffee, took a deep breath, and began to write. Images of Gram were like a ping-pong game in his head. He would fend off one memory and another would immediately take its place. Amid this disordered state of mind, Dan finally wrote his story. Before he left the newspaper office, Dan called Rosalina and told her of his grandmother's death. Talking to her calmed him, and he felt able to deal with whatever he would find once he got home.

The Kerr home was crowded with people when Dan arrived. The Medical Examiner had arrived, and the undertaker was hard on his heels. Presently, the doctor emerged, a stethoscope bulging from his left pocket. He spoke directly to Mr. Kerr and his brother, "Natural causes and advanced age were the manner of death. Nothing suspicious and no need for an autopsy. My condolences to you." With that, he was gone.

As the family sat at the kitchen table making funeral plans, Dan thought of Aunt Julia. "Has anyone let Aunt Julia know about Gram?" he asked his parents. No one had, so Dan decided to call her and deliver the bad news himself.

"Hello," said a raspy voice audible to all in the kitchen.

"Hi, Aunt Julia, it's Chip."

"Chippy, what a surprise. How are you?"

"I'm ok, but I'm calling to tell you that Gram died this afternoon."

A pause, audible breathing on the phone line. "Margaret's dead? Then I won the bet!"

"The bet? What do you mean?"

"We had a bet to see who would live the longest. I won!"

"Aunt Julia, how can you win a bet you can't collect?"

"It doesn't involve money, just pride. Well, well, I always knew I would win. I'm lucky that way. And, you know what? I'm going to call Jack Callahan and give him my hat that you said is like Captain Hunch's hat and have him put it on Margaret for the wake. I know he'll do it."

"I don't think that's a good idea, Aunt Julia."

Aunt Julia risked an amused cackle. "It would be a riot. Everyone would be laughing their heads off. Well, I have to go now, Chippy. I can't keep Jack waiting too long. Make sure you let me know when the wake and funeral will be. 'Bye."

Dan hung up and turned towards the stunned people at the table. Pup had come during Dan's conversation with Aunt Julia and spoke first. "Aunt Julia is off her rocker. She's seeing too much of Jack."

Mrs. Kerr, not at all amused, said, "What a disgraceful thing to say. Julia needs to learn some respect and learn it soon. Chip, I can't understand why you are so fond of her. She has a tongue like a viper."

Dan felt compelled to defend Aunt Julia. "You know that's just her way, Mom. She doesn't mean half of what she says. Don't worry, Gram will not be wearing Aunt Julia's Captain Crunch hat."

Pup snorted. "What's all this about a Captain Crunch hat?"

"I think it was at Mimi's wedding," Dan mused. "Aunt Julia was wearing this monstrosity of a hat and it reminded me of Captain Crunch, that's all."

Pup stood. "Well, I have to go back to work. Thanks for the coffee, Mom. Let me know what the arrangements are. I'd like to be a pallbearer if that's ok."

Mrs. Kerr gaped at her oldest son. "Of course, it's all right. All the pallbearers will be grandsons." With a light brush of a kiss on his mother's cheek, Pup was gone. Dan figured the business Pup had to attend to could be settled most expeditiously at the local pub, but he didn't mention this to his mother.

Mr. Kerr and Uncle Ron would be seeing to the practical aspects of the funeral with the undertaker tomorrow, but today, the more personal details had to be settled. The family had to choose three readers, six pallbearers, music for the Mass, and make arrangements for the collation to follow. Mrs. Kerr called each of her daughters in search of readers. Mimi declined, Cissy flatly refused, Bridy graciously accepted, Gabby couldn't decide, and Biddy was at work. Pup would be a pallbearer, along with Chip, Bart, Neil, but that was only four. The unspoken name of Champ hung in the air, but no one acknowledged it. Mrs. Kerr took a deep breath. "Ok, that's four. I'll ask Carl, but we still need one more."

Mr. Kerr sensing a decline in his wife, hastily interjected, "What about Patrick? He's old enough to be a bearer."

"Of course, Patrick. That's it for pallbearers. Now we still need two readers. Chip, will you be a reader?"

It was not until this moment that Dan realized that he wanted to speak at the funeral. He didn't want the occasion to pass without some acknowledgement of his grandmother. "I will read, but I also want to give a eulogy."

His mother looked confused. "A eulogy? I thought only famous people had eulogies."

"Anyone can have a eulogy. I'll only speak for a few minutes. I want everyone to know what an incredible lady Gram was."

Now Dan had a more practical detail to attend to; he didn't have a suit to wear to the funeral. Armed with his new credit card, Dan headed for the men's tailoring shop downtown. The last time Dan had been in that store was to pick up a tux for the senior prom. The owner of the store was the same man. Dan was measured and chose a dark pinstriped suit. In addition, he bought three shirts and two ties. As he paid the bill, the old man asked, "Do you have a pair of black shoes to wear with the suit?" Dan, of course, did not. "No, I don't. Where can I buy a nice pair of wingtips?"

"I used to carry shoes, but not anymore. There's a good shoe store over in Huron. You can't wear a new suit with old, scuffed shoes."

An hour later, Dan's wardrobe was complete. Now he really had to sit down and write the eulogy that had been floating around in his head since his grandmother died. He needed to fit those pieces into a coherent whole. He retreated to his room to write and found it unexpectedly difficult. Then he remembered what one of his writing teachers had said. *Make a list of whatever words you can to describe the subject. Pick a few and start writing.* Dan's list included words like endurance, toughness, tenderness, discipline, sacrifice. Now all he had to do was apply those words to his grandmother. An hour later, he had one paragraph written. He stared at his word processor and read. "My grandmother was an extraordinary woman whose life bridged three generations. She was tall of stature and firm of conviction. She had an opinion about everything and everyone, some laudatory, some scathing. There was no middle ground with Gram. Everything was either very good or very bad. She lived through the Great Depression when discipline and sacrifice became an everyday reality. Less than a decade later, both of her sons answered the call to duty during the Second World War: my Dad, Bert, to Central Europe and my Uncle Ron to the Philippines. There was never a day during that time that she didn't wake up to the reality that she may never see her sons again. Constant worry dominated her life until both returned home safe and healthy."

Dan began another paragraph. "As a kid, I loved having both sets of grandparents as my neighbors. Gram used to say, 'If the Kennedy's can have their compound, the Kerrs can have theirs.' Every Saturday night, my two sets of grandparents would get together to play cards. Those games were only ended by the sudden, untimely death of my maternal grandmother, followed by my devastated grandfather less than six months later. My two grandmothers had been best friends and Gram grieved her loss deeply."

Paragraph Three: "Gram's anchors in life were her faith and strength, two words that were synonymous with her. No matter how difficult her circumstances were, Gram found a way to cope and then move on. Her home was full of statues and holy cards and she would pray every day for anyone who had died, even twenty years previously. Gram loved attending church and she wouldn't miss Mass even in a blizzard; she would just walk instead of drive."

"My siblings and cousins and I were very much aware, even as children, that Gram was the boss in her house, no exceptions. She loved a good joke, even a slightly ribald one, but if she heard one of us use inappropriate language, there would be hell to pay. Gram insisted on good manners and respect for adults. She wanted things done right and done well. Every Thanksgiving anyone who ate dinner had to do something either before or after dinner to help out, even if it was only carrying plates from the dining room to the kitchen. Her dinners and desserts were legendary."

Closing: "Margaret Moriarty Kerr's life was a mosaic. She was tough but tender, imperious but tolerant, serious but funny. All of these seemingly disparate pieces came together to inform the life of my grandmother. In short, she was a great lady with many moving parts which kept everyone who knew her on their toes. Gram has gone to God, and I will miss everything about her: her cooking and baking, her sparring with Aunt Julia, our talks over coffee, her astute appraisal of events, both local and national. Gram lived life to the hilt and now it's time for her to be reunited with all the people who went before her. I hope heaven is prepared."

Dan looked over what he had written with as critical an eye as possible. He only had a few minutes to speak, so he had to keep his eulogy as concise as possible. If he had time tomorrow morning, he would give it one more look, but he doubted anything would change.

After a quick supper, the family gathered for the wake. Dan didn't expect a flood of people given his grandmother's age, but he would be happy with a decent showing. Mr. Kerr decided to keep the receiving line as brief as possible with only himself and Uncle Ron and their respective spouses, no grandchildren. Dan was disappointed; he wanted to be able to speak to people, especially those he hadn't seen in a long time. He decided to station himself near the door to greet people as they came in.

In a small city like Coltonwood the older residents tended to know each other by sight, if not by name, and a lot of people who knew Gram only casually came to her wake. Of course, Dan knew that going to wakes was de rigeur to Irish people. It was almost like a spectator sport; people reacquainted and greeted each other as though they hadn't met in years. All of this was amusing to Dan as he watched people come in and stay; it was a party in honor of Margaret Kerr and she would have loved it. Rosalina came with both kids in tow. Bryant extended his hand to Dan. "I'm sorry about your grandmother, Mr. Kerr."

Dan knew Bryant was just parroting what his mother told him to say, but Dan was touched by the boy's sincerity and the firmness of his handshake. "Thank you, Bryant. I really appreciate that you came to the wake."

With that, the boy suddenly became inarticulate once again, "Well, yeah, ok." Bryant turned and gave way to his sister who looked wide eyed at everything around her.

It was obvious that Marla had never before been to a wake and she was struck dumb by the whole experience. Dan gently took her hand and shook it. "I'm very happy to see you, Marla. Thank you for coming to my grandmother's wake." The little girl squirmed and was guided gently aside by her mother.

Rosalina kissed Dan and murmured her condolences. Dan held her hand for a long time. "Thanks for coming, Rosalina, and for bringing the kids. It really means a lot to me."

"They wanted to come, both of them, even though it's the first time for each of them. I knew Mrs. Kerr slightly. She used to come into City Hall for various things, so I knew her somewhat. She certainly had a long and fulfilling life." Rosalina looked Dan up and down. "Nice outfit. You ought to run for mayor, then we could work together."

"Now that I would like, working together, but I don't know about being mayor."

"You couldn't do any worse than the current officeholder."

Dan laughed. "Now you sound just like my grandmother."

The two hours of the wake flew by. People began to filter out and soon it was just the family and Gram. Dan was pleased with not only the numbers but also by the ambience of the wake. People laughed and joked, reminisced, hugged and kissed. It was exactly as Gram would have wanted it.

Dan was up early the next day. He looked over his eulogy and decided to leave as written. He printed it and practiced reading it aloud. Should he give his parents a sneak preview? No. He wanted their honest reactions after hearing him speak in church. The mood at the funeral home was totally different than it had been the previous evening, somber and quiet as opposed to the noisy, party-like atmosphere of the wake. As Dan knelt and looked at his grandmother for the last time, he thought he should be sadder than he felt. Now that the shock of her death was behind him, the reality was that deep inside, Dan felt an emptiness in his heart that no one would ever be able to fill. Yet, he also felt a muted joy that Gram was at peace, and she had left this world on her own terms. She had lived as she wanted even on the day she died. Gratitude and love moved him to reach and touch his grandmother's arm and whisper, "Thank you, Gram. Raise hell in heaven."

On the way out of the funeral home, Dan gallantly offered his arm to Aunt Julia, who gratefully accepted and leaned heavily against her nephew. "Are you all right, Aunt Julia?"

"Absolutely, Chippy. I'm just peeved that Margaret is wearing a dress that really doesn't become her. And Jack Callahan was a little heavy-handed with the rouge. I'm going to call him tomorrow to complain. He better not do any such thing to me."

The Funeral Mass was low-key but inspiring. Dan was surprised to see so many people already at the church when the family arrived. He expected pretty much only family and neighbors to attend, but there were a smattering of people he didn't know throughout the massive church. During the rite, Dan was unaccountably nervous. A speech course was required when Dan was in college, and he did well. But his audience then was people he knew only casually. Now he had to speak in front of family and neighbors who knew him and his weaknesses all too well. Worse was he had to wait until the end of the Mass to give his eulogy. Dan walked to the pulpit on rubbery legs and gazed out at the congregation before he began to speak. The lights in the church cast a peculiar glow on the paper and he wished he had triple spaced his talk. With a deep breath, he began. Dan remembered to look up at certain points and was amazed that people were actually listening. His gaze sought out Bart and this time Dan didn't lose his composure at his cousin's resemblance to Champ. Mrs. Salina was smiling wickedly at Dan, and he had all he could do not to smile or laugh. Dan remembered how many times he had looked at the congregation when he was an altar server. He felt humble and small as he stood, the center of attention, in this magnificent church.

A light snow had begun to fall as the Kerr family exited the church. Bart stepped up to take Aunt Julia's other arm lest she slip on the stairs. In his haste to get the perfect outfit for the funeral, Dan had forgotten one essential item, a coat. His new suit was nicely cut, but not at all warm. He dreaded the ceremony at the cemetery, which he hoped would be mercifully short. It was. The priest led the people in prayer, sprinkled some ashes on the casket, then it was over. Aunt Julia remained in the car; she was too afraid of falling. As she informed Dan, "If Margaret thinks I'm going to break a hip for her, she's crazy. I'll wait here."

The Mercy Meal at the house after the funeral was packed. Ten people had lived in that house, and it never seemed crowded, but now it was wall to wall people. Mrs. Salina had skipped the cemetery and she and Salina had gone back to the house to put on the coffee and put out the food. The first pot of coffee was gone within five minutes. Another coffeemaker was procured to meet the demand on this December morning. Dan was reminded of the Salina house on Christmas Eve. People were everywhere. The funeral home had loaned the family chairs, and each one was occupied. Dan grabbed a cup of coffee and a sandwich and ate standing up. Numerous people told him how moved they had been by his tribute to his grandmother. Pup was holding forth, going from room to room greeting people, telling stories, kissing all the women. Dan had seen Rosalina at the church, but there were so many people at the house he had no idea where she was. Mimi and Neil brought Shannon with them in some sort of baby carrier thing. Dan picked her up. He was amazed at how much she had grown. Evidently Shannon had been dozing and didn't take well to being disturbed. She screamed and Mimi had to take her to one of the bedrooms until she quieted.

"I see you have a way with babies." Dan turned to see Rosalina smirking at him.

"Yeah, and I'm her godfather, no less. I'll remind her of this someday."

"The funeral was beautiful, and your eulogy was inspiring and deeply personal. I'm sure your grandmother was pleased. You were the man of the hour at the church, but John, Pup as you call him, is stealing your thunder now."

"He's been doing that my whole life. I think he should run for mayor."

"So do I. But he'd be my boss."

Dan winced. "I'm not sure I'd like that."

People eventually began to filter out. Dan was sorry to see them go. He also felt guilty that he was having too good a time after his grandmother's funeral. Somehow, he also knew that Gram would not be angry. She always liked a good party almost as much as she enjoyed a good wake or funeral. The Kerr family was wired that way.

Very little of the food remained after the last guests had departed. Mrs. Salina had made a lasagna and every bit of it had been eaten. The finger sandwiches were gone, as was the garden salad. All that remained was a little potato salad. The beer that Pup had supplied was almost gone, so Dan grabbed one now that he could relax. He pulled up a chair next to Gabby.

"How's Stanley? I didn't think he ever let you out of his sight."

Gabby, offended, sniffed, "He had to work. He couldn't come."

"Pity. When's the big day? All the Kerrs will come out of the woodwork for that. I'm palpitating already at the thought of it."

"We haven't set a date yet, so you can stop palpitating. I'm not sure we will get married. It's too much fuss and bother."

"I want to be around when you explain that one to Mom. She thinks you're getting married in the spring."

"I never told her that."

"Yes, you did at Thanksgiving. You were supposed to talk about the wedding, remember?"

"No, and I'm sure you're mistaken."

"I'm sure I'm not."

Dan groaned at the thought of another Kerr crisis looming on the horizon. Perhaps Gabby was just being difficult or looking for attention, two lifelong traits of hers. Either way, it wouldn't be pretty. Dan changed out of his suit to take Aunt Julia home. As usual, Aunt Julia had bonded with Salina's wine and was unsteady on her feet. Bart had left to catch a plane, so Dan would have to ask someone else for help in getting her home. Cissy and family had already left, and Pup and family were preparing to leave. Neil volunteered to help. Dan really needed two more strong arms in case Aunt Julia had to be carried rather than escorted. The two guys managed to get Aunt Julia home safely despite the deepening snow. Her parting words were, "Margaret missed a great party."

Back at home, Mimi was anxious to leave due to the weather and Bridy and Gabby had to decide whether to leave and drive in the snow or stay overnight and leave early in the morning. Bridy decided to stay; Gabby couldn't make up her mind. Uncle Ron and Aunt Alice had already returned to Gram's house; they would leave in the morning.

"You should stay, Gabby. It's too dangerous to drive in the snow. Wait until the morning and leave early like Bridy. That's what you and Stanley did at Thanksgiving. I can't be worried all night about you. Just stay, have an early breakfast, and leave. Call Stanley and tell him you're not going to drive in the snow."

Dan noticed that Gabby didn't remind her mother to call her Sheila. "Well, all right. But I'll have to leave early. I have to work tomorrow."

Mrs. Kerr swooped in for the kill. "And speaking of

Stanley, when are you two getting married? You said we'd discuss it at Thanksgiving, but we didn't. Spring is not that far away, and you need to make some plans."

Gabby glanced at Dan as though he were a co-conspiritor. Gabby wet her lips and looked away from her mother. "Actually, Mom, I'm not sure I want to get married. Stanley and I are happy the way we are. Why ruin a good thing? We are adults; we can do anything we want."

"I see. In my book, adults get married. Kids play house, which is what you're doing."

"Mom, it's my life and I'll live the way I want. Period. I can't help it if you and Dad don't like it."

As usual, when there's a family standoff with no apparent remedy, Mr. Kerr would step in and do his best to de-escalate hostilities. He took Gabby's hand and spoke quietly. "Gabby, your mother and I would like you to marry Stanley. We're an honorable family and we like to do things the right way. If Stanley is your choice, then we will accept him and consider him our son, as we do Neil and Carl. We liked having Stanley here for Thanksgiving. He's a decent guy."

The speech worked. Gabby's expression softened, and even her posture relaxed. Perhaps this was all Gabby was looking for—the reassurance that Stanley would become a part of the family and not an outsider or a pariah to be shunned. "Well, I always did want to have a church wedding, but I don't know if that's what Stanley wants."

"The best way is to talk to him and ask what he wants. You'll have to do a lot of talking once you're married, so you might as well start now."

Gabby smiled. "Thanks, Dad. Stanley and I really do need to have that talk. I've never been a talker, as you know. It's hard for me, especially with serious issues. I prefer not to talk and just let things happen. Talking is something I have to work at every day. I hate being quiet, but that's who I am."

"There's nothing wrong with being quiet," her father reassured her. "But sometimes you need to lay your cards on the table and let your feelings be known. It may not be easy, but it is necessary."

Biddy, who had been taking all of this in, announced through a yawn, "I'm never getting married. Ever."

*****

Christmas was now just a couple of weeks away. Dan bought Rosalina some jewelry and video games for the kids. He had always given presents to his parents and all his siblings, plus his nieces and nephews, which put a considerable dent in his finances. Luckily for him, work at the paper had been steady, so he had a reserve in the bank. Dan had also treated himself to a MasterCard, which he vowed to use only in an emergency, like buying a suit for the funeral.

Mr. and Mrs. Kerr decided to keep the holiday low key since the recent death of the elder Mrs. Kerr. The family would host an open house on Christmas Day and spend Christmas Eve with the Salinas as they had for decades. This posed a dilemma for Dan. He wanted to spend Christmas Eve with Rosalina and the kids, but he also didn't want to miss the celebration at the Salinas' home. He took his father's advice to Gabby and lay his cards on the table. He paid a visit to his old friend, Mrs. Salina, to ask if he could bring a non-neighbor to the gathering. Mrs. Salina's reaction was typical. "AAAYYY, why do you even ask? You know I can't say no to you."

"I just wanted to make sure. I didn't want to end up in your doghouse."

"Doghouse? What you mean by doghouse? Stunada. I only have cats not dogs. No doghouse here."

"It's just an expression. So, it's ok, kids and all?"

Mrs. Salina rolled her eyes. "Go home. I'll see you on Christmas Eve."

As the holiday drew nearer, Dan became increasingly nervous about his mother's appointment with the neurologist, which was to take place in January. He found himself watching her every move, her reactions, her speech now that some semblance of normalcy had returned to the Kerr household. All seemed well until a few days after the funeral, Mrs. Kerr asked Dan if he could write the acknowledgement cards for people who sent cards to the family. "My handwriting is not as good as it was and I have trouble making letters, so it would be good if you could do that for me. Your father's handwriting is unreadable, so you'll have to do it." Dan was somewhat irked that the task was delegated to him and not to be shared by Biddy, but he would do as his mother asked. He recognized most of the names on the cards, so writing the notes was not all that difficult. Occasionally he would ask his mother something about one of the people he was writing to, and she would usually respond that she didn't remember, whatever the question happened to be. Maybe she did and maybe she didn't, but Dan was worried that her forgetfulness and inability to write in cursive might just be real. Mrs. Kerr was not forgetful about Gabby's presumed wedding in the spring. If anything, this presumptive event kept her buoyed for days on end. She would talk about guest lists, different venues for the reception, what priest might perform the ceremony. To the best of Dan's recollection, his mother considered his sisters' weddings to be nuisances and usually complained about the cost of everything. Now she was as excited as he had ever seen her.

Dan and John Murphy were extremely busy at the food pantry. Donations poured in and once again, the pair had to work long hours to meet the demand and find room for all the food. At the end of another long day, Dan and John would sit and drink coffee and just talk. Dan still had a hard time believing that his former nemesis had become his closest friend. It was to John that Dan confided his worries about his mother's health and the dreams about Champ. Dan told John about a dream that he had had shortly after his grandmother's funeral. In it, Gram was prevailing on Dan to save Champ; Champ was drowning in the Salinas' pond during the Christmas Eve skating party. Dan would dive into the water, but he couldn't see or grab hold of Champ. No one else at the party helped. They continued to skate as though nothing was wrong. Dan gave up this attempted rescue when he became so cold he couldn't feel his feet or his fingers. Still, Gram insisted that Dan had to save Champ.

On Christmas Eve, the Kerr clan crossed the street once again to celebrate with the Salinas. Mr. and Mrs. Kerr would skate, much to the delight of their children. Champ had been the best skater, but Bridy was a close second. She would whiz around the ice sometimes with one leg on the ice, the other held gracefully behind her. Mrs. Salina once asked her why she didn't join the Escapades. Rosalina, Bryant, and Marla joined the festivities. She and Dan skated as a couple and Dan was impressed by her agility on the ice. Since the temperature hovered around ten degrees, the skating party broke up earlier than usual. All repaired to the house for snacks and wine. Mrs.

Salina had long ago given up the custom of cooking seven fish on Christmas Eve. No one minded since her Italian delicacies pleased all palates.

Christmas Day at the Kerrs was supposed to be quiet. Dan cooked breakfast for the family and the Salinas, or most of them anyway. Gabby and Stanley were due to arrive in the afternoon and Mimi, Cissy, and Pup were home with their own families. Despite the missing members, Dan happily flipped pancakes and scrambled eggs with home fries and bacon. Some of the guests also enjoyed Mimosas, a new tradition in the Kerr family. All ate heartily and Dan once again felt the satisfaction of watching people enjoy the meal he cooked. The afternoon was to be a buffet for anyone who wished to visit. The food had just been set out when Gabby and Stanley arrived. They walked through the door hand in hand, both beaming.

Gabby all but shouted, "I'd like you to meet my husband, Stanley."

1982

CHAPTER 9

"CAN YOU HELP ME WITH THIS TABLE, BRYANT?"

Bryant nodded his silent assent. Dan and Rosalina were getting ready for their party to welcome 1982. Their house, Gram's former home, was still undergoing renovations, but enough of the house was done to enable them to have some family and friends to their New Year's Eve party.

"Rosie, where's the tablecloth for this table? I want to use this for the wine bottles."

"In the drawer of the hutch in the dining room. Where it always is," teased Rosalina.

Dan and Rosalina married last August. In January of last year, Dan was given an unexpected boost for his career. One of the editors at the paper had quit without notice, and Matt asked Dan if he would fill the position. Finally, Dan had a full-time job with benefits and a considerable increase in salary. Now that he had a secure future, Dan could ask Rosalina to marry him.

In addition, now that he had a steady income, he would make a bid on his grandmother's house. Dan wasn't optimistic, since he knew that Pup had been sharpening his teeth for the house ever since Gram died. Pup had many things in his favor: he had plenty of money and good credit at local banks. He also owned a company that could do all the work that the house needed to update it. Pup was a formidable opponent and would stop at nothing when he wanted something.

Dan had almost given up, but in early February, Pup collapsed at a job site and suffered a nearly fatal heart attack. Mr. Kerr called Dan at work to tell him that Pup had been taken by ambulance to the hospital. Elaine had called and told her in-laws what had happened. Dan got permission to leave work, and he met his parents and Elaine at the hospital. They waited, knowing nothing, for nearly an hour. Presently a young doctor approached and told Elaine that Pup had one hundred percent blockage in two of his coronary arteries and bypass surgery was the only thing that would save his life. Elaine, disabled by shock and stunned at what had happened, consented immediately. The doctor said the surgery would take several hours and they might as well go home. They all went to the Kerr home to wait for the phone call from the surgeon.

Dan called Rosalina and told her what had happened to Pup. She joined the family after she got out of work. Her kids were with their father, so she was able to wait with Dan. The family ordered takeout, but hardly anyone ate. Mrs. Kerr was on the verge of collapse herself and sought refuge in her room with her rosary. Dan wondered how on earth his mother would be able to accept the inevitable if Pup died. He pushed the thought out of his head. Three interminable hours later, the surgeon called to say that the surgery had been a success and Pup would survive. Dan ran upstairs to tell his mother the good news. Mrs. Kerr sat bolt upright on the bed and scanned Dan's face as he spoke. It was almost as though she was afraid she wasn't hearing the truth that Pup really had survived and would be fine. Dan helped her from the bed and downstairs. The family devoured the food that they had ignored before the doctor's call.

Pup's life had changed in an instant. He was under doctor's orders to lose at least thirty pounds and refrain from fried food and alcohol. The doctor also strongly suggested that Pup give up work during his recovery. The strongest admonition, however, was to stop smoking. Elaine, of course, seconded the doctor's orders and promised to hold Pup to them. Pup grunted, but he was a changed man. Never had he expected something like a heart attack to happen to him. Pup's success had gone to his head, and it took a near death experience to get his balloon to land. He always had to learn the hard way.

Pup's illness had put Dan's plans to ask Rosalina to marry him on temporary hold. When it became clear that Pup would live, Dan made his move. He asked Rosalina to dinner at the same restaurant where they had their first date, and over filet mignon and Italian wine, Dan presented Rosalina with the ring he had bought the day before. In typical Rosalina style, she smiled and teased, "What took you so long?"

Dan, misunderstanding, said, "To do what?"

Rosalina rolled her eyes. "To propose, of course."

Now that their engagement was official, Dan and Rosalina had to grapple with the question of where they were to live. Dan did not want to live in the house that Rosalina had shared with her ex-husband, to sleep in the same bed. To his immense relief, Rosalina confided that she had wanted to sell her house for a long time, but never actually took the time to do so. Dan wanted to buy his grandmother's house, but he knew Pup did as well. But now that Pup had suffered a life-threatening illness and had to make some changes in his life, Dan saw his chance. The two brothers met to discuss the sale of the house, and surprisingly, Pup agreed to let Dan buy it with the stipulation that Pup's company would be the contractor to do the renovations. Handshakes all around sealed the deal.

Now Dan's dilemma, although a pleasant one, was who to ask to be his best man. His first choice was his cousin Bart, but Bart had recently been sent to a new post on the West Coast and he didn't think he'd be able to get away. Bart didn't want to commit and then back out at the last minute. Dan decided to ask John Murphy, his closest friend. John was reluctant at first.

"I appreciate the offer," John said to Dan, "but I won't be able to stand next to you. Isn't that what the best man does?"

"Maybe so, but you can still hand me the rings and hear the ceremony, can you not? It doesn't matter if you're sitting or standing if you can do those two things."

"True. I'm really honored, Dan, that you asked me."

"Why wouldn't I? You're my best friend, aren't you?"

"If you say so. Just kidding. What about your brother? Shouldn't he have first dibs?"

"I've thought about that, but Pup and I aren't that close, and he's a lot older than I am."

Perceptive as ever, John said, "Are you afraid he won't live until August?"

"The thought has crossed my mind, yeah, but that's not the real reason I decided to ask you."

John looked thoughtful. "How will I get into the church? There are no ramps to the upper church. I don't want people carrying me inside. That can wait until I'm in a box."

"Rosalina and I don't want a huge to-do. We may not have it in the upper church, but those details remain to be ironed out."

Dan and Rosalina exchanged vows in the chapel of St. Tom's Church on August 15, 1981. Dan invited all the Kerrs, including all the children. Only Champ and Gabby were among the missing. Rosalina's immediate family and the Salinas and Aunt Julia rounded out the guest list. Champ, for obvious reasons; Gabby used her usual excuse that Stanley had to work and she couldn't go alone since she was "with child." Rosalina's parents hosted the reception in their backyard. Dan and Rosalina then left for a brief honeymoon on Nantucket.

New Year's Eve was always a good time to reflect and, as Dan looked back, he realized what an upheaval had occurred in his life. He was now married; he had a steady, good paying job, and he was a stepfather to two kids. In addition, Pup had suffered a nearly fatal heart attack and Gabby and Stanley were expectant parents. Mimi and Neil were also awaiting the birth of the seventh Mullaney. Life was good. Dan's only real regret was that he had to give up his volunteer job at the food pantry. Aside from a couple of hours on Saturday morning, Dan just didn't have the time. Pup had wanted to take his place, but he couldn't do any of the heavy lifting. Dan felt as though he had abandoned John, so he ran articles in the paper asking for some much-needed help for John. Some people did respond, but John was pretty much left to run the place alone.

Pup and Elaine had arrived early for the party at Dan and Rosalina's home. Elaine and Rosalina chatted in the kitchen while Dan and Pup held forth in the living room. It had been an eventful year for both brothers, life changing for Pup, who reflected on the changes as he sipped his Ginger Ale. "You know," he began. "I never thought anything like a heart attack would happen to me, especially since I'm still young. But now I'm glad it did. I miss drinking beer and eating whatever I wanted, but now that I've lost weight, I realize I never would have made these changes if I didn't have something drastic happen. I guess everything happens for the best."

Dan sighed. "I was afraid that we would lose you and Mom that day. She never could have adjusted to losing two sons, especially her favorite."

"You're always saying I'm her favorite. I never felt that way."

"You are, but that's beside the point. We're starting another year and still we know nothing about Champ. This is an everlasting treadmill that we're walking. I want to get off."

"Me too. I thought about making a trip to VietNam since I now have time on my hands."

Dan gaped at his brother. "To do what, search rice paddies and jungles? There's nothing there. Save the money and take Elaine to Cancun or some other resort. You could both use it."

"Yeah, it was just an idle thought. I'm not used to having time on my hands. I want to go back to work."

"You do work. You're still the head of your company. That's work."

"True, but I mean real work with a hammer and saw. I want to work beside the guys I employ, to use my hands. I was always better with my hands than with my head."

Dan wanted to steer his brother away from this talk of work since Dan knew once Pup did go back to the nuts and bolts of building, he would soon return to smoking and drinking. "I'm glad you are able to visit Mom and Dad more. They like it, especially Mom. How do you think she's doing these days?"

"She's ok. Of course, she's on her best behavior when I visit, so I can't comment beyond that. She probably is forgetful, but who's to say that she has a disease? Even the neurologist couldn't say for certain that she had dementia, which flies in the face of the diagnosis of Dr. Francesca, whose specialties are hysteria and overreaction."

"I disagree. Mrs. Salina is one sharp lady and I believe what she says. The doctor's diagnosis of inconclusive is just a cushion that doctors use when they don't know."

Pup shifted in his seat. "Maybe. But I think if Champ is ever found, dead or alive, we'll know for sure if Mom is losing it or not. Let's go join the ladies."

Dan had put his culinary skill to the test by making sweet and sour chicken, Swedish meatballs, and three bean salad for the New Year's Eve bash. The Salinas were among the guests and Dan thought he made it clear that they were to come as guests, not as the caterers. Yet Francesca made Italian wedding soup and Salina brought several bottles of homemade wine. Both sets of parents came, as did John Murphy, after being duly hauled up the stairs by Dan and Neil. Aunt Julia declined, citing the cold and the snow and ice. "This is probably the only party invitation Aunt Julia ever turned down," observed Pup.

"It's better than breaking a hip and ending up in a nursing home," his father reminded him.

Dan loved being a host, all the more since he was entertaining guests in his own home. Rosalina also loved a good party, and she was a considerate and gracious hostess. They had invited the mayor, but he had several other parties to attend, so he declined. Bryant went to a party at a friend's house with the firm understanding that he was to be home before midnight. During the course of the evening, most of the food was disposed of, as was most of the wine. Mrs. Salina kept everyone laughing with anecdotes of her childhood in Italy and her early years as a married woman. Francesca was a born comic; her timing and delivery were natural and smooth. She contrasted markedly with her husband, who tended to be dour, that is, until his wine brought him up to some level of jocularity. They played off each other beautifully.

At midnight, Dan turned on the tv and they all watched the ball drop in Times Square and then clinked glasses to welcome 1982. The party was now anticlimactic, and the guests requested their coats and departed for home. Dan and Rosalina left the cleanup for the morning and called it a night. As he carried a sleeping Marla to bed, Dan realized he had finally found the happiness he always hoped for, yet his heart still felt the emptiness of missing Champ.

In the new year, Dan spent most of his time and energy trying to ingratiate himself with his stepchildren. Both had been evasive and distant since Dan and Rosalina married. Dan wondered if they were just missing their home and their friends in the neighborhood or if they resented him and considered him an interloper at best and a father replacement at worst. Marla softened first after her mother had taken her to friends' homes for all day visits and school started. She still had her school friends and soon she succumbed to the inherent silliness of being twelve and prepubescent worship of Michael Jackson. Bryant was another matter entirely. He had always been taciturn, but now his silence seemed to take on a deeper layer of sullenness. Even though Dan and Rosalina attended every one of his football games regardless of the weather, the boy remained implacable. Dan was exceedingly puzzled by his stepson. Bryant was a good student and athlete. He did his chores at home without complaint, but there was always an undercurrent of suppressed angst about him. Rosalina kept telling Dan to give him time. He'll come around. Dan seriously doubted he would ever have any kind of relationship with the boy.

The shift in Dan's relationship with Bryant happened one warm day in February when Dan asked Bryant to help him clean out the garage. The teen complied readily enough, silent as usual. When he spoke, Dan was so surprised that he wasn't sure the boy had spoken at all. He stared at Bryant. "What did you say?"

Bryant cleared his throat. "Dan, would you teach me how to drive?"

In his surprise, Dan said exactly the wrong thing. "Sure, as long as we use your mother's car."

Bryant flushed, and he looked away. "Never mind."

Sensing he was about to lose the boy forever, Dan recovered quickly. "I was only kidding. I'll teach you how to drive. We can start tomorrow afternoon."

Bryant smiled. "Thanks, Dan. My Mom wouldn't have the patience to teach me."

The next day, man and boy were in the high school parking lot. Bryant handled the car with ease. He obviously knew the basics. "You drive very well. Have you driven before?" Dan asked.

"No, but I've been watching people drive my whole life. It's easy. Can I drive home?"

"No, you can't. You don't even have your LP yet, so you can't drive on the street. Have you gotten the book to study from the Registry?"

"Not yet. I wanted to make sure you could teach me first. My Dad said he'll buy me a car once I learned how to drive."

So that was it, thought Dan. Senior, as he and Rosalina called her ex, was trying to buy the boy's affection by dangling a huge carrot under his nose. Dan suddenly felt sorry for Rosalina. This game of good cop, bad cop has likely been going on since the divorce, but now the toys are bigger. Dan and Rosalina would discuss this tonight.

"I feel like a trip to Dunkin Donuts. How about you?" Dan turned expectantly towards Bryant.

"Yeah. I'd love an iced coffee."

As they sipped coffee, Dan tried to draw the boy out more. "Are there any girls you'll ask out when you have your license and a car? You're a jock. Girls swoon for jocks, especially football players."

Dan expected a mumbled reply, but Bryant spoke up clearly. "Yeah, several. I have lunch with one girl every day, but it's hard to go out when you don't have a car."

Dan's heart squeezed as he thought of Champ. "My two brothers were jocks in high school. They had more dates than brains. I wished I could charm girls like they did, but I was a geek, not a jock. I went out with some girls, but I had to work hard for a date. Those two just snapped their fingers and the girls came running."

"Do you miss your brother? The one who's MIA?"

Dan had to look down at his coffee cup and swallow the emotion that threatened his voice and moistened his eyes. "Yes, I do. Every day. Not knowing what happened to him is the worst thing."

"I like your other brother, the one you call Pup. He's a cool guy. Why do you call him Pup? He's not a dog."

"My neighbor, Mrs. Salina, named him that when he was a little kid. He was always getting into trouble and I guess that in the old days, troublesome kids, especially boys, were called pups. Anyway, the name stuck and after that, every kid in the family had a nickname."

"You're Chip."

"Yes, I am, for better or worse."

"I really like your family. They're all nice. I can't stand Dad's new girlfriend. I hate going there every weekend. I can't wait until I'm eighteen so I can stop these visits that are so pointless."

"You have to see your father."

"I know, but I don't have to see his girlfriend. Even Marla, who's a real twit, can't stand her either. Bettina, the girlfriend, takes Marla to the mall all the time to buy her new clothes."

"Have you told your mother any of this?"

"No. She can't do anything about it anyway. Bettina makes such a big stinking deal about our visits. She's so phony nice. She makes me sick. She's such an airhead. She can't boil water so we have to go out to eat every weekend. It gets old after a while; you know what I mean?"

While Dan couldn't help being thrilled that Bryant had not only begun talking but had confided in Dan who would have to break this confidence and tell Rosalina all the Bryant had told him.

Rosalina listened in silence as Dan related what Bryant had told him. "My ex has been playing this game with the kids ever since we split up. He's so insecure he sees you as a threat, and since he's so controlling and manipulative, he uses the kids as his pawns. I was wondering when they would catch on. I'll talk to him, but I know it won't do a bit of good. Senior does exactly what he wants and the more it displeases me, the more he'll do it. I'm sure he's hoping that I'll try to get the court to change the custody decree, then he'll hire a lawyer and whine that I'm trying to keep his children away from him. I wish there was a way I could limit the visits, but that doesn't seem likely or practical."

"I'm sorry that you have to deal with all of this. I'll have Pup break his legs if you'd like."

Rosalina smiled. "I wish it were that easy. I didn't want to marry him to begin with, but I had to. Back then, if a girl got pregnant, she had to marry the father, like it or not. We got married the summer after we graduated from high school, so Senior lost out on his scholarship and had to go to work instead to support his family. Once he wasn't the adored football hero anymore, just another working stiff, he didn't take too kindly to his changed circumstances. I left him twice and twice he begged me to come back. Like a fool I did, and he'd be nice for a while, but eventually he would lapse into his usual behavior. I'm just sorry now that the kids have to be dragged into this mess."

Dan looked with fierce admiration at his wife. Only a strong woman could deal with this constant trouble. Rosalina made something of herself so she could leave her husband and forge a new life for her kids. In her own way, Rosalina was as strong as Gram. She accepted what she couldn't change, but changed what she could. Dan also realized how easy his life had been and felt slightly ashamed. The best he could do would be to stand by Rosalina and catch the reflection of her strength and character.

Dan took his wife into his arms. "You are a woman who could use some comfort."

"And you are just the man who can provide it."

CHAPTER 10

DURING THE WINTER OF '82 THE KERR CLAN expanded once again with the arrival of Liam James Mullaney and a son to Gabby and Stanley yet to be named. Dan wondered how a couple can await the birth of a child and not have settled on a name when the child was born. Evidently, Gabby wanted to name their son Dennis Francis after Champ, but Stanley objected, saying that name was unlucky given Champ's fate. The name expert, Stanley, saved the day by deciding to name the boy Dylan Robert after Stanley's favorite singer. Typical, thought Dan. Stanley objected to Gabby's choice to clear the way for his own.

Late in February, Dan checked the post office box, something he hadn't done in months. To his surprise, there was an envelope inside. Dan ran to his car and tore open the letter, which informed him that Champ's dog tags had been found and verified to have belonged to Champ. Dan stared at the letter and read it over and over. Could it be? Would Champ's body be located after all this time? Dan returned to his office and called Rosalina and then Pup. Each reaction was typical. Rosalina was elated; Pup was irked and skeptical.

"Chip, you pulled me out of a meeting to tell me this?"

"Don't you want to know? This is a significant development after years of nothing."

"I still think this is nothing. How do they know the tags belong to Champ? Maybe they belong to another guy with the same name. This is bogus. Call me when we have a body to bury."

Dan couldn't believe his brother's anger. It didn't make any sense.

"Sorry I called you, since your business is obviously more important to you than your family. Maybe you should go to Nam and find the body yourself."

Pup's tone softened. "Have you told Mom and Dad?"

"Not yet. I intend to tell Dad, but not Mom. I don't know how she would react."

"Good move. I have to go."

A few days later, Dan made sure his mother was out of the house when he went over to tell his father about the letter. He had made arrangements with Mrs. Salina to make sure Mrs. Kerr was occupied elsewhere when he went to see his father. Dan bought two coffees and made his way down the street.

Upon entering the house, Dan found his father asleep in his recliner, the paper in his lap. The house was quiet and much too warm. "Dad," Dan called to his sleeping father. No response. A little louder Dan called, "Dad." Mr. Kerr adjusted his position in the chair. Finally, Dan yelled, "Dad, wake up. I have coffee for you." Mr. Kerr looked up at his son with rheumy but alert blue eyes. "Hi Chip. Why are you here at this time of the day?"

"I have something to tell you and show you."

"Is it about Champ?"

"Yes, it is. Just listen for a minute, ok?"

Mr. Kerr sipped his coffee and waited to hear what his son had to say. "I never told you, but a few years ago I wrote to the government office that deals with locating missing soldiers. I gave them Champ's information and waited to hear from them. I heard nothing until a few days ago. I received a letter informing me that Champ's dog tags have been located and verified to have belonged to Champ."

Dan waited for his father's reaction. Mr. Kerr sipped his coffee tentatively and finally spoke.

"This agency is sure the tags are Champs and not someone else's?"

"That's what the letter said."

"And this is a bona fide government agency?"

Dan felt his irritation rising again. "Yes. It's legit. I was hoping they had found the remains, but this is something at least."

Mr. Kerr shook his head. "I want to believe you, Chip, but without Champ's remains, I'm still skeptical. It's been so long. I really have a hard time believing that anything would turn up after all these years. I still have my dog tags, you know."

"Yes, in the second drawer, under your socks. Why are you saving them?"

"I don't really know why I'm saving them. A memento maybe? I know it doesn't make a great deal of sense. War is hell. I don't know why I didn't throw them away when I returned home. Are you going to tell your mother?"

"No. That's why I asked Mrs. Salina to invite her for coffee so I could talk to you privately. I called Pup, but he doesn't believe the tags are Champ's. I don't want to incite another Kerr family war over this."

Mr. Kerr sighed and sipped his coffee. "I really wonder if we will ever know this side of the grave."

Dan wondered the same thing.

During the spring, Dan and family found themselves partaking of that family sport known as looking at colleges. Since Bryant was in his junior year and doing well both academically and athletically, it seemed the natural thing to have him shop around and choose a college. Bryant had decided he wanted to go away to school, but not too far away; he wanted to stay in New England. If Bryant expressed interest in colleges in Maine or Vermont, Rosalina and Marla would go along for a family weekend away. If Bryant wanted to go to campuses in Massachusetts, usually he and Dan would go alone. Dan came to enjoy these trips. Not only had he not seen a lot of New England, but he also saw these excursions as golden opportunities to get to know Bryant better. The kid who would hardly speak a sentence the year before had become quite talkative, save for occasional bouts of adolescent pouting. Bryant also seemed to enjoy the time alone with Dan when they could converse freely, man to man, so to speak.

On this Saturday, Dan and Bryant were driving to UMass Amherst, one of Bryant's prime choices. The day was wet and cold, but the two had stopped for breakfast after an hour of driving and were feeling full and warm. Bryant had indicated that he wanted to become an architect or a builder like Uncle Pup. As they traversed the Mass Pike, Bryant turned to Dan. "Did Uncle Pup ever go to college?"

"No, he didn't," replied Dan. "He learned the basics of carpentry from our grandfather. You know that room in my parents' house, the one in the cellar? Well, my grandfather and Pup converted that from a dark, cobwebby mess to a downstairs bedroom. Pup then honed his skills in the service. He never went to college because he learned a trade and made it into a business."

Bryant looked at Dan. "Where did you go to college, Dan?"

"I went to Fordham University, a Jesuit college in New York."

"What's a Jeszoowit college?"

"A Jesuit college is run by the Jesuits, an order of priests that are known for their teaching ability."

"Did you like it there?"

"Yes, I did. It was quite a change from little Coltonwood. I'm glad I had the experience. Back then, most students didn't visit potential schools. They looked at the catalogs and decided. What you're doing makes much more sense. Actually seeing the place and talking to people can help you decide where you want to go."

Bryant was quiet for a while and then said right out of the blue, "Do you miss your brother? The one lost in VietNam? The other day, Grammy called me Champ and went on talking about something I had no clue about. I think she really thought I was your brother."

Dan's heart's heart rate suddenly accelerated. "She called you Champ? Are you sure?"

"Yeah. She's called me that before, too. Do I look like him?"

"No, you don't, but he was an athlete like you. That's what probably makes her think of Champ. He was a three-sport athlete, as you are."

"Grammy's a funny lady. The other day when I was there mowing the lawn, she took something out of the freezer. It was a radio wrapped in foil. It still worked too, one of those transistor radios from the old days."

"Oh, my God," thought Dan. His mother was putting radios in the freezer. What else had she done? He could see how she could mistake Bryant for Champ, since her last clear memory of Champ would be when he was just about Bryant's age. And yet, the doctor's report was inconclusive. Now what?

Bryant loved the UMass campus and just about decided on the spot to go there. "Let's wait and see a few more before you decide, ok? We still have Connecticut and Rhode to go."

"No problem."

As Bryant paged happily through the college's catalog, Dan kept turning over in his mind what Bryant had said. Should he take his mother to another neurologist? Why hasn't his father spoken about his wife's bizarre behavior? Is it so common that he's become accustomed and doesn't see it anymore? Should he share this with Pup or another one of his siblings? Dan worried steadily about his mother's condition, yet he couldn't come up with any solutions.

Dan's dreams about Champ had all but disappeared, but on the night of the college visit, he dreamed of his brother. In the dream, Champ was two people; he was himself and he was Bryant. No one except Dan seemed confused by this double identity. At one point in the dream, Champ sat at the kitchen table and was eating strawberry ice cream, which he had loved.

He was listening to the transistor radio as it blasted sixties music. Then Champ/ Bryant looked at Dan and said, "Why do I have to listen to that old music? I want to hear something that I like, something modern." Then the scene shifted, and Champ and Bryant dressed for football tossed the ball back and forth. Then Champ aimed the ball at Dan's head, and he woke up drenched in sweat.

Dan said nothing to Rosalina about the dream, but he wondered if the dreams would return as they always had in the past. He told her about what Bryant told him about his mother. Rosalina looked seriously alarmed. "Your mother reminds me of what happened to my grandmother. She started saying and doing things that didn't make any sense. She had dementia. I wonder if the same is true of your mother, despite what the neurologist said. I think Francesca is concerned about the same thing." Hearing the word dementia and Rosalina's linking his mother's behavior with that of her grandmother who had dementia gave Dan considerable pause. He decided to call Bridy and discuss it with her. At least she would be reasonable, unlike Pup or Gabby or Cissy. That night, Dan called his younger sister and they spoke at length about their mother's issues. Ultimately, they decided to give it more time and watch more carefully.

A week or so later, Dan was deep into a book when Marla ran into the house yelling, "Mom, Dan, the firetrucks are at Grammy and Grampy's house." Dan flung the book away and he and Rosalina and Marla ran to the Kerr home. As they were about to run into the yard, Dan saw Mrs. Salina racing across the street. In her haste to get inside, she hip checked two firefighters into a hedge. Under different circumstances, Dan realized the scene he just saw would be funny, but not today. Dan burst through the back porch door and saw his mother looking dazed, sitting on the porch glider. She looked pale, but otherwise all right. But where was his father? His car was in the driveway, so he must be home. "Mom, where's Dad? Is he in the house?"

Mrs. Kerr raised tired eyes to her son. "I don't know."

"What do you mean, you don't know? Is he home or not?"

"I don't know."

Thoroughly exasperated, Dan began to run through the house dreading what he might find. He and Rosalina and Marla search the entire house. No sign of Mr. Kerr. At that moment, the object of the search pushed open the porch door. He had been out for a walk.

The kitchen was filled with smoke from a scorched pot on the stove. Dan recognized his mother's pan that she used to cook potatoes. The firefighters had quenched the small blaze with a fire extinguisher. They lugged two large fans into the kitchen to clear the smoke. One of the firefighters pulled Dan aside and told him the cause of the fire had been a pot on the stove that evidently had no water, or the water had boiled away. Inside were the remnants of whole potatoes, charred almost beyond recognition. The pot, a staple in the Kerr household, was twisted, and the bottom had been burned away. The stove top was blackened, and the burner had melted in the heat of the fire.

Mrs. Salina stayed after the firefighters left and announced that the Kerrs were invited to dinner at the Salina residence, no excuses accepted. The kitchen was still somewhat smoky, so Mr. and Mrs. Kerr would have had to go out to dinner anyway. The six of them crossed the street to the Salina's where they were greeted by Salina, who held a bottle of homemade wine in each hand. All partook of the wine, except Marla, who had to be content with Pepsi. All the while, Dan eyed his mother carefully. Aside from looking somewhat pale, she seemed fine and spoke as soon as she accepted a glass from Salina. "This is such an imposition, Francesca. You shouldn't have to make dinner for five extra people on the spur of the moment. It's not fair."

Mr. and Mrs. Salina both spoke at the same time. "Mia casa, tua casa. My house is your house. Neighbors help neighbors." Mrs. Salina, wooden spoon in hand, bustled about the kitchen. "I make lasagna for many people. If I didn't have that, I would throw on a pot of spaghetti. Salina and I like the company. Otherwise, we fight all through supper."

The wine helped the mood, but the tension was palpable. Dan wanted to speak to Mrs. Salina alone, but he couldn't very well do that with his parents sitting right there. No one spoke of the fire. Instead, the mayor became the topic of conversation. The town was set to vote on a recall petition to remove His Honor from office. Dan and Rosalina both liked the mayor and felt the petition was politically motivated and totally unnecessary. Since he was an editor at the local paper, Dan's head was spinning from all the stories the paper had published about the recall. The last thing he wanted to discuss was politics, but Salina was relentless in his carping about the mayor. Mrs. Salina brought the discussion to a prompt end by serving the lasagna and dispatching Salina to the cellar for more wine. Dan's legs were rubbery by the time he and Rosalina and Marla left for home. As they were walking through the door, Mrs. Salina whispered as discreetly as she could, "Don't worry. I'll keep an eye on her. We talk later."

Once home, Dan retreated to the warmth and security of his favorite recliner and he and Marla watched some silly sitcom on tv. Not ordinarily a fan of tv, Dan just wanted something to take his mind off the fire and his worry about his mother. Dan was comfortably dozing when the phone rang in the kitchen. A few seconds later Rosalina came into the den. "Pup's on the phone and he's mad. You better talk to him." Dan groaned and heaved himself out of the chair. The last thing he wanted was an argument with Pup, but he would just have to face the music.

"Hello," Dan said cautiously.

"Why the hell didn't you tell me the fire department had been at the house? I heard it from a buddy of mine who's a firefighter."

"I'm sorry, Pup. I should have called you. Mom was cooking potatoes but forgot to add water before she put the pot on the stove. She turned on the burner and went out onto the porch and evidently fell asleep. A neighbor passing by saw smoke and called the fire department. Marla told us that the fire department was at the house, so we ran down the street to see what was going on. The firefighters just used an extinguisher to put out the fire, but there was a lot of smoke, so Mrs. Salina invited us to dinner since Mom wouldn't be able to cook. With all the excitement, I forgot to call you."

Somewhat mollified, Pup asked, "How could Mom forget to put water in the pan when she's cooking potatoes? That doesn't make any sense. Where was Dad while all of this was going on?"

"He was out for a walk. We searched the house for him, but then he came home all frazzled when he saw the firetrucks. Mom seemed out of it when we first got there and didn't know where Dad was. She could have burned the house down. Something is definitely wrong; I don't care what that doctor said. Mom has a problem, and we need to find out what it is. We got lucky this time; we may not be so lucky the next time."

Pup exhaled a long sigh. "Yeah, this is serious. We had better take her to another doctor. Maybe that doctor will know something. Have you called anyone else?"

"No. I'm exhausted. I didn't have the energy to make all of those calls. Could you call Mimi and let her know before she hears it from someone else?"

"I can do that. I'll ask around and see if I can get the name of a good doctor, even if the doctor is in Boston."

"Thanks. I'll be talking to you."

That was better than I thought it would be, thought Dan as he hung up. Now he knew to apologize first and put Pup on the defensive instead of arguing with him. He returned to the den and another stupid show was on. Dan didn't care. He just wanted to relax as much as his muddled mind would let him. Dan's time of solitude was short-lived. The phone rang again.

Rosalina rushed into the den. "It's your father. He says he has to take your mother to the hospital."

This time, Dan sprang from the chair and sprinted to the kitchen. "Hello, Dad. What's wrong with Mom?"

"She is slurring her words and she can't lift her right arm. She needs to see a doctor right away. I don't want to drive since I had so much wine at Salinas'. Could you take us?"

Dan also had had too much wine. The last thing he wanted to do was drive. "Why don't you call Pup? He's home and ask him if he could drive you. Better yet, I'll call and ask him."

"Ok, but make it quick. I don't like the way your mother looks."

Dan swore after he hung up the phone. Rosalina, surprised by the oath, looked up anxiously. Dan told her what had happened as he dialed Pup's number. Elaine answered and Dan wasted no time in making his request. "He's down cellar with the boys playing pool. I'll get him right away."

"Thanks, Elaine." Dan could hear Elaine in the distance yell to Pup, "John, your mother needs to go to the hospital. Dan wants to know if you could drive her and your father." A breathless Pup picked up the receiver. "What happened now?"

"Dad just called and said Mom is slurring her words and can't raise her right arm. It sounds like a stroke to me. Dad and I had too much wine at dinner, so he was asking if you could drive them."

"I'm on my way."

Dan realized how fuddled he was when Rosalina asked the obvious question, "Why didn't you call the ambulance?" The thought had never crossed Dan's mind. "Too late now. Pup is on his way over."

Rosalina drove to the hospital and the long vigil of waiting for news began. The ER wasn't busy, and Mrs. Kerr was taken to a room immediately. Dan, Rosalina, Pup, and Mr. Kerr anxiously sipped coffee and waited for the doctor to let them know what had happened. Mr. Kerr was nervous and fidgeting, which made Dan nervous. His father was usually calm and in complete control, but not tonight. The four of them made small talk to pass the time, but Dan grew more and more anxious the longer they sat.

Finally, a doctor who looked to be the same age as Bryant, approached. "Are you the family of Theresa Kerr?" He asked.

Pup answered. "We are. What can you tell us?"

"We did some tests. It appears that Mrs. Kerr had a TIA or Trans Ischemic Attack which is a mini stroke. She will be admitted so we can do more tests to be sure of the diagnosis. Any questions?"

Pup spoke up. "Does that mean that she might have a bigger stroke at some time?"

"Yes, it does. Usually a TIA is a warning and the precursor of a much more serious stroke in the future."

"But isn't there some medication which could prevent a bigger stroke from happening? You make it sound as though it's inevitable."

"We need to be sure of what we're dealing with first before we talk about medication."

Dan could see Pup's frustration with the doctor had morphed into anger. "What else do you need to do before you know?"

"We'll do more blood work and some imaging tomorrow. In the meantime, your mother will have some clot blocking medication tonight and we'll run the tests first thing tomorrow."

"Why can't you do them tonight?"

"Because we need to see how well the medication is working and keep checking the blood work. Your mother isn't in any immediate danger. Her vitals are good, and she's bright and alert. You can call the hospital any time to ask about her condition."

Pup looked about to snap at the doctor when Mr. Kerr spoke up, "Doctor, is my wife going to die?"

Dan looked at his father, who was pale and trembling. The doctor said gently, "Not at this time, Mr. Kerr. What the future holds, of course, I can't say. We'll design a treatment plan for her and give her the best care we can. I wish I could be more reassuring, but we can only do what is in our power to do."

The family thanked the doctor and left the hospital. Both sons supported their father, who spent the night with Dan and Rosalina. The next morning, Dan called the hospital and inquired about his mother's condition. A nurse on the floor told him his mother had had a good night and was resting comfortably. Mr. Kerr came downstairs a few minutes later, unshaven and pale. Dan wished he could stay with his father, but he had to go to work.

"How are you feeling, Dad?" Dan asked as he passed a cup of coffee to his father.

"I'm all right. Can't wait to get home and shave and then go visit your mother."

"I called the hospital, and a nurse told me Mom had a good night and she's resting comfortably."

"Good. Maybe she'll go home today. That would be good."

"Now, don't rush it, Dad. Give the doctors time to do all the tests so they can give us some answers."

*****

Dan got a call at noon from his father: "Your mother is going home right after lunch."

"Did you talk to the doctor?"

"Yes, I did. He said your mother is fine and able to go home."

"He must have said more than that, Dad. What did the tests show?"

"He didn't mention the tests. He said that he tweaked her medication. Is that a word, tweaked?"

"Yes, it's a word."

"Never heard it before. What does it mean?"

"It means he changed the medication, raised or lowered the dose. Let me talk to Mom."

"Hi, Chip. I'm going home."

"So I heard. Did you see a doctor this morning?"

"Yes, a woman doctor. I'm glad there are women doctors now."

"What did that doctor say?"

"She said I'm fine and able to go home."

"What's that doctor's name?"

"I'm not sure. I'll have to ask."

Totally exasperated, Dan said, "Mom, I'll talk to you later, ok?"

"Ok. See you later."

Dan's next call was to Mrs. Salina. "AAAYYY, how's your mother? I go visit her today."

"No need. She's going home."

"Already? She just got there."

"I know, but she's going home. Could you check on my parents this afternoon? I couldn't get any information out of either of them. They're both so happy that my mother is going home that they've completely forgotten why she had to be there in the first place. Please keep an eye on them until I can get there tonight."

"AAAYYY, stunada. I keep both eyes on them."

"Thanks, Mrs. Salina. I knew I could count on you."

Flustered and harried as he was, Dan had to prepare for a meeting of the editorial board to take place in his office that morning. After a frantic hour of work, Dan had his notes prepared when the phone rang. Thinking it was his father and hoping it wasn't, Dan picked it up.

"Hello," he said cautiously.

"Chippy, it's so good to hear your voice."

"Aunt Julia? I really can't talk right now. I have a…"

"Don't worry. I'll only take a minute of your time."

The editorial board filed through the door.

"Aunt Julia, I can't…"

"Chippy, since you are cursed or blessed with a writer's memory, I knew I could ask you. Do you remember what color dress I wore to the last christening? I would hate to wear the same color this time. That would be unspeakably gauche."

"Aunt Julia, I have people in my office. I can't." Still Aunt Julia persisted. "Cissy is going to take me shopping for a dress. But I can always buy a color I don't have and that would solve the whole problem. Every occasion calls for a new dress and hat, even though most women don't wear hats now. Imagine! In my day, you weren't properly dressed unless you were wearing a hat and gloves. Style and class are both going to hell in a handbasket." Dan heard the sound of the doorbell. "Oh, there's Cissy."

"Cissy," Aunt Julia screamed into the phone. "Do you want to talk to Chippy?"

Dan felt the flush that started at the base of his neck float up to his ears at the smirks and smiles of the editorial board, who were clearly enjoying this unexpected show.

"Chip?" He heard Cissy say.

"Cissy, please tell Aunt Julia I can't talk now. I have a meeting going on in my office. Tell her I'm sorry and I'll talk to her later."

"Ok. No problem. Bye."

A sincerely abashed Dan addressed the people in his office. "Forgive me, gentlemen. That was my aunt; she's in her nineties and decided for some reason to call me at work. Shall we get on with it?"

Sutcliff, an editor, spoke for the group. "No problem. We wanted to hear more."

Dan flushed again at the titters and guffaws that followed. "No, thank you. You heard enough."

Later that evening, Dan called Cissy. "Am I missing something or is Aunt Julia losing it? I had no idea what she was talking about."

"You're the one who's missing something or losing it. Aunt Julia was talking about Dylan's christening, which is happening in two weeks."

"No one told me about any christening."

"Mom was supposed to tell everyone. Pup and Elaine are hosting the after party. I'm surprised Pup didn't mention it to you."

"Thanks for telling me. I'm going to call Pup right now."

So furious was Dan that he had to dial Pup's number twice before he got the connection. He didn't mince words. "Why the hell didn't you tell me about the christening? I had to hear it from Aunt Julia. I thought she was nuts, so I called Cissy and she confirmed it and said the party is at your house. Don't you inform your guests when you have a party at your house, or do we guess the date and time?"

"Calm down, Chip. Mom was supposed to call everyone, not me. Evidently, she, for whatever reason, hadn't gotten to you yet. You know she's not herself these days. Aunt Julia just beat her to the punch, that's all."

Chip drew a deep breath. "Now I know there's something wrong with Mom. She loves christenings and talks about them for weeks before and after. We have to have her evaluated again as soon as possible. This is not normal."

"Agreed. I've been asking around about doctors, but no bites yet. Don't worry. I'll find one."

"Ok. What time is the christening and the after party? I don't want to be late."

"The baptism is at one. The party is right after. This will be my big day. I'm the godfather, you know."

"Congratulations. Who's the godmother?"

"Gabby's high school friend, Susan something. You remember her? She used to come over to the house a lot. I've forgotten her last name."

"Yeah, I remember her somewhat. I don't know her last name either. Talk to you later."

The following Saturday morning, Dan paid his parents a visit. They were at the kitchen table sipping coffee when he arrived. "Hi, Mom. Hi, Dad. I thought I'd stop in for a few minutes. How are you both feeling?"

Mr. Kerr spoke for both. "We're doing fine and going shopping this afternoon to get some new clothes for the christening. We both need shoes and I need a new tie."

Mrs. Kerr reached across the table and touched her husband's hand. "Dear, the christening was weeks ago. We don't need to go shopping for anything. Liam is going on three months." Then to Dan. "Have you seen him lately? He's growing like a weed. I think he's going to look just like Champ. I wish Champ wasn't so far away so he could see Liam."

Dan and his father exchanged a look, both incredulous and speechless at what they had just heard. Dan decided to disregard what he heard about Champ, but to address the issue of the christening. "Mom, the christening is for Gabby's baby, not Liam. It's easy to confuse them since they were born so close together. You should go shopping this afternoon. You have to look your best."

His mother's vacant stare totally unnerved Dan. "When did Gabby have a baby? Why didn't anyone tell me? I'm the grandmother and no one told me, not even you, Bert."

"Gabby told you herself, dear. She called and told us she had a boy."

"What's his name? I seem to recall talking to Gabby recently. The family is getting so big I'm losing track. I will need a new dress for the baptism. When is it, again?"

"It's a week from Sunday, Mom. His name is Dylan Robert."

"Dylan? That's not a saint's name. He can't be baptized unless he has a saint's name. Doesn't she know this? I thought I raised a good Catholic family, but apparently not."

"Relax, Mom. Not everyone has a saint's name anymore. More modern names are acceptable now. Stanley chose the name after his favorite singer, Bob Dylan. He just reversed the first and last names."

"The baby is named after a singer? I'd better call the priest and ask if that's appropriate. That would be awful if he couldn't be baptized. The family would be disgraced."

"Dear, Gabby made the arrangements with the priest. He knows all about the name. There won't be any problem," Mr. Kerr tried to reassure his wife.

"Well, I suppose if she talked to the priest,"

Dan spoke up. "It's ok, Mom. It will be a great time."

The day of the christening was pouring rain. After church that morning, all Dan wanted to do was put on his oldest jeans and an equally old sweatshirt and watch football from the comfort of his recliner. However, he was forced to don dress pants and a jacket for the return trip to church. Pup and Elaine and their boys were there, as were Mimi and Neil and their entire brood. Dan wondered where his parents were and the rest of his sibs. Presently Cissy and Carl arrived with Aunt Julia who had just recently consented to the use of a wheelchair for her outings. As Carl pushed her to her seat, she gave Dan a sly wink. He wondered what kind of mischief she would be up to at the after party.

At ten past one, the rest of the family still had not arrived. Dan began to worry that something had happened at the last minute. He turned to watch the front door when the massive wooden door opened and in stepped his parents, Gabby and Stanley with Dylan, Bridy and Biddy who held the hand of a guy Dan had never seen before.

The ceremony took less than ten minutes. Pup stood beside the parents and the godmother with solemn dignity, obviously relishing his new role as godfather. After Dylan was officially welcomed into the Catholic Church, everyone had to endure the endless picture taking. Elaine slipped out to go home and make sure all was ready for the party. Since Elaine had taken the car, Pup had to hitch a ride with Dan and Rosalina. They all watched as Carl did his best to get Aunt Julia out of her wheelchair and into the car, reasonably dry. Dan couldn't help since he only brought an umbrella and not a slicker with a hood. Bryant was out of the car and running to help before anyone could react. He took the chair from Carl and put it in the truck. It took him less than a minute, but in the short time, he was drenched as was Carl. Bryant returned to the back seat next to Marla who squealed, "Ooh, you're soaked. Stay away from me."

Bryant, nonplussed, replied, "Shut up, you little twit. I didn't see you doing anything to help." Pup, used to sibling squabbling, leaned across Marla to address Bryant. "Good job, Bry. Now you'll be Aunt Julia's new favorite instead of Dan. Now that's an honor."

The party got off to a good start. Pup and Elaine presented their guests with hot and cold food, even wait staff to serve and clean up. The house was equal to the number of guests, and everyone could find a table at which to eat. Dan and Rosalina went to the lower level to eat and watch the kids play pool. As Dan went back for seconds, Biddy approached him with the guy who was with her in church.

"Chip, I'd like you to meet Dexter, my man."

Dexter was natty in a pinstriped blue suit, complete with vest and watch chain. His hair was cut severely and he gave off the quiet confidence of a successful person. His handshake was strong, and he looked Dan in the face as they shook hands.

"I'm happy to meet you, Dan, or should I say, Chip? Elizabeth told me all about the family nicknames. I think I have them all straight in my mind."

Dexter's smile was genuine, as was his demeanor. Dan liked him immediately.

"What do you do, Dexter?" Dan asked.

"I work for a distributor of cosmetics. That's how I met Elizabeth. She tells me you're a newspaperman."

"Yes, I work for the local daily. Most people cringe when I say that, but since you're not a local, I guess I can get away with it with you."

Dan saw his mother on the couch laughing and talking and obviously enjoying herself. She had been trying to eat, but so many people were approaching her it was a difficult business. Matty, Cissy's youngest boy, ran to his grandmother to present her with a sandwich.

"Thank you, Michael," Mrs. Kerr said.

The boy looked at her with unnaturally wide eyes. "I'm Matty."

Mrs. Kerr's startled look lasted only for a second. "Of course you're Matty. I always confused my children, now I confuse my grandchildren. Will you forgive me, Matty?"

"Yes, Grammy. I brought you a sandwich to eat."

"Thank you, Matty. That was very nice. Would you like half?"

The boy dutifully took the sandwich and crammed the whole thing into his mouth at once.

"Be careful, Matty," warned his grandmother. "You could choke doing that."

Dan had observed this interaction between grandmother and grandchild and he immediately sought out Bridy. He had to talk to her, but Bridy was surrounded by people. Dan didn't want to be rude and interrupt. Instead, he sought out Aunt Julia, who was surprisingly deep in conversation with Stanley. As he approached, Dan heard Aunt Julia say, "Stanley, if you plan to move here, you really should learn the name of this place. We live in Coltonwood not Cottonwood. Don't worry, I won't tell anyone about your gaffe." There was no need for Aunt Julia to inform anyone since at least half the people in the room heard her remark. Stanley reddened and suddenly felt the urge for another gin and tonic. Dan approached now that Aunt Julia was free. "Chippy. I was wondering when you were going to come and talk to me. Lovely party, don't you think? Pup pulled out all the stops this time. Cissy took me shopping, and I found this dress and hat just for today. I love to dress up, don't you?"

"Actually, I'd rather be in a sweatshirt and jeans, Aunt Julia. I have to dress up for work and I can't wait to get home and change. But you look lovely as always." Dan felt an arm around his waist, and he turned to see Bridy beside him.

She reached for Aunt Julia's thin, deeply veined hand and kissed her cheek. "Forgive me, Aunt Julia. It seems everyone wants to talk to the celebrity from the big city, but I had to get away so I could tell you how lovely you look."

A pleased smile creased Aunt Julia's face. "You look lovely as well in your sleek black cocktail dress and pearls. The two of us could teach the women here how to dress. I've forgotten where you live."

"I live in Manhattan."

"That's right. I lived in New York for years and loved it. There's no place quite like it. I could turn a few heads in my day, I'll tell you. All the men loved my style, the women not so much."

"Maybe so, Aunt Julia, but I don't think many of them could outdo you."

As the two women conversed, Dan admired his little sister. He was much impressed by her sophistication and poise; she had such an air of confidence about her, but she was neither brash nor haughty; her confidence was born of success tempered by her innate affability and friendliness. She was still a young woman, but her tenacity enabled her to swim with the sharks in the super competitive world of fashion design. She was another Aunt Julia minus the acid tongue. She was, without doubt, the most successful of the Kerrs. When Bridy finished her chat with Aunt Julia, Dan gently guided her to a corner of the room where they could speak confidentially.

"Bridy, I'm very concerned about Mom. She seems to slip farther away every day and I don't know what to do to help her. Any ideas?"

"We should somehow get her to go to the Neurological Institute in New York. It's only a few blocks from my apartment that no one in the family has seen, by the way."

"I know. We'll have to change that, but in the meantime, we really need to find a doctor who can at least give us a diagnosis. But going to New York is out of the question. To Mom, a trip to New York would be the equivalent of driving cross-country."

Before Bridy could reply, Pup motioned for both to get into the kitchen, where Gabby and Stanley were going to cut the cake. The proud parents, each with a hand on the knife, cut into an enormous sheet cake; a cake big enough to feed a small army. In the confusion of cake and coffee, Bridy and Dan were separated and could no longer talk, but Dan wanted to seek out Gabby and talk to her for a few minutes. Gabby, flushed and radiant as a new bride, was the center of attention, even more so than her newborn son. Dan saw his chance and poured her a cup of coffee, with which he gently nudged her arm to get her attention. "Got a few minutes for me?"

"Of course. I've been trying to find you all afternoon. Guess what? Stanley and Dylan and I are moving back here."

Dan hated to spoil the surprise, but he said, "I already know."

"How? I haven't told anybody yet."

"Maybe not, but Stanley told Aunt Julia. Unfortunately for him, he called Coltonwood Cottonwood and Aunt Julia corrected him within earshot of everyone in the room, myself included."

"He would upstage me. I wanted to make the big announcement to everyone."

"Why are you moving? Does Stanley have a job offer from some company around here?"

"No, he doesn't. We're moving because I'm tired of the big city. Also, now that we have the baby, our apartment is much too small, and we can't afford to buy a house in New York. It seemed to make sense to move back here where Dylan will have a yard to play in like we did. He wouldn't have that in New York. Pup is going to build the house in his latest development. He actually offered to do that. I still can't quite believe it."

"When will you move?"

"Probably not until the fall. Pup's company will begin work on the house either next month or in September. Our lease will be up at the end of October, so we'll have to find a place to live until the house is ready. I'm really excited to be coming home. I'm not a city person like Bridy. I've had enough of traffic and neon lights."

Without really knowing why he said it, Dan asked as gently as he could, "Are you happy, Gabby?" He didn't miss the slight hesitation or the averting of the eyes.

Gabby faced her brother. "Yes, I am happy, but I never realized what an adjustment marriage is. I want to be happy like Mom and Dad are happy, but I don't feel that yet. Maybe after eight kids I will."

Stanley poked his head around the doorway. "Come on, Sheila. We have to get moving. It will be dark soon."

"All right. Is the baby all set to go?" The question hung in the air as Stanley disappeared, only to reappear a second later with Gabby's coat, which he helped her put on. Gabby skipped the big announcement, preferring only to tell her parents as she tucked her now fussy baby into his carrier. Stanley made a big show of thanking Pup for the party, but made no mention of the house. Mrs. Kerr, seated at the kitchen table, stared quizzically at Gabby. "When will you be back?"

"We'll be here either for Thanksgiving or Christmas. We have a lot to do between now and then. Dylan will be really big the next time you see him."

"Yes, he will be. Drive carefully; you have precious cargo to protect. Do you want to take the rest of the cake? Don't leave it with Pup. He's too fat already."

The aggrieved party countered, "I'm not fat, Mom. I'm what you call pleasingly plump, and I'm going to have at least one more piece of that cake."

"You still need to lose weight, Pup. Your belly is much too big."

Defeated, Pup mumbled, "Yes, Mom."

With the departure of Gabby and Stanley and Dylan, the party was clearly over. Mr. Kerr appeared with his wife's coat and handed it to her. A puzzled Mrs. Kerr eyed her husband. "I'm not going anywhere. I don't need my coat. The only place I'm going to is bed very soon."

"We have to go home, dear. We're at Pup's and Elaine's house."

"Oh, so we are. I could have sworn I was sitting at my own kitchen table. Thank you, Pup and Elaine, for having us over. You certainly went to a lot of trouble to entertain us."

A worried glance passed among the Kerr children. Dan felt that empty feeling in his heart again. He and Rosalina gathered their family and headed home. As he drove, Dan remembered the question he asked Gabby about happiness. Despite the worried feeling he had about his mother, he silently reflected on his own life. He was happy. Love, he thought, cannot be defined or explained. It can only be felt in the deepest recesses of the heart.

CHAPTER
11

DAN LOOKED FORWARD TO THANKSGIVING, but not for the usual reasons. It would be different this year since he and Rosalina would be spending the day at her sister's house. He didn't really mind since Rosalina was always so good about attending and enjoying Kerr family events. His uneasiness stemmed from the fact that he hardly knew these people. Time to man up and bite the bullet. At least, he would be with some of the family at Cissy's afterward for dessert. What Dan craved most of all was the time off from work. After the big day was over, he had the entire weekend to spend as he chose. Such were his thoughts as he prepared to leave work the Friday before the holiday. He had just turned off the lights in his office when the phone rang. It was his father. "Chip, I'm worried about your mother. She left at two o'clock to do some shopping for Thanksgiving, and she's still not home."

Dan groaned. "Dad, that was three hours ago. Why is she going grocery shopping for Thanksgiving? Cissy is having it."

"I don't know. She said she had to pick up a few things."

A million scenarios, none of them good, raced through Dan's head. "All right, Dad. I'll go home and change and go look for her. Did you call Mrs. Salina or Mimi or Cissy? She could have gone to any of those houses to visit."

"She's not at Francesca's. I'll call Mimi and Cissy."

"Ok. I'll go home and change. You stay beside the phone in case she calls."

"Chip, I'm so worried. She's never done this before. Where could she be? Maybe she had an accident and we don't know."

"I doubt that, Dad. It's pretty hard to have an accident in Coltonwood without someone seeing something."

Dan called Pup, who hadn't yet left for Texas. "Pup, Dad just called me. Mom has been missing for three hours. He has no idea where she is."

Pup swore. "Not again. This is getting ridiculous. What are you going to do?"

"Well, Dad said she was going grocery shopping. So why don't we search all the parking lots of the stores in town and see if we see her car? You do Stop and Shop, I'll do IGA and we can meet at the A and P parking lot."

"Sounds like a plan. And if she's not in any of those places?"

"Then we call the police."

Dan rushed home and hurriedly told Rosalina what had happened. She had left work early to cook a big dinner that Dan would probably miss due to yet another Kerr emergency. Bryant offered to go with Dan and once again Dan was grateful to the boy, but his mother was mad. "You haven't finished your dinner yet."

"I had enough. Let's go, Dan."

Dan and Bryant searched the parking lot, slowly driving down each aisle and looking at each car. No sign of the one they wanted to see. Dan drove around a second time and left to meet Pup at the A and P. Pup hadn't seen the car either. They returned to their father's home to find him distraught and haggard. For a second, Dan wondered if his father had heard bad news, but from whom?

"Dad, we didn't see Mom's car at any of the stores. Did you call Mimi and Cissy?"

"Yes, she isn't at either place."

Pup interjected, "Then we call the cops and report her missing. I'll call since I know all of them."

Dan didn't like the way his father looked. "Dad, why don't you come home with me? Rosie cooked a big meal and we can eat while we wait. Have you eaten yet?"

"No. I'm not hungry. Go home if you want. I'm staying here."

Dan went home to eat and let Rosalina know the latest, which was nothing. Rosalina took some dinner for Mr. Kerr if she could coax him into eating.

At nine o'clock the agonized wait ended. The police had found Mrs. Kerr in her car twenty miles away. The officer said he found no sign of groceries in the car or the trunk. The car was on a back road out of gas. Mrs. Kerr would be taken to the hospital since she appeared to be tired and confused, but otherwise all right. The car would be towed to the Coltonwood Police Station, where the family could reclaim it.

The doctor at the hospital told the Kerrs that Mrs. Kerr was dehydrated and confused, so she would be admitted for fluids and observation. Mr. Kerr asked if they could see her, but the doctor said she was sleeping and best not to wake her. She would be discharged in the morning if she had an uneventful night. They swung by the police station to pick up the car, momentarily forgetting that the car was out of gas. That would have to wait until after the holiday.

Dan was brooding and preoccupied as he drove to his in-law's house an hour away. He didn't mind Rosalina's sister, Evalina, but he couldn't endure her husband, Orin. Dan thought Orie, as he was called, a loud, boorish lout given to drinking beer and chain smoking. Dan had met him on two previous occasions and just couldn't find anything good about the guy. Worse yet, Bryant and Marla were staying in Coltonwood where they would have dinner with their father's family. Rosalina chatted happily as he drove, but Dan was not listening. He just wanted to get through the day as best he could and get home.

The day didn't start off badly. Orie greeted them, Bud Light in hand, but he wasn't too oiled, so he actually seemed cordial. Rosalina joined her mother and sister at the kitchen table for a glass of wine, which meant the men had to find another place to talk. Dan, his father-in-law, and Orie repaired to the den to watch football. Dan liked football, so he concentrated on the game while the other two men argued about politics. By halftime, Orie had consumed three beers and grown louder and more offensive. Dan was saved when Evalina called them to the table.

Being the traditionalist that he was, Dan expected to see the usual Thanksgiving fare, but the only thing he recognized was the turkey. He had to ask Rosalina in a muted tone what some of the other dishes were. Rosalina, obviously amused, pointed out swiss chard which to Dan looked like something someone had pulled out of the ground and cooked. Then he spotted the artichokes. Really? Artichokes on Thanksgiving? Then Rosalina pointed out the okra. Dan remembered that Miriam had cooked okra on occasion. He also remembered that he didn't care for the taste. No potatoes? No squash? No yams? What kind of dinner was this? He knew that he would be expected to sample everything, so as each dish was passed, he took some and cringed inwardly. He loaded up his plate with turkey and poured gravy over everything so he could swallow the abominations on his plate. Dan took more than his share of cranberry sauce and olives.

As they ate. Orie commenced a loud harangue about the President. "How the hell can an actor, and a bad one at that, run this country? Besides, he's old. He should be impeached so a real politician can take over."

Dan liked Reagan, but he didn't want to throw gasoline on the fire by disagreeing with Orie, which he knew was exactly what Orie wanted.

"Oh, shut up, Orie. No one wants to talk about politics on Thanksgiving. Give it a rest. You sound like Archie Bunker, the biggest idiot on the planet." This was from Evalina.

Orie exploded. "I have an opinion and the right to express it."

"Just shut up and eat your dinner."

With that, Orie picked up his plate, knife and fork and stomped out of the room, shouting curses over his shoulder as he did so.

One of the kids, Sheldon, said, "Way to go, Mom. Now Dad's going to be mad for the whole weekend. Can't you just ignore him?"

"No, I can't. I'm tired of his constant complaining. He ruins every holiday dinner. I'm sick of it."

"Well, if you weren't such a nag, he'd be much better. Haven't you learned how to get around him yet? You know he's all bluff. He's just looking for attention."

Now Evalina was raging. "How dare you talk to me like that, young man? You're insolent and disrespectful, just like your father. I was hoping you would turn out better. Instead, you're a carbon copy of him and that's no compliment."

Earl, Dan's father-in-law, brought his fist down on the table. "Now stop this. We didn't come here to listen to arguing and fighting. How can anyone enjoy their food with all this going on? Save your family fights for your own time. I won't have them on mine."

The family quieted down, and everyone finished their meals. Dan had been so busy eating that he cleaned his plate, hardly aware of what he was eating. He looked around for a roll or some kind of bread, but there was none. He picked up the platter of turkey and helped himself to more. The meal was pretty good after all.

Dan suddenly felt bad for Rosalina; she must be embarrassed by this ridiculous display of volatile histrionics on the part of some of her family. True, the Kerrs did their share of fighting, but it was forgotten the next day. In this family, the fighting was personal and long remembered. Dan breathed a silent prayer that these people lived an hour away from him and Rosalina.

Dinner ended and Dan and Rosalina were on their way earlier than expected. The drive was quick and easy. No one was on the road in the middle of the afternoon on Thanksgiving. Once home, they had an hour to just relax and unwind from the day. With all the fireworks at the in-laws, Dan was able to forget about his preoccupation with his mother's condition. Now that he was back in familiar territory and with less than an hour to go before he joined the family for dessert, that worry wormed its way into his head. Amazingly enough, worry about his mother had almost entirely replaced his distress about Champ. Dan was no longer troubled by dreams or obsessive thoughts about his brother. He couldn't decide which was worse.

Dan and Rosalina joined Bryant and Marla at Cissy's house for dessert. The kids had their father drive them there rather than home. Dan loved how his stepchildren had taken to his family. Bryant was sprawled on the couch watching football with Michael and Carl; Marla was looking for something to do that didn't involve family, food or football. The girl was disappointed. Dan asked how dinner had been for them. Bryant replied without opening his eyes, "I can't stand my father's family. They're so boring." Marla, who never agreed with her brother about anything, seconded this opinion. "They're all a bunch of dorks." Dan smiled inwardly.

Dessert was in the dining room and Dan saw his parents seated and looking happy, but tired. It had been a long day for them and still more to come. Dan hoped this second round would be quick and everyone could go home happy. Dan was feeling good until his mother looked right at him and asked, "Why are you so late? You missed dinner."

"Mom, I told you that Rosie and I were going to her sister's house for dinner this year. We're actually early for dessert."

"When did you tell me this? I can't recall."

"It doesn't matter, Mom. How was your day?"

Mr. Kerr answered for his wife. "It was great. Cissy went to a lot of trouble to cook such a big dinner. We had a wonderful time."

Dan exchanged a glance with Rosalina, but said nothing. He went to the kitchen looking for Cissy, who was taking pies out of the refrigerator. "Need any help?"

She turned, and the look wasn't friendly. "Of course, I can use some help. I've been on my feet all day and no one has helped me in the least. You can put these pies on the dining room table." Before Dan could do as he was instructed, Matty ran to him and embraced his uncle's legs. "Uncle Chip, I'm so happy to see you. I waited all day for you. So, you have any nolies?"

"Matty, I don't have any cannolis, I'm sorry to say. You'll have to settle for a hug." Dan wrapped his arms around his little nephew, who smelled faintly of cranberry sauce. Cissy caught the embrace and reproved her son. "Matty, men don't hug; they shake hands."

The chastised child backed away from Dan as though pushed. Dan was instantly angry with Cissy. "He's only seven. Why can't he hug his uncle? You're ridiculous sometimes, Cissy. Do you know that?

"Are you telling me how I should raise my child?"

"Of course, I'm not. I just think there's no reason to be so severe over something so innocent."

Dan loved Matty's spontaneous, joyful nature that his mother was doing everything in her power to stifle. He wanted to throttle his sister but instead picked up a pie and carried it to the dining room. That done, he sought out Matty. "Want to go see the lady with the cannolis? Nobody will miss us."

Matty's face lit up. "Yeah."

"Ok. Get your jacket and we'll slip out quietly." Matty loved this illicit slipping away and he and Dan drove to Mrs. Salina's in hopes of snagging some of her leftover pastry.

"AAAYYY, what's wrong? Why are you here? Is it your mother?"

Dan smiled. "Nothing's wrong. Matty wanted some cannolis, so we drove over."

"No cannolis today, only pies and cookies." She handed a small, frosted cookie to Matty, who shoved the whole cookie into his mouth. Mrs. Salina stuffed at least a dozen into a bag for Matty to take home. She said to Dan. "How's your mother today? Good, I hope. I had my daughters and their men for dinner. They eat and leave. No cleanup, no thank you. Next year, Salina and I will go on a trip. They can cook their own dinners. AAAYYY, stunadas."

Dan thanked his former neighbor and headed back to Cissy's house to find the hostess in an uproar. "Where do you get off taking my child out of this house without my permission? Who do you think you are?"

"Relax, Cissy. I just took Matty over to Mrs. Salina's to see if she had any cannolis. I should have asked you, but it was a spontaneous thing, and I just did it. Sorry."

"Sorry, sorry. You're always sorry. I have a good mind to never let you see my son again. I'm his mother. I say where he can and cannot go. You stay out of my family's business. You understand me?"

Now Dan realized the trouble he had caused. The crux of the situation was that Cissy was right. He had no business taking Matty without alerting one or both of his parents. What had started as a spontaneous burst of fun had developed into a full-scale war. Dan knew how agitated his sister could be when she entertained. He had unwittingly tapped into that agitation and given her an excuse to vent her anger. He also knew she wouldn't give up until she had vented her spleen completely.

The raised voices brought Bridy and Carl from the dining room. Carl, long used to his wife's constantly shifting moods, tried to placate Cissy. "Come on, Cecilia. Chip apologized for what he did. Can't you let it go at that? Why do you have to make a federal case out of everything? He's your brother. He meant no harm."

"Don't you realize he took our child without asking either of us? I don't care if he is my brother. He had no right to do that. If you had any sense, you'd be mad too." Carl, disgusted, shook his head and left the room.

Dan tried again to mollify Cissy. "I don't know how many times I can say it. I'm sorry, Cissy. I was wrong. It's just that I like to spend time with Matty and…"

Cissy exploded. "He's not your child. He's mine. Will you ever understand that? Carl and I decide what our children will do and with whom. You should just mind your own business and tend to Rosalina's kids or have some of your own. What the hell do I care what you do? Just leave my kids alone."

Just then Matty flew into the kitchen and flung his arms around Dan. "Get over here," Cissy snapped.

Matty ignored her and said, "All you do is yell. You yell at Michael, you yell at Daddy, now you're yelling at Uncle Chip. All you do is yell at everybody." With that, the child cried piteously in Dan's arms. The kids in the living room stared pop-eyed into the kitchen while Rosalina had stopped making small talk in the dining room.

Mrs. Kerr walked quietly over to her nearly hysterical grandson. "Do you want to see Grammy?"

"Noo," wailed Matty. "You don't even know my name."

Time stood still and finally Dan hoisted the boy into his arms and said, gently, "Let's go have some pie. Tell me what kind I should have. Your mother made so many and they're all so good, I can't decide what to eat. Will you help me, Matty?"

The little boy sniffed and wiped his nose. "That one," he said as he pointed to a blueberry pie.

"That one it is."

Cissy entered the dining room, coffee pot in hand. "Coffee's ready. Let's eat."

Dan thought about the day as he ate. What happened at his sister-in-law's house was like watching a play performed by bad actors. He could forget it and move on. What happened at Cissy's was different; he couldn't put it aside or try to put the best face on it. His anger had coalesced into pity—for his sister, for Carl, but mostly for the kids. They were the innocent victims of their mother's unwillingness to seek help for her insecurities that led her to take out her frustrations on her family. Her oldest, Michael, was becoming just like her. He was sullen and withdrawn, uninterested in life. Matty still had joie de vie to share, but it would be just a matter of time before he too became like Michael. Dan knew he could do nothing. It really wasn't his business and he couldn't interfere even for the sake of helping.

The silence around the dinner table was relieved by the unexpected appearance of Biddy and Dexter. They had spent the day with friends and hadn't planned to spend any time with the Kerrs. Dan was thrilled. Biddy sparkled with life, especially since her engagement to Dexter. Never was unexpected company so welcome. Everyone at the table perked up, even Mr. and Mrs. Kerr who were both visibly exhausted. Despite the arrival of Biddy and Dexter, Dan wanted to end this coffee klatch as soon as possible. Dan was finishing his second piece of pie when the phone rang. A moment later, Cissy approached him. "Gabby's on the phone. She wants to talk to you."

Dan rose and walked to the kitchen to take the call. He couldn't imagine what Gabby wanted on Thanksgiving. "Hello? Gabby, what is it?"

"Hi, Chip. It's nothing bad. I just need to know if you and Pup could come to New York next weekend to help us move. We decided to leave earlier than January when there could be a lot of snow. Can you do it?"

"You know that Pup's in Texas, so I can't speak for him. I'll ask him. Do you need us on Saturday and Sunday?"

"No. Just Saturday will be fine. See you then."

As he hung up, Dan knew there was more to this story than Gabby was willing to admit.

CHAPTER 12

PUP RELUCTANTLY AGREED TO ACCOMPANY Dan, and the two set out for New York at six o'clock the following Saturday. Traffic was light and they made good time. Pup knew the city and could navigate the narrow streets with an ease that amazed Dan. They saw the U-Haul that Stanley had rented double parked outside a three decker. Gabby had forgotten to tell her brothers that her apartment was a third-floor walkup which required the ascent of a torturous winding staircase. Gabby and Stanley got by with the bare essentials, but Dylan had furniture for his every need. After one trip from the apartment to the truck, Pup was ready to quit when two sturdy young men strolled by on the sidewalk. Pup flashed some cash, and the young men were more than glad to do most of the heavy lifting. The truck was loaded in record time and Pup invited everyone, including the young men, out to breakfast. The men gracefully declined after Pup greased their palms and shook hands. They walked to a small breakfast and lunch place and ordered a hearty breakfast. As they ate, Gabby explained that Stanley and his boss had had a difference of opinion, leaving Stanley unemployed. Therefore, rather than look for something short term, it made sense to move now so Stanley could secure employment in Massachusetts. Stanley heartily seconded this plan. By prior arrangement, Gabby and Stanley and Dylan would live with Mr. and Mrs. Kerr until their house was ready. Breakfast done, Stanley climbed into the truck, Gabby and Dylan rode with Pup, and Dan had to drive Stanley's car back to Mass. Dan didn't know the city as well as Pup and he was extremely uneasy that he would lose sight of the truck and Pup and be hopelessly lost in New York City. He cursed Gabby and Stanley for this hasty decision to move so soon, and for not making better arrangements for the removal of their belongings. Traffic in New York proved to be a nightmare, even on a Saturday. Fortunately, Stanley and Pup drove slowly, and Dan was able to follow them out of the city with no issues. He didn't relax until they crossed the New York border.

Dan rather liked having Gabby and Stanley living with their parents; now he had a spy of sorts observing what went on from day to day. Every time he would ask his father how his mother was, the usual reply was fine or just fine. Dan knew that probably wasn't the case, but he didn't have any real evidence to the contrary. Now he could ask Gabby for an honest assessment of what was happening in their parents' home. Dan looked ahead with dread to his mother's appointment with the neurologist in January since he pretty much knew what the doctor would say. With all of that in the back of his mind, Dan called his father and asked to see him the following Wednesday when his mother would be at her coffee time with Mrs. Salina. Armed with coffee and a cinnamon bun, Dan ambled down the street to his parents' home. His modus operandi was to park in his own driveway and walk the short distance to his boyhood home. He didn't want to leave his car in the driveway lest his mother see it and wonder why he was there.

A light knock was answered immediately by Mr. Kerr. "Come in, Chip."

"Thanks. Is Mom home?"

"No. She's at Francesca's. I see you brought coffee."

"And a cinnamon bun."

"What's the occasion?"

"We need to talk about Mom's car."

"What about it?"

"Bryant needs a car and would like to buy it."

"It's not for sale."

"Dad, you can't keep it. Mom can't drive legally anymore. Do you want a repeat of what happened a few weeks ago?"

"Your mother only drives locally and not all that often. She needs a car to shop and visit."

Exasperated, Dan remonstrated, "Dad, Mom can't even drive to the First National, and that's only two minutes from here. The last time she did that, she ended up twenty miles away. Do you want that to happen again? Why do you think the Registry revoked her license? She's not supposed to be driving. If you keep her car, what's stopping her from driving?"

Mr. Kerr looked thoughtful and took a deep sip of coffee. "I suppose you're right, Chip. But I hate to take away her independence. She loves being able to go out and do what she wants. It would be awful to deprive her of that."

"I know that Dad. Yet you have to be realistic. Mom's driving days are over."

Just then, Gabby strolled into the room carrying Dylan. Dan flushed when he realized he should have bought three coffees and another bun. "I'm sorry, Gabby. I should have bought you a coffee. I guess I'm just not used to your being back."

Gabby smiled. "No biggie. I can make my own coffee just as well as not. What brings you here in the middle of the afternoon? Can you hold Dylan while I make coffee?" Dan took the sleeping baby and snugged him into the crook of his arm.

"I came to try to convince Dad to sell Mom's car to Bryant."

"That's a good idea. Dad, Mom really shouldn't be driving. She gets too confused."

Mr. Kerr looked angry. "Well, two against one; I guess I better give in."

"Dad, we're only saying this for Mom's own good. Besides, if she drives and gets pulled over, she'd get a citation for driving without a license. The police aren't going to let her go just because she's a nice old lady. She'd get a ticket like anyone else."

Dan glanced at Gabby who sat quietly with her hands around her coffee cup. Despite the tension in the room, Dan noticed how good Gabby looked. She was relaxed and content. Obviously, moving back was good for her. He also noticed how much Dylan looked like his mother. He had the same shape of face and even the same expression.

"Ok, I surrender. Bryant can have the car."

"Thanks, Dad, but Rosie and I don't want you to give him the car. We want him to pay for it. He has some money he's been saving."

"Your mother and I don't need the money."

"That's not the point, Dad. We want him to pay for it and for the gas and maintenance. We'll help him with the insurance since it's so expensive for boys his age. He really needs it to get to work and school."

"And when will you tell your mother?"

"When we pick up the car."

"She's not going to like it. You better be prepared for a fight."

"Why don't you hint around that Bryant needs a car?"

"No, sir. This is your job, not mine."

Dan worried for days about how his mother would react. Since the car was in her name, she would have to sign the bill of sale. If she was having a good day, she would probably refuse. If she was having a bad day, maybe it would work. On Saturday, Dan and Bryant went over to the house with the two hundred dollars Bryant would pay for the car. Mr. and Mrs. Kerr were seated at the kitchen table finishing their morning coffee. Dan glanced at his father, who just shrugged. Bryant relieved the uneasy silence. "Thank you, Grammy, for letting me have your car. I really need it."

Mrs. Kerr looked at her husband. "What's this about, Bert? Are you selling my car? How will I get around?"

Mr. Kerr took his wife's hand. "We don't want you to be pulled over by the police since you don't have a license anymore. Bryant needs the car to get to school and work. We can go out to dinner, or you can buy yourself whatever you want with the money. Besides, you'll be helping Bryant. He just needs you to sign the paper to make it legal."

Mrs. Kerr looked doubtfully at the paper Bryant handed her. "I'm not going to sign this. I can't take money from my grandson. He can have the car if he needs it that much."

Dan exhaled a massive sigh of relief until his mother continued. "I don't need to sign anything. It will still be my car, but Bryant can take it whenever he needs it. What's this about the police? I've never been stopped in my life. I'll have another set of keys made so Bryant can have his own. He can leave it here. We have more room here than you have, Chip. Do you need it today, Bryant? We can share the car. It will be our car."

"I was outflanked," was the way Dan described the incident with the car to Rosalina. "I never thought that my mother would refuse to sign the bill of sale. She fooled me again."

Rosalina couldn't help but smile. "Your mother is smarter than you think she is. But what can you do? Just go with the arrangement for now. Winter is here and Bryant will need the car more and more. After a while, he will keep parking the car here and your mother will get used to that. It won't be a problem until next August when Bryant goes to college and won't need the car anymore. But that's a long way off. A lot of things can happen in the meantime."

And so it stood. Bryant needed the car more and more, and Mrs. Kerr didn't mind except when she wanted to go Christmas shopping. Her husband managed to soothe her and promised to take her the next day. Often as not, Mrs. Kerr forgot she wanted to use the car.

Dan's biggest family problem now was what to do about Christmas. Pup and Elaine had done their share of entertaining and it wasn't fair to ask them to be hosts again. They earned their right to be guests. Hosting Thanksgiving almost put Cissy over the edge, so it didn't make sense to ask her to host

Christmas. Mimi's family was large and some of the kids still very young, so having the entire Kerr brood at her home wasn't fair either. Biddy lived in a small apartment in another town, so that wouldn't work either. Bridy could do nothing since she would be visiting for the holiday. That left Dan and Rosalina. They agreed that any party they would have would be Christmas Eve, not the day after. With that in mind, they drafted the guest list which included both sides. They decided on a buffet rather than a sitdown dinner.

 Dan went all out buying presents for everyone. Rosalina would receive a diamond necklace with matching earrings, along with a Florida getaway planned for February. Bryant would receive Celtics tickets. Marla, two tickets to a Michael Jackson concert. The entire family would also get Red Sox tickets for a game next summer. Now that Dan had a good job, he could spend freely and not worry about the expense. He also bought for his parents, Bridy, and Biddy. He stopped buying for his other siblings and their kids. Too many people now that the family had grown so much.

 City Hall closed at noon on Christmas Eve, so Rosalina would have time to cook the steamship roast that would be the centerpiece of the dinner. Dan also wanted a turkey, which he would cook at his parents' house. They invited the Salinas, but all had to forgo the skating party since the pond hadn't frozen. Mrs. Salina refused to come without a lasagna. Dan graciously gave in to her request. Rosalina prepared Irish potatoes and candied yams. Neither set of parents was to bring anything. Dan had insisted on this since he knew his mother would want to cook, but her cooking skills had dwindled so much it would be better if she did nothing.

 The buffet would be in the kitchen so everyone could eat in the dining room. The dining room table had to be moved to one side to make room for a folding table so everyone could eat in the same room. Pup and Elaine were to bring hors d'oeuvres and wine and Cissy an apple pie. Bridy, who had arrived earlier in the afternoon, made egg nog. Mimi and Neil would remain at home since they had young children, but some of the older kids would be there. Biddy and Dexter were spending most of the night with friends, but promised to drop in early and see everyone. Gabby and Stanley made peanut brittle and Christmas cookies.

Everything seemed ready. Then Rosalina asked where they could put the hors d'oeuvres. The kitchen table had to be used for the buffet and the dining room table for eating. All the counter space was taken. They would need another table and another red tablecloth. Dan called Mrs. Salina. The response was predictable. "AAAYYY, why you call now? Is the party off?"

"No, it's not. We need another table and a red tablecloth. I can send Bryant over to pick them up."

"I have both. I'll send Salina over. He can leave some wine while he's there. I think you need some right now. I'd come too, but the lasagna is still in the oven."

"Thanks, Mrs. Salina. I knew I could depend on you."

Crisis over, thought Dan, until Bryant announced that there were not enough chairs for everyone to sit in the dining room. Another call, this one to the Kerr residence. "Dad, could I borrow some of the dining room chairs? We need at least five more. Bryant can pick them up."

"Of course," said Mr. Kerr. "Take as many as you need. We never use them anyway."

Second crisis was averted. Salina arrived with the table and the tablecloth and the promised wine. He would return later with his wife. Dan set up the table on one side of the kitchen away from the table. Bridy had brought some new Christmas candles that complemented the table very well.

All seemed in readiness until Rosalina asked Marla if she had wrapped Aunt Julia's present.

"I don't know, Mom. I wrapped a lot of presents," came the reply in Marla's testiest teenage voice. She was irritated that none of her friends could join her at the party. "Did you look under the tree? That's where presents go on Christmas."

"Don't give me that attitude, young lady," rejoined her mother. "I'm in no mood for any of your nonsense. Go look under the tree."

Marla flounced out of the room and returned with a huge, wrapped box, which she waved triumphantly at her mother. Fingering the tag, she read, "To Aunt Julia. See, I wrapped her present. I don't know why you have to question everything I do. You don't do that to Bryant."

Trying to avoid an argument, Rosalina merely gave Marla the look that meant to say no more. Marla got the hint and fled to her room. Dan shrugged. He was slowly getting used to living with a teenage girl who had recently taken to using more sass than sense when talking to her mother. Dan couldn't remember if any of his sisters had acted like this with their mother. Probably, especially Mimi and Cissy. Cissy still had the attitude. He hoped Marla would outgrow hers.

Bryant delivered and set up the chairs in the dining room. The doorbell rang and Pup and Elaine arrived with shrimp, chicken wings, and tabouli. Dan was a little ticked that they had brought so much. What if the guests filled up on the appetizers and had little interest in the main course? How like Pup to overdo it even when it's not his party. He never missed an opportunity to remind the family how well off he and Elaine were. Bridy arrived with the homemade eggnog and Gabby and Stanley with the peanut brittle. Dan was intrigued that they chose such an unusual offering to bring. Stanley explained that his family had always made peanut brittle on Christmas Eve. He had learned how to make it years ago. "It's a real party pleaser," smiled Stanley. Dan thought, party pleaser? Give me a break.

Cissy and Carl and the boys arrived soon after. Dan remembered to tone down his welcome to Matty. Dan knew that Cissy was still ticked about Dan's abrupt abduction of her son on Thanksgiving. She and Dan had not spoken since. With the arrival of the two sets of parents, the party was officially underway.

CHAPTER

13

THE FEBRUARY SUN WAS BLINDINGLY BRILLIANT as Dan drove his parents and sister Gabby into Boston to the specialist in one of the hospitals in the city. Three weeks earlier, Pup and Cissy had made the same trip to have their mother evaluated by a neurologist. As he drove, Dan tried to quiet his mind, but Pup's story about what happened at the first visit kept sabotaging his peace of mind. He kept hearing Pup telling him that the doctor had asked Mr. Kerr, Pup, and Cissy to leave the room while the evaluation was in progress. It would take two hours, the doctor had said. The three left for lunch in the hospital cafeteria when the beeper that doctor had provided went off, forty-five minutes into the evaluation. Pup, confused, thought it was an accident. But when it went off a second time, he left his father and sister in the cafeteria and went to investigate. He returned minutes later with his mother. The doctor had stopped the testing because Mrs. Kerr had become hopelessly confused and he thought it unnecessary and heartless to make her continue. "I can form a diagnosis with what I have," the doctor assured Pup.

Now they were on their way to hear that diagnosis, the verdict of a distinguished expert in the field, someone who could offer an unbiased opinion of Mrs. Kerr's forgetfulness and confusion. Dan wanted to know, but he dreaded what he would hear. He grew increasingly uneasy as they approached the hospital. During the drive, Mrs. Kerr had asked why they were going to Boston to see the Swan Boats in the winter. "We're going to the hospital, Mom," Dan had reminded her. "Don't you remember when Pup and Cissy and you and Dad went a few weeks ago?"

"We did? Why?"

"So, you could see Dr. Soriano, the neurologist."

"That's not my doctor's name."

"This doctor is a specialist, not your regular doctor."

"I'm not sick. Why do I need to see another doctor? Besides, I have a hair appointment today that I don't want to miss."

Dan knew he had to stop this senseless dialogue, so he lapsed into silence; his heart sinking lower as he pulled into the entrance of the hospital. He and Gabby led their parents along the confusing maze of hallways that led to the doctor's office. Dan hoped this specialist wouldn't keep them waiting for two hours for a few minutes of his time. Already Dan was biased against the doctor whom he had never met.

The wait wasn't long and soon the Kerr family sat in the office of this world-renowned doctor, who would tell them the news they all expected but hoped not to hear. The doctor was pleasant enough and addressed Mrs. Kerr before anyone else. "How are you feeling today, Mrs. Kerr? Do you know where you are and why you're here?"

What stupid questions, Dan thought. Of course, she doesn't know where she is or why. Otherwise, we wouldn't be here. Cut to the chase, doc.

And he did. The doctor addressed the family. "Based on the testing that I was able to perform on Mrs. Kerr, I have come to the conclusion that she does indeed have dementia. At this point, it's still in the incipient stages, but progression is inevitable. She will, over the course of time, lose her ability to do routine tasks and eventually fail to recognize even family members. At this stage, she is easily confused and unable to concentrate. That's why I had to terminate the testing during her first visit. She is unable to comprehend even basic directions and complete basic tasks. She has extreme difficulty with word retrieval and short-term memory. I know this is not what you want to hear, but the hallmarks of the disease are unmistakable."

Everyone was silent as they absorbed this news. The doctor continued. "At this point, I would recommend that Mrs. Kerr be watched carefully, as she might wander off and get lost. Do not let her drive or even cook. Her sleep schedule will be disrupted and she could awaken for the day in the middle of the night since she has lost all sense of time. She may begin to hide objects or put things in unusual places. Eventually, she will lose her ability to associate. I would recommend at that point that she be placed in a nursing home since she will require constant monitoring and care."

At the words nursing home, Mr. Kerr broke out harshly, "My wife is not going to a nursing home. Never. My children and I can take care of her at home. How dare you even suggest such a thing?"

The doctor, unfazed, retorted, "I understand your feelings, Mr. Kerr, and I certainly won't invalidate them by arguing against them. However, given the progression of the disease that your wife has, the time will come when you will not be able to meet her constant needs. No one wants to place a loved one in a nursing home, but it may become inevitable and the best choice for everyone, especially Mrs. Kerr."

Mr. Kerr sniffed disparagingly, "Never."

Dan broke the uncomfortable silence that followed by asking, "Is there any medication that can help my mother?"

The doctor sighed. "There are some experimental meds that we could try, but all they can do is retard; they cannot reverse. In many cases, they may not work at all. This disease continues to confound medical science, so there really isn't any effective treatment and there may not be for several years to come. I could prescribe one of these meds, but I don't want to give you any false hope that it will work. Your mother will continue to decline, but I cannot say at what pace. It could be months; it could be years. A terrible thing is happening, and it will be awful for all of you to watch. If there was anything I could do or say that could change the situation, I would. As a neurologist, I see this terrible disease every day and I see the terrible toll it takes on my patients and their families. All that I can say is that I'm sorry."

Despite himself, Dan was impressed by the doctor's humility and his respect for the inexorable disease that people expected him to conquer; his honesty in the face of his helplessness as a medical professional to provide answers to people who desperately sought his help. What a lonely professional world this man was forced to inhabit. Dan stood and extended his hand to the doctor. "Thank you, doctor, for your candor and sympathy. We really appreciate your honesty in telling us what you knew we didn't want to hear. Is there anything else?"

The doctor stood. "Thank you. This is the part of my job that I hate. I became a doctor to help people, but then I found myself in mortal combat with an enemy that cannot be vanquished or conquered. One of my aunts has dementia, so I know how devastating the disease is on a personal level. I wish all of you, especially Mrs. Kerr, all the best as you struggle to make sense of your new normal. I wish I could have been of more help."

Dan fetched the car and picked up his parents and Gabby at the front door of the hospital. He could tell from his father's expression and his body language that he was furious. Dan unthinkingly switched on the radio as he pulled out of the parking lot. "Turn off that damn radio," Mr. Kerr called harshly from the back seat. "This is no time for silly music."

Dan complied and looked in the rear-view mirror at his parents. They were holding hands; his mother looked bewildered and lost. His father was not finished. "I suppose that you agree with that high priced quack that we should put your mother in a nursing home. You dragged us all the way down here for nothing. Your mother's tired and so am I. From now on we only deal with local doctors, not these high falutin' specialists who don't know shit from shinola."

That last remark shook Dan and Gabby, who exchanged a shocked look. Dan could count the number of times he had heard his father curse on one hand. Now he understood the depth of his father's anger. "Dad, just because the doctor told us what we didn't want to hear, does not make him incompetent or uncaring. The fact is that Mom has an illness that is no one's fault, not yours, not mine, not the doctor's, not Mom's, not anyone's. You can't ignore what we've seen for ourselves or pretend everything is ok. We have to deal with this as a family. Being angry at me or the doctor doesn't help anyone, especially Mom."

After a tiny pause, Mr. Kerr broke out savagely, "Your mother will never be put into a nursing home. That would happen over my dead body. I'll never forgive you if you do."

Seething, Dan tried to keep his voice level. "Dad, this is not the time or the place for this discussion. We can make whatever decisions need to be made when they need to be made. You're acting like Mom is going to die tomorrow. Besides, I'm trying to drive. Please let me do that."

Mr. Kerr subsided grudgingly. Dan glanced at the speedometer and was amazed to see that he was going over eighty. He looked around for any blue and gray cars, but there were none in sight. He could feel a terrible headache beginning at the back of his head. This cannot get any worse, Dan thought, and then it did.

Champ's voice whispered, "Find me. I want to go home." Dan groaned inwardly. Of all times for Champ to assert his presence. "Find me," the voice said again. "I want to go home." Taking a fresh grip on the wheel Dan noticed that the sun was as bright and the sky as blue as when they drove down, but now the Kerr family's world had crumbled; the illusion that they had desperately clung to had dissipated. Their mother and wife did have the dreaded disease that some people call dying twice. Confirmation of what had initially been just a suspicion made Dan miserable. It was true.

Since Dan was driving so fast, he reached the exit from the Pike in record time. The silence and the tension in the car were becoming unbearable. "Does anyone want to stop somewhere and get lunch?" Dan asked, just to hear a sound. His father answered. "We'll have lunch when we get home." Dan turned to Gabby. "How about you?"

Gabby turned to look, but merely said, "No." Dan then realized that Gabby had not said one word either in the doctor's office or in the car. Whatever fears she was grappling with, Gabby kept them inside as was her wont. So much for the raucous Kerr clan, mused Dan.

A half hour later, Dan had taken his parents and sister home and he headed for his own home. Once home, he realized he was ravenously hungry. He rummaged in the refrigerator and found some ham and cheese and French bread. He cut an enormous hunk of bread and slathered it with mustard and several layers of ham and cheese. A beer and some chips completed his meal. Dan really expected one of his siblings to call but the phone remained silent. He popped another beer and settled in his recliner to call Pup, who answered on the first ring.

"Hey, we just got home. Not good news. Mom has dementia and Dad is in complete denial. He's really mad at the doctor and at me for taking Mom to Boston. If you start arguing, I'm hanging up. I've had enough for one day."

"Whoa, no arguments from me. I pretty much knew it wasn't good after the first visit with the doctor. Did he prescribe medication?"

"No. He said it wouldn't do any good. Of course, he mentioned the possibility that Mom might have to go to a nursing home. That's what got Dad so riled up. Dad even swore on the way home. It was not a pleasant trip. I have no idea what the future holds, but it won't be good. Then to make matters worse, I started thinking about Champ. I'm on my second beer. Could be many more to follow."

Pup chuckled. "I wish I could join you. Did the doctor give any kind of plan for the future? Cissy and I were really impressed by him. He knows his stuff."

"I was impressed also. Of course, Dad thinks he's a bumbling incompetent idiot, but he thinks anyone who disagrees with him is hopelessly stupid. This is going to be tough. I feel bad for Gabby. She has to live with Mom and Dad. You know, she said absolutely nothing while we were with the doctor and nothing on the way home. She's turning inward like she used to do."

"I'll bet her husband will have plenty to say. I don't envy them having to live with the folks."

"Me either. Well, I just wanted to let you know how it went. Can you call Mimi and Cissy? I'll call Bridy and Biddy."

"Will do. Later, bro."

Dan wanted another beer, but when he glanced at the clock, he realized Marla would be home from school soon. She might not like seeing him drinking in the middle of the afternoon and her mother would like it even less. Sighing, Dan decided to catch up on some work. Just as he opened his briefcase, the phone rang.

"Hello."

"AAAYYY. Bad day today?"

"Hi, Mrs. Salina. You might say that. How did you know?"

"I just come back from your parents' house. Your mother looked like she didn't know where she was. Your father was stompin' around like a caged tiger and talkin' to himself. Not good, if you ask me."

Dan then told his neighbor the story of the trip to Boston, the doctor's diagnosis, and his father's tirade in the car during the trip home. Mrs. Salina listened without interrupting.

When he finished, she asked, "What you goin' to do? Your mother gets a little worse each day. Been seein' that for some time now."

"We need to talk this over. Pup called me and I told him, but no one else except Gabby knows. She didn't say one word the whole time we were in Boston. I felt like I was alone. I was the one who got all the abuse, and she didn't even defend me."

"The girl is scared, and she should be. All of this will fall on her. She lives there. She knows what goes on. She's there with that husband of hers. Ask them some time what it's like."

Mrs. Salina's bluntness unnerved Dan a little. Never one to mince words, Mrs. Salina obviously knew the situation better than he did. "You better start talkin' soon. Like tomorrow."

Dan knew better than to ignore Mrs. Salina's advice, so he called each of his siblings to see if he could somehow get them all together for a dreaded family meeting. Usually these gatherings were social occasions with other family members present. It would be different this time, and the politeness that would be generated by other peoples' presence would be nowhere in sight. This would be a sibling battleground with all the gloves off. Dan braced himself for the worst. All agreed that even spouses would not be there. This would be strictly a Kerr kid meeting.

Pup offered to host the summit at his home, on his territory. This worried Dan a bit, but it was the only practical solution. The meeting was set for the end of March on a Saturday night when everyone would be free. There was a little soreness between Pup and Dan over an incident that had occurred a few weeks before. Marla had gotten her license and her mother had let her drive her brother's car to school, unbeknownst to Bryant. When he came home for spring break, he had sole use of the car. On his first night home, after an obligatory but hurried meal with the family, Bryant left to meet his friends. Rosalina received a call about an hour later from the police. Bryant had been stopped because the vanity plate had been attached to the back of the car and the license plate to the front. It turned out that someone at school had decided to prank Marla and switch the plates. That someone was her cousin, Chase, Pup's son. The boy had apologized and was appropriately punished, but Dan was still miffed about the whole situation.

The first person Dan saw when he arrived at Pup's house was Chase, and Dan could have sworn the boy had a smirk on his face. Dan gave him a curt wave and hurried to Pup's spacious basement, where the meeting would be held. Pup wasted no time in starting once everyone had arrived. Never one to mince words, Pup got right to the point. "We need to talk about Mom."

To which Cissy hastily added, "And Dad. They're in it together."

Pup ignored this and turned on Gabby. "You live there. What's going on?"

Gabby shifted uncomfortably in her seat. "Well, Mom is different."

Pup flared. "We've established that. We need to know how different."

"Well, she forgets things. She doesn't seem to know how to cook anymore."

"That's not good," offered Dan. "That's one of the things the doctor mentioned is that Mom would forget how to cook."

"What else?" demanded Pup.

"Well, Mom doesn't talk as much as she used to. When

she does talk, she usually is talking about something that happened in the past. And she thinks Bryant is Champ, and he's come home. She wonders why he doesn't visit."

Dan groaned inwardly. He had suspected this, but couldn't accept it. Now there it was in black and white.

After a pause, Cissy broke out savagely. "This is all your fault, Chip. Mom and Dad were fine before you insisted Mom had to see that fancy pants doctor in Boston. Mom has gone right downhill since then. You can't deny that."

Before Dan could regain his composure and speak without shouting, Mimi said, "It's no one's fault, Cissy. Mom has an illness and Dad just can't see it or accept it. Don't start playing the blame game. That won't get us anywhere. We're not here to point fingers needlessly."

Cissy subsided, sulking.

Pup surveyed the room. "Anyone else have any ideas?"

Mimi looked thoughtful and then offered, "I read that people who have dementia often respond to music. Mom has a lot of albums of musicals. Why don't we play them once in a while and see how she reacts?"

Pup looked disgusted. "Yeah, maybe we could take the act on the road like the Osmond family. We'd be a sensation."

Mimi whirled in her seat. "Don't give me any of your sarcastic crap, Pup. We're all in this together and don't you forget it."

"Yes, Sister. Please pardon me, Sister. I'll make sure I go to confession next weekend."

"That's it, I'm leaving," said Mimi as she reached under the table for her purse. "If you manage to come up with some sensible ideas, someone let me know. Next time, we'll have to choose a more suitable leader. Good night." The door slammed.

Everyone was quiet, then Pup spoke. "The hell with her. Where were we before we were so rudely interrupted?"

No one said anything. Pup then turned to Biddy. "So, Bid, what's your take on all of this?"

"Don't call me Biddy. It's either Elizabeth or Liz. Biddy makes me feel like a five-year-old."

"Very well, Elizabeth. What do you think?"

"Are you insulting me?"

"Who, me? Never. I'm asking for your opinion. It could be that the youngest is wiser than the oldest."

"I think you are insulting me. I don't have to take any of your crap either. Who made you the leader? I'm going home."

As Biddy was headed out the door, Pup called, "Good night, Liz."

The remaining people looked at each other but no one spoke until Pup said abruptly, "This meeting is adjourned."

On his way home, Dan wondered how it had come to this. He had expected fireworks, but not personal attacks. The night was warm and Dan thought he saw lightning play across the sky. As he was exiting his car, he heard thunder ripple in the night. Only then did it strike him that it was odd to be having summer weather in March.

Dan told Rosalina all about the meeting. "We've had our share of fights over the years, but I've never seen it become so personal and vicious. Pup was on everyone's back. Mimi walked out, and so did Biddy. Bridy and I were the only ones spared Pup's wrath. What do you make of all this?"

"Didn't you tell me once that John was your mother's favorite?"

"Yeah, he was. She always took his side, no matter what he did. The rest of us got punished, but Pup had a free ride."

"Ok. Think about this for a minute. John is scared that he's losing his mother, and it's coming out as anger. Some people use humor, some people withdraw, some people deny, but everyone deals with a loss in a unique way. And the family is still trying to come to terms with Dennis's disappearance. That's a lot for one family to handle."

"Do you know that Mom thinks Bryant is Champ, that he's back?"

"Does she? I don't think Bryant is aware of this. If he is, he never mentioned it to me."

"I don't know what to do about that either. Do we continue to pretend or just ignore the whole thing?"

"I think that's the least of your worries."

With that, Dan reached for the only constant in his life, his wife.

Easter would come in another week and this year would be totally different from any other Easter for the Kerrs since each family would celebrate individually, not as a group as in previous years. Dan and Rosalina and Marla would be with Rosalina's parents for the majority of the day. Mr. and Mrs. Kerr would be going to Mimi's for dinner without Gabby and Stanley, who wanted to go to brunch at a restaurant. Dan had stopped in on Saturday with a lily for his mother, only to see that Pup had beaten him to it with a lily as tall as a small oak tree. While Mrs. Kerr was grateful for a second, she kept asking about Easter baskets for the kids. Dan didn'tt know if she meant himself and his siblings or the grandchildren. He comforted himself by thinking that at least his mother knew it was Easter.

The next day, Dan and Rosalina visited again. While Rosalina kept his parents engaged in conversation, Dan pulled Gabby aside for a private chat. Gabby, Stanley, and Dylan had just returned from a day in Boston. "We ate at a great restaurant," she told Dan. "Then we walked around the Freedom Trail before Dylan got tired and cranky, so we came home. It was wonderful to have a day to myself with my family. No cooking, no watching Mom, no listening to Dad. I should do this more often."

"What do you mean by listening to Dad?"

"You know. He's always asking how I think Mom is doing. Does she seem better today? Did I notice that Mom read the paper this morning? Every day it's the same thing. Dad lives in his own fantasy land and he's trying to get me to buy into it. Some days I have to flat out lie."

"Has Mom done anything really crazy?"

"No, she hasn't. Yet. Stanley is great with her. He gets up early and cooks breakfast. Whatever Mom wants, he cooks. I have no idea what time she gets up, but she's always up before

Dad and me. Stanley seems to have a knack for communicating with Mom."

Stanley, Dan was thinking. Of all people, Stanley. But at least he serves a purpose if what Gabby was saying was true and not her attempt to make Stanley look like the salt of the earth.

"I can't wait to get out of here, Chip. Stanley and I want to move before the end of the summer. We're looking for a house we can afford since Pup never built us one like he promised. I want out before Mom gets really bad. I've done my bit, regardless of what the others might think. More than my share."

Dan cringed at Gabby's words, but he had to acknowledge that she was speaking the truth. He had to ask: "Do you think Mom will be in a nursing home soon?"

Gabby looked away; her face was sad. "Yes, I do. She's forgetting how to get dressed. Sometimes she knows me, sometimes she doesn't. She can't concentrate on anything for any amount of time. Dylan is a good distraction, but she tires easily, so even he doesn't keep her engaged for long. In a way, it's like having two toddlers in the house. Each one demands constant watching. Dad's really tired but he won't admit it. He's become an old man from looking after Mom. Thank God for Mrs. Salina. She's so good. She comes over a lot and keeps us laughing, if nothing else. This can't go on for too much longer, Chip. Something has got to give."

The Kerr sibs had declared a tacit cease fire, perhaps in the spirit of Easter, and each visited their mother as often as possible. Dan had not followed through with his threat to call Cissy and let her have it after the last family meeting. He was very glad that he had forgotten his anger when he heard from the family conduit of gossip, Gabby, that Cissy and Carl were having marital problems. Despite that, things were relatively good until one day, when Dan was involved in a heated editorial meeting about a controversial story, his secretary, Rachel, interrupted the meeting to tell him that he had an emergency call from his father. Dan took the call with extreme trepidation.

"Hello, Dad. What's going on?"

"Your mother's missing. We searched the whole house and the cellar. She's not here."

"Did you call the police?"

"No. Can you come over?"

"Dad, I'm at work and I can't just leave. Call Pup and see if he can go over."

Predictably enough, Mr. Kerr exploded. "This is all Stanley's fault. He didn't lock the door. I'm going to kick that guy out of the house."

"Dad, you don't know that for a fact. Call the police and keep me posted."

Dan hung up, totally exasperated. Rachel, who had become a trusted friend and knew about Dan's family issues, offered her sympathy. "I'm sorry this has happened again, Dan. If you want to leave, go ahead. I can manage until you get back." Dan smiled at this support. Rachel had no problem telling the mayor or any other bigwig to call later, or this isn't a good time to see the managing editor. She always had Dan's back.

After much indecision, Dan returned to the meeting, and it wrapped up relatively quickly. He then left and went to the family home. His heart sank when he saw a police car in front. He hurried in to find a fresh-faced officer talking with Mr. Kerr, Gabby and Pup. Dan got the gist of the story as the officer prepared to leave for another call. A school bus driver had called the dispatcher who had called the police to report an elderly woman in a robe and slippers was "harassing" students at a bus stop. She was asking if they had seen her son. The police found her immediately and had received other calls to report a crazy lady wandering around inappropriately dressed. The police took Mrs. Kerr to the hospital to be checked out.

Once again, Dan, Mr. Kerr, Pup, and Gabby, with Dylan in tow, went to the hospital. After a brief wait, the doctor who had attended Mrs. Kerr briefed them. "I saw your wife and mother about an hour ago. Physically, she's fine. She was cold and hungry, but otherwise good. She could tell me her name, but not her address. She had no recollection of why she was outside in a robe and slippers or how she got there. I'm going to discharge her since there is no reason to keep her in the hospital. You should consult with a neurologist about her mental state. It's not good. I saw in her record that this is not the first time she's wandered and ended up here. You've been lucky twice, but the next time, you may not be so fortunate."

No one said what everyone was thinking, so the doctor said, "I'll complete the discharge papers and she'll be ready to go."

Now what?

Not a day went by that Dan didn't wrestle with the futility and frustration of his mother's situation. His father's solution had been to change all the door locks, which Mr. Kerr soon came to realize was not a great idea when he had to have keys made for each of his children. Dan spent his days in mute desperation, waiting for the other shoe to drop. It was coming, but in what guise? He remembered the fire, the aimless drive on the way to the supermarket, the latest escape in a robe and slippers. Since there was not an immediate remedy, the status quo would have to prevail, at least for the immediate future.

Mimi called him one day at work. "Someone just told me that there is a facility in East Millertown that is for elderly people who have memory problems. Maybe we could be able to get Mom in there. I have the name of the person to contact. I'll call her and find out more."

The following week, Mimi and Dan had an interview with the woman in charge of admissions at this place. Mimi gave a brief history of Mrs. Kerr's memory issues and the woman listened without comment. "We think this place could be a good fit for our mother," Mimi concluded.

The woman, a Ms. Heartstone, pursed her lips and shuffled some papers on her desk. "I hate to disappoint you, but this place is not appropriate for your mother. This is an assisted living facility, which means we take people who are still able to fend for themselves with some help from the staff. We do not treat people with dementia or other serious cognitive issues. Our staff is not trained for that. Please forgive me for being blunt, but your mother should be in a nursing home. She needs twenty-four/ seven care that family members, no matter how well intentioned, cannot provide. I know that you are looking for an alternative to a nursing home, but there really isn't one. I can give you the names of some homes in the immediate area."

With nowhere else to turn, the Kerr family would have to continue to face each day and hope that nothing drastic would happen.

A few days later Dan sat dejectedly in his office, debating whether he should take some time off to reassess his priorities and his life. His phone console buzzed. "Call for you on line one, Mr. Kerr," came the operator's voice.

"Hello. Dan Kerr."

"This is your lucky day, Dan. I have the biggest scoop of your career."

It took Dan a few seconds to realize he was listening to his old buddy, John Murphy.

"Hey, sorry, man. I'm so out of it these days, I don't even recognize the voices of old friends. So what's this big scoop?"

"You have to come here to find out. Right now. I won't tell you over the phone."

After a quick glance at his watch, Dan decided he could spare an hour away. "Ok. Give me ten minutes."

Dan told Rachel he would be leaving for an hour or so. His ever-faithful secretary gave him a knowing glance. "Good. You need more time off than an hour, but it's a start."

Dan's footsteps echoed on the marble floor of City Hall as he walked briskly to his friend's office. "Ok. What's the big scoop?"

John Murphy pushed a coffee and a bismark in Dan's direction. "Holy cow. Is this the scoop?"

"Well, part of it. I wanted to reassure myself that you hadn't been stolen by the *New York Times* or the *Washington Post*. I even bought a paper this morning to see if you were still the management there."

"Thanks for this. You don't know how much I need this. Or maybe you do."

Dan relished the bismarck and the coffee while John talked. When Dan finished his treat, John said casually, "I do have a big scoop for you. I'm getting married, and I'd like you to be my best man."

John had been so quiet about his budding romance that Dan decided not to question him. What he wanted Dan to know, he would tell him. "Wow! That's fantastic, John. Of course, I'll return the favor you bestowed on me. When is the wedding?"

"We want to wait until the fall. That will give you plenty of time to get ready."

"I'll be ready, don't worry," said Dan as he extended his hand to his friend to shake. He had never seen John looking so happy.

After his impromptu coffee with John Murphy, Dan decided on a sudden whim to check the post office box. He had become very lax about looking after so many months of seeing nothing. Expecting more disappointment, Dan inserted the key. There was a letter waiting. Frantically, Dan wondered if he had opened the wrong box by mistake. He knew it was real when he saw the U.S. government address in the upper left corner.

He fled the post office, willing himself to not open the envelope. Dan fumbled with his keys, hardly able to unlock the door. Once seated, he tore open the envelope, almost tearing the letter in half. His hands shook as he ripped the letter from the envelope. His eyes rapidly scanned the entire letter at once. Dan only saw fragments - "official forensic examination," "the remains have been identified as those of Pfc Dennis F. Kerr," "a cargo plane will return the remains to Logan Airport," "on behalf of the United States of America, Pfc Kerr's family has its deepest sympathy."

Dan's heart hammered in his chest and beads of sweat dotted his forehead. After such a long time of expectant waiting, Champ would finally be coming home.

CHAPTER
14

NOW THAT THE LONG-AWAITED MOMENT had come, Dan didn't know who to tell or what to do. Who should know first? His wife, his parents, his best friend John Murphy? Dan felt like a fifth grader who had to give a presentation but forgot his notes. After a deep breath to steady himself, Dan drove to the inevitable destination, his family home, to tell his parents that Champ had been found. Dan pulled into the driveway and spotted his parents seated in lawn chairs, enjoying the warmth of May. He cast about frantically in his mind for the right words. None came. Instead, tears wet his cheeks and his voice became incoherent. Mr. Kerr looked pointedly at his son and knew the worst. Mrs. Kerr, baffled by Dan's strangled utterances, merely stared as Dan choked out "Champ," "cargo plane," "deepest sympathy."

Hurriedly, Mr. Kerr found another chair for Dan whose legs were wobbly. He felt a headache in his forehead. With infinite tenderness, Mr. Kerr took his wife's hand. "Theresa, Champ is coming home. His body has been found. Chip got the letter."

Mrs. Kerr turned rheumy eyes to her husband's face, uncomprehendingly. "But Champ is already home."

"No, dear. Now it's official. He's back."

Dan couldn't bear the vacant look in his mother's eyes. His mind whirled as he remembered the dreams, the flashbacks, the utter hopelessness that Champ would ever be found. Now he sat with his parents on a lovely May afternoon and the world had shifted.

The news about the finding of Pfc Kerr's remains sent shock waves through Coltonwood. The small city had never experienced anything like this, dating back to the Civil War. Dan, as the managing editor of the local paper, had to dispatch reporters to cover the story of the tragedy that had rocked his family. One reporter had wanted to interview the parents, but Dan scuttled that idea; the reporter could interview him but no other family members.

On May 24th, the Kerr family boarded a luxury bus provided by the Veterans Agent in town to head to Logan Airport to be reunited with Champ. They departed from behind City Hall for the forty-five minute ride to the airport. The mood inside the bus was somber and people spoke in whispers. The bus sailed down the Pike to Boston in record time. At the airport, the family were met by an official from Mass Port who escorted them to the tarmac where the military transport plane bearing Champ's body had just touched down.

The hearse from Callahan's Funeral Home drove slowly and stopped in front of a lift that would lower the coffin from the rear door of the plane. The day was hot and a tropical wind blew across the airport that lifted and dropped Dan's damp white polo. No one spoke. To the right, a contingent of military men marched in slow cadence to the front of the lift where they remained at attention. The rear door of the plane opened, and four military men carried the flag draped government casket to the end of the lift. Ever so slowly the lift collapsed its way to the ground until it was low enough for the pallbearers to reach the coffin. With heartbreakingly slow precision, the pallbearers passed the coffin along until it reached the two men at the end. Each grasped the handles and carried Champ's remains to the waiting hearse. The bearers again passed the coffin each to the next until it was fully inside the hearse. They did an about face and respectfully marched back in the direction they had come.

Dan stood mesmerized by the scene before him. No one spoke. Dan thought that the Kerr clan had never been so silent, even in church. Dan craned his neck to look at his parents. A military officer was speaking to them and presently took Mrs. Kerr's arm and led her and the rest of the family back to the waiting bus. Dan glanced at his watch. The entire event had only taken fifteen minutes.

The hearse appeared along with some motorcycle policemen from the Boston Police who were to provide an escort along the Mass Pike. The toll booths were ignored and traffic parted to let the procession through. When they exited the Pike, the Coltonwood Police met them and provided the escort back to City Hall, where the family left the bus and headed for their own cars. The hearse continued on to the funeral home.

The Kerr family then proceeded en masse to the family home. They were greeted by Mrs. Salina who had just brought over two pans of lasagna and four loaves of Italian bread. Her husband supplied several bottles of his homemade wine. As the family sat to dinner, the mood was more festive than funereal. Now that Champ was home, the family's ever-present tension melted and everyone heartily partook of the repast their neighbor had provided.

Now that his brother's remains had been returned, Dan could turn his attention to the necessary arrangements that needed to be made. To that end, he went to his office to make sure that everything would run smoothly in his absence. Not that he needed to worry. Rachel, his super-efficient secretary, would make sure that the business of the *Clarion* would continue even without the managing editor.

When Dan arrived at his office, Rachel informed him that the mayor had called and wanted to talk to Dan at his earliest convenience. The paper had been consistently critical of the mayor's administration, which had made life difficult since Rosalina was the mayor's secretary. "Is this official business?" he asked Rachel.

"I don't think so. He wants to see you about your brother."

Dutifully, Dan reported to City Hall to meet with His Honor. Rosalina looked up from her desk at his entrance. "Yes?" she said, feigning impatience.

"I'd like to see the mayor," retorted Dan, feigning deference.

"Do you have an appointment?"

Dan was about to make a sarcastic rejoinder when the inner door opened and the mayor advanced towards Dan, his hand outstretched. "I'm so sorry about your brother, Dan. Come into the office." Dan glanced over his shoulder at Rosalina and gave her a furtive wink.

The mayor spoke first. "Please, Dan, sit down. Make yourself comfortable."

Dan sat, warily eyed the mayor, who took his place behind his enormous desk. "As the mayor of this city, I would like to officially honor your brother."

"How so?"

"I'd like to have his body lie in state here at City Hall so the people can pay their respects."

Dan shifted uncomfortably in his chair. "The wake will be open to the public. Everyone who wants to can attend."

"Ok, but some people might not feel comfortable doing that."

An obscenity rose in Dan's mind, but he didn't let it escape his lips. Instead, he said, "I can't give you an answer right now. I have to consult with my family. However, I will tell you that under no circumstances will my parents be any part of a public memorial. This is hard enough for them as it is. And if they say no?"

"So be it. I just wanted to mention the idea. It's not etched in stone."

"We're meeting today to discuss the arrangements. I'll mention this. That's all I can say for now."

"Fair enough. I'll wait to hear from you."

Later that afternoon, the Kerr family gathered to decide the particulars of Champ's wake and funeral. Dan dreaded yet another family meeting, but this one was necessary. He waited until all of his siblings had arrived before he broached the idea of a public memorial. The reactions were predictable. Pup was all for it. "That's a great idea," he gushed. "Champ deserves some public recognition."

Cissy was the first to pounce. She sneered in Pup's direction. "You would think this is a good idea since you're the mayor's buddy. I don't think Champ's death should be made into a public spectacle just to make the mayor look good."

Biddy chimed in, "I agree. Would we have to be there at City Hall?"

"Absolutely not," countered Dan. "I made it clear to the mayor that no one from the family would be there glad handing people."

"You can bet the mayor will be there," offered Mimi. "He will use this occasion as political fodder whether we say yes or no. This mayor is as devious as they come. He's got something up his sleeve. I don't want to see Champ or any of us used by this guy."

Pup listened impatiently to his siblings' disapproval. "Why are you people always so skeptical of everyone's motives? Champ is the first MIA soldier from Coltonwood to return home. Why not give him his due?"

Dan turned to his parents. "Mom, Dad. What do you think?"

All the Kerr kids smiled as their father responded with his classic line. "This discussion is at an end. The answer is no."

The family met with the funeral director and planned Champ's arrangements. Dan mentioned the mayor's plan to Jack Callahan who looked thoughtful and then replied, "I don't like the idea. It may seem like a nice gesture but it's unnecessary. You're having four hours when people who are interested can pay their respects. Anything else would be superfluous."

Pup eyed the funeral director suspiciously and, with a voice that dripped sarcasm, said, "And more work for you, ha, Jack? You don't want to do more than you have to."

Before Jack could reply, Mimi said quietly, "Pup, that's enough. Stop sounding like an idiot."

One day later, Dan and Rosalina drove to Logan Airport to pick up Dan's cousin Bart. During the drive, Dan wondered aloud about the mayor's motives in wanting to publicly honor Champ. He looked at Rosalina. "You know him better than I do. Do you think the mayor was sincere when he offered to honor Champ?"

"I do think he was sincere. The mayor isn't a bad guy, but he is a politician, and he thinks like a politician, so there was probably some self interest in the offer, but for the most part I do think he meant to honor your brother in the right spirit."

"If you say so."

"You don't believe me?"

"I believe you. I just think that everything the guy does is to help his political ambitions. He's a political animal through and through."

"Of course he is, just like you're a journalist through and through. The mayor is a human, believe it or not, he has his good side and his bad side, just like everyone else."

It was amazing Dan thought how Rosalina could abruptly end any conversation she found distasteful.

Forty-five minutes later, Dan, Rosalina and Bart were on the Mass Pike headed for a restaurant. Since Bart had announced that he would love a big steak, Dan exited the Pike in Natick and they made for Ken's for dinner. The place was crowded, and they had to wait a half hour for a table. All during the drive and now at the restaurant, Dan had wanted to talk about Champ, but neither Bart nor Rosalina seemed inclined to discuss him. Rosalina asked Bart a lot of questions about his job, and Bart was more than happy to oblige. As for Dan, he combed his mind to dredge up every possible memory of Champ even though the same ones kept playing in his head like a never-ending movie. At one point, he found himself irked at Rosalina and Bart and their easy conversation despite the circumstances. Yet Dan had to admit that they were not to blame. Rosalina never knew Champ and Bart and Champ, though cousins, never had much use for each other. Champ's open dislike of guys who were not into sports bordered on disdain. Bart, like Dan, preferred more cerebral pursuits like reading and writing. Bart had very few memories of any personal interaction with Champ and, therefore, nothing to talk about.

They ordered a bottle of wine with dinner and Dan consumed most of it, despite the fact that he was driving. As he poured his fourth glass, Rosalina said, "It looks as if I'll be driving home. Do you realize how much wine you've had?"

Dan ignored her. Bart and Rosalina exchanged a look. "Easy, Chip. You have consumed most of the bottle," said Bart.

The wine loosened his tongue and before he could stop himself, Dan hissed, "You two are acting like you're old high school friends at your class reunion. I'm dealing with the death of my brother, and you two are acting as though nothing has happened. Naturally, I'm a little pissed at both of you."

Rosalina and Bart looked stunned. At last Rosalina said quietly, "You're absolutely right, Dan. I apologize, but I didn't want to talk about death the whole time that we're here. You need a break from that."

"You haven't talked about it at all. No acknowledgment of the reason why we're here. Don't you think that's rather insulting? You're acting like Pup and that's no compliment."

A few seconds passed and Rosalina said, "I said I'm sorry and I am. It wasn't my intention to hurt your feelings. Would you like to talk about Champ?"

"I don't need to talk about Champ. What I need is to hear you talk about him. He lived. He went missing for ten years and every minute of that time I wondered about him. Was he dead or alive? Do you know what that's like? To not know? To live with that uncertainty? I NEED TO TALK ABOUT THAT WITH YOU. DON'T YOU UNDERSTAND THAT?"

"You just said you didn't need to talk about Champ. I think we need to skip dessert and go home."

Rosalina put her arm around Dan, and they left the restaurant, a bewildered Bart trailing in their wake.

Later that evening, when Dan had recovered his equilibrium, he apologized to Rosalina and to Bart. Despite the apology, Dan could not verbalize how he felt inside: that his mind was consumed with anger, regret and sadness. A cauldron of emotion had taken root since Champ's remains had been returned. Dan didn't understand the violent feelings that roiled and seethed within him. There was no way he could convey this to another person. He would tell Rosalina that he wished he had more time with Champ to resolve their differences, but that was all he could do. Otherwise, he groped within his mind and heart to put a name to what he felt. Never in his life had he experienced such inner turmoil and he was at a complete loss. Yet, things needed to be done, and the family looked to him, fairly or unfairly, to get them done.

Dan had arranged the accommodations for visiting family. Bart would stay with him and Rosalina. Bart's parents would stay with Pup and Elaine. Aunt Sue and her two sons, Anthony and Girard, would stay with Mr. and Mrs. Kerr. Bridy would stay with Cissy and Carl. Once the relatives had been placed, Dan turned his attention to the eulogy and other funeral business. Since Champ's pallbearers would be service members, the family would have to choose honorary pallbearers. Dan chose his brother Pup, brothers-in-law Neil, Carl, Stanley and Dexter and himself. Technically, he had enough, but he wanted to include Mike Dello Russo, the VietNam vet permanently scarred by his service. Pup objected.

"Why are you including him? He's a bum and a degenerate. I'll bet he doesn't even own a suit."

Dan countered. "I'll loan him a suit if he needs one. He served his country just like Champ did, but no one honors his service. People in this town just see him as lowlife, a pathetic scumbag with no ambition. That's totally unfair. I went to school with him. He was a good student who could have had a bright future. Instead, he chose to don the uniform and now he's scorned by his hometown, by the people he grew up with who've judged him and found him unworthy. He's the object of pity and abuse, and that's pathetic."

Pup was quiet for a long moment. "What you say may be true, but why does he have to be a pallbearer when we have enough within the family? Isn't that pitiful rather than honorable?"

"You would see it that way, but I don't. Mike deserves this and the only way he won't be a bearer is if he declines the invitation."

Pup grunted. "We'll see what Dad has to say."

"Dad's a veteran. He's been in a war. No problem there."

Now Dan had to turn his attention to the eulogy. His thoughts had been so convoluted that he had not been able to piece together even an opening. But time was running out and he had to force himself to put something on paper. Unable to sleep, he found himself at his desk, yellow legal pad before him, pen in hand, yet unable to write a word.

Instead, his mind wandered to his other siblings and the ways that had dealt with Champ's disappearance. Only Mimi and Bridy had been able to successfully channel their heartache into constructive outlets. Mimi had her large family to raise and her time was given totally to them and her husband. Bridy moved to New York City and built herself a fulfilling career in the unforgiving world of retail. The others had turned inward and never really dealt with their pain and loss. Pup was a perfect example with his obsessive need to be recognized and acknowledged by everyone as having the best job, the biggest house, the largest bank account, and by his voluminous consumption of food and drink. Cissy had morphed into an unhappy bitter woman who took out her frustration with herself and her own inability to come to terms with Champ's situation on her husband and children who had to live with her insecurities and temper tantrums. Gabby took refuge in a fantasy fueled by Stanley that she had dealt with her loss and had gotten on with her life, with no repercussions whatsoever. Biddy had been a child when Champ went missing and she suffered from a lack of attention from her parents, especially her mother, that left her unsure of herself and unwilling to take on any serious responsibility. As for himself, Dan felt that he had managed to deal with the uncertainty by moving away and throwing himself into his work. With Rosalina's help, he had managed to build a good life, at times even forgetting about Champ. Worst of all was the effect on their mother. Dan winced as he remembered his mother wandering around town like a lost soul clutching her rosary beads. His father cooked and kept house while his wife worked her way through the grief of losing a child.

Dan had to get started writing the eulogy. He was out of time. Before Champ's remains had been found, Dan had written many so-called eulogies in his head; now he couldn't recall a single word of any of them. Every time he tried to write, Dan's thoughts kept circling around the fact that Champ had been an athlete. Yet, there had to be more to Champ than just his athleticism.

Dan had asked his siblings for their recollections and reflections, but they too just kept mentioning Champ's exploits on the field or the hardwood. Dan got no help from them. He couldn't ask his mother because she thought Champ was found years ago and can't understand all the fuss now. His father was more help to a certain extent. He wanted Dan to focus on Champ's military service. Dan intended to do this, but Champ had only been a soldier for a brief time before he went missing.

Dan recalled all the conflict between Champ and himself. Stabs of guilt pierced Dan as he remembered that he thought of Champ as little more than a dumb jock. He used to make fun of Champ who never read a book or showed the slightest inclination to do well in school. Of course, Champ did read *Sports Illustrated*, but did that really count? Champ would frequently ask Dan what certain words meant, and Dan would laugh and tell Champ to look them up. Dan would never admit that he didn't know the meanings of some of the words either.

Dan made a tentative start. "My brother was a hero, but not in the way he wanted. He would have preferred to wear the uniform of the Patriots rather than that of the U.S. Army. All of his dreams centered around his love of sports. He wanted more than anything to play professional sports. Champ was a good baseball and basketball player, but his real love was football.

However, his dreams were shattered in his senior year when he tore his ACL in the second to the last game of the season. He would never play football again. Champ then made a fateful decision: he would join the Army and serve his country."

"For almost ten years, my family and I have waited in excruciating anxiety and uncertainty to hear some word of Champ's fate. Not a day went by when we didn't wonder, hope, pray to know what happened to our brother. What this meant for our parents I will leave to the imagination. Of course, we got on with our lives, but the cloud of expectant waiting never lifted."

"Now, with Champ's return, we have found some measure of peace. Now we grieve a life taken much too soon. We wonder what Champ would have done with his life had he returned from Nam alive. The world of possibilities open to a young man has shrunk to the size of a grave; his potential stolen by a senseless war of which he is just another statistic."

"We honor him today because he faced the loss of his dream and he was not afraid to wear the uniform and fight for his country. His dream of being a hero really did come true but not in the way that he or anyone wanted. Today we honor his courage, his steadfastness, his sense of duty."

"Champ, you are a hero. A real hero doesn't catch passes or ram through the defensive line. A real hero dodges bullets, slogs through rice paddies, and watches his buddies die. There are no cheers for this kind of hero, no victory parades. Your family and friends will take you today to your final resting place, proud of the man you were."

"Welcome home, my brother. Your family and your hometown salute you today and we will never, ever forget you or the sacrifice you made for your country. Rest easy, bro."

Dan was surprised and pleased with what he had written. The words came easier than he thought they would. Had he said enough? Would his parents like it? His father would. Dan would read it to Rosalina for her input. It would have to do unless he had another brainstorm which was about as likely as snow in July.

In his preoccupation with arrangements, Dan suddenly realized the day of the wake that he had forgotten to ask Mike Dello Russo if he would be an honorary pallbearer. Since he had no idea how to get hold of Mike, Dan went to the Sunoco gas station where Mike had worked. The owner was reluctant to tell Dan anything until Dan explained his reason for wanting to find his old friend. "He lives at the hotel," the owner told Dan. "That's all I know." Dan didn't need any further explanation. The hotel was actually known as the Chesterfield Hotel, a courtesy title for a rundown brick building downtown where people who were down on their luck lived. Dan was able to open the outside door and scanned the mailboxes for Mike's name. It was there. He lived in Number 47. Dan pushed the button and a tired voice said, "Yeah?"

"Mike, it's Dan Kerr. Could I talk to you for a few minutes?"

"Hey, Kerr. Sure. Come on up."

Although the door was ajar, Dan still knocked and identified himself. "Hi, Mike. How you doin?"

Mike Dello Russo, a skeletal wraith of a man, shrugged. "As you see me. What do you want to talk to me about?"

"You know that my brother Dennis's remains have been returned and his funeral is tomorrow. I'd like you to be an honorary pallbearer."

"Me? Are you kidding? Look at me. I can't be an honorary anything. I don't even own a suit."

"I can loan you a suit. My family and I want you because you've had the same terrible experiences as my brother. You served honorably and we think you deserve recognition for that."

Mike considered for a minute. "Where is the funeral?"

"St. Tom's at eleven o'clock."

"I haven't been there in years. What would I have to do?"

"You just have to walk behind the casket with the other honoraries. Some guys from the military will do the heavy lifting."

"Who are the others?"

"My brother John, my brothers-in-law Neil, Carl, Stanley, Dexter and John Murphy and me."

Mike paused for a long minute. "All right, I'll do it. I'll need a suit."

"Do you have a tie and a shirt and shoes?"

"I'll need a tie also. I have a white shirt and black shoes that I never wear because I don't go nowhere."

"Fantastic. I'll bring over the suit in about an hour." Dan extended his hand. "Thank you, Mike."

CHAPTER 15

AS HE DROVE HOME, DAN WAS CONSUMED WITH a searing anger reminiscent of the anger he felt about Champ's disappearance. To his way of thinking, Mike was just as much a victim as Champ, perhaps more so. Champ had met his maker. Mike lived every day in a living hell. On a whim, Dan stopped at a drugstore and bought some essentials for Mike which he obviously lacked: soap, shampoo, shaving cream and a package of disposable razors, toothpaste and a toothbrush. Dan resolved that once the services were over for Champ, he would visit that worthless Veterans Agent and ask him why he isn't doing anything for veterans such as Mike. They had been ignored and forgotten now that their service was over. His errand done, Dan went home and picked out a dark suit and a tie and returned to a grateful Mike with the clothes and the essentials. Now Dan had to get home fast, change and head to the wake.

Less than an hour later, Dan and Rosalina, Bryant and Marla rode quietly to the funeral home. When all the family had arrived, Jack Callahan instructed everyone as to where they should stand, "Usually by age." But Pup usurped the head of the line from Mimi, saying he knew more people in town than she did and could introduce them to the rest of the family. Who cares, thought Dan. Pup always had to be the top dog, even at his brother's wake. So, the Kerr family stood to one side of the flag-draped coffin, a soldier standing at attention at the head and the foot. The soldiers rotated every forty-five minutes. When it was Dan's turn to kneel at the casket, he felt empty, unable to feel any kind of emotion. He said a brief prayer and steadied himself to greet people.

They came in droves. Mostly townspeople but also the mayor, the city councilors, the school committee. All came to pay tribute to a soldier most never knew. They just wanted to be there. Dan noticed a very pretty woman as she advanced down the line. He thought she looked familiar, but he couldn't place her. The woman extended her hand to Dan and said, "I'm Kathleen, but you know me as Sister Ursula." In his happy surprise, Dan almost yelled, "Sister. I thought you looked familiar. I can't believe I'm seeing you."

Kathleen smiled. "As you can see, I'm not a nun anymore. I left the convent years ago. Now, I'm married and I have two sons. I am still a teacher."

Dan recovered slowly and said, "Do you live in town? I'd love to visit you."

"No, I don't. I live a few towns over. I teach at Riverdale Elementary School. You can come see me anytime."

Dan then introduced Kathleen to Rosalina as "My all-time favorite teacher."

The two women shook hands and Rosalina chuckled, "I haven't seen Dan this excited since we got married. You must have really been something."

Kathleen smiled again. "He was certainly one of my all-time favorite students. Daniel was wonderful."

Still in shock, Dan shook hands mechanically with other people as they made their way through the line. As he wondered how his parents were doing, he noticed a commotion at the head of the line. He didn't miss the alarm in his mother's voice when she said, "Why are all these people in my house? I can't cook for all these people."

Mr. Kerr tried his best to calm his wife, but she grew even more frazzled. Dan saw his dutiful neighbor, Mrs. Salina, as she left her seat among the clutch of neighbors and made her way behind the receiving line to assist Mr. Kerr. Most of the people paying respects froze in place and they watched this disturbance.

Jack Callahan appeared from nowhere to help. He and Mrs. Salina gently helped Mrs. Kerr into another room. Bridy slipped away to see what was happening with her mother. Calm was soon restored, and the line moved once again.

The peace did not last long as Aunt Julia and her personal care attendant pushing the wheelchair appeared. As she made her way through the line, Aunt Julia bellowed, "Where's Theresa? How could she miss her own son's wake? Awful."

Aunt Julia leaned into an abashed Mr. Kerr as he tried to explain his wife's absence.

"Oh," wailed Aunt Julia. "I'm glad she's here, at least. Otherwise, the family would be disgraced in front of the whole town."

Dan noticed several people who tried not to laugh at Aunt Julia's impropriety. The oldest member of the Kerr family shook hands mechanically with most of the family, but not with

Dan, her favorite. "Chippy," she squealed. "You're looking well, but your tie is a little bright for the occasion. Tone it down for tomorrow."

"Yes, Aunt Julia," replied a red-faced Dan.

Then Aunt Julia noticed another member missing. "Where's Bridget? She's not here either. Disgraceful."

Before Dan could explain why Bridy wasn't there, Aunt Julia pounced on Biddy. "That hairstyle does not flatter you one bit, young lady. You look like a floozy. The very idea, and at your brother's wake, no less."

Poor Biddy looked around wildly for help. Once again, Jack Callahan appeared from the shadows and hurried Aunt Julia and her attendant into an adjacent room. Biddy fled with her shocked fiancé hard on her heels. Although Dan usually enjoyed Aunt Julia's sallies, even he was stunned by her vicious personal attacks, which everyone in the two rooms heard.

The crowd didn't thin until the last hour. The exhausted Kerr family could finally take a deep breath and sit for a few minutes. Dan's legs felt like wood from so much standing. Jack Callahan passed out bottles of water and Dan drank deeply. Only then did he think to wonder about his mother. Did she go home? Was she all right? He couldn't bear to think of the next day. This would mean another dreaded family meeting to decide if Mrs. Kerr was up to attending the funeral. Dan groaned at the thought of it.

When no new people waited to greet the family, Dan slipped away to find Jack to ask about his mother. "She went home with Francesca Salina," Jack explained. "She was so agitated and confused, so there was no other option."

When the hours were finally over, the family left for their parents' home where they would have a meal. Dan and Rosalina and their kids went home and changed before heading to the Kerr family house. The night was steamy and breathless with impressive heat lightning that split the sky. The house was packed with Kerrs, old and young. Pup was grilling steaks and burgers in the backyard despite the heat. Mrs. Salina and two of her daughters unwrapped huge bowls of potato salad, green salad, and macaroni salad. Chips and crackers and dip were placed all over the downstairs to placate the hungry people who wolfed down everything in sight. The house was packed to the rafters with humanity. Salina appeared with his arms full of his homemade wine and the occasion became downright festive.

Anyone who didn't know the circumstances surrounding this gathering might wonder at and find this reveling after a wake offensive. Yet this family was celebrating life, not death. With Champ's return, his parents, siblings, cousins, aunts, uncles had been released from a stark prison of uncertainty and doubt. The dark cloud of constant wondering had been lifted and each could breathe fresh air again and see the sun. The relief that washed over each of them at Champ's return was in full flower on this hot summer night. Champ was home and his family celebrated after ten long years of waiting.

The approaching dawn roused Dan from a fitful sleep. Suddenly, he wanted to walk. He slid silently out of bed, being careful not to wake Rosalina. Dan pulled on a tee shirt and shorts and slid his feet into flip-flops. He headed downtown. The old buildings on Main St. still stood, but most of the storefronts had changed. Dan walked past where his father's shop had been. As he walked, Dan remembered the days when he and Champ would work at the store, flattening cardboard boxes for later disposal at the dump or running the vacuum cleaner around the showroom carpet installed by Mr. Kerr to make the space look like a living room. Mrs. Kerr had called it a foolish investment. All those feet, wet and otherwise, would ruin the carpet in short order. She was right.

The early morning air was sweet, not yet heavy with the oppressive humidity that would hang like overripe fruit on the rest of the day. Dan's head was clear. He waited for the nerves that he thought would precede the eulogy he was to deliver, but they remained at bay. He walked to the end of Main Street, arriving at St. Thomas Aquinas Church, which would be the location of Champ's funeral in a few hours. He lingered by the railing where his childhood nemesis, Johnny M, had sat so many years ago and watched Dan as he walked to the side entrance of the church. Dan still had some trouble believing that the same Johnny M who had terrorized his childhood was now his best friend. Disordered thoughts banged in Dan's head. As hard as he tried, he couldn't remember his brother's face.

Dan returned home by a different route, only to find his family up and frantic. They all looked up from the table at his entrance. Rosalina handed him a cup of coffee as she almost yelled, "Where have you been? I was ready to call the police and report you missing. Why didn't you leave a note?"

"I'm sorry. I just needed to clear my head, so I went for a walk."

"Fine. Just let me know the next time you decide to go wandering."

In less than an hour, Dan and family were on their way to Callahan's Funeral Home. They were the first to arrive, which gave Dan a pinch of worry about his parents, especially his mother. Soon, however, the entire Kerr entourage began to arrive. Soft music played in the background as the family sat silently awaiting the time when they would accompany Champ on his last journey. Dan looked around for Aunt Julia, but she was not in sight. Neither was Mike Dello Russo. Dan hoped that Mike didn't have a last-minute change of heart about being an honorary pallbearer. Four limousines ferried the Kerr family on a slow, sinuous drive to the church. On the sidewalks, people stood, some with hats doffed, some with hands over hearts, some waved American flags. All stood respectfully silent as the body of the first soldier from Coltonwood who had gone MIA but returned rolled its way by in the hearse. Dan and all the family gaped at the crowds. They never expected anything like this.

Servicemen from all branches carried Champ into the church, where he had been baptized and confirmed. His family followed the flag-draped casket down the aisle.

The church was full and stifling. True to his word, Mike Dello Russo waited in the vestibule of the church to walk behind Champ's casket. He fell into line with Dan, Pup, the four brothers-in-law, John Murphy, Bryant, and Patrick. Pup waited for Elaine, and they eased their way into the front pew with Mr. and Mrs. Kerr. Pup pulled rank again ahead of his two older sisters. As hard as he tried, Dan was having trouble concentrating due to the oppressive heat. The venerable grande dame of churches had to rely on fans for air circulation, but they had to be turned off so people could hear the service. He could see Pup from where he sat, and he noticed his older brother was red-faced and sweating. Dan wished he had not bowed to fashion decorum that dictated that he had to wear a long-sleeved shirt with a suit, regardless of the temperature. He remembered virtually nothing of the priest's homily or the rest of the Mass. After the distribution of Communion, which took a long time due to the crowd, it was Dan's time to speak.

He walked calmly to the pulpit and remembered to bow to the altar. Dan took a second to survey the crowd, many of whom had fled after Communion. He began to speak, vaguely aware of his increased heartbeat, which he attributed to the heat. He kept his voice even and deliberate as he spoke the words he had come to know by heart. As he spoke, Dan's mind returned to the time that he and Champ had been altar servers and people had to kneel at the altar rail to receive Communion. He thought about how many funerals he had served, the Solemn High Masses of the Latin liturgy that seemed to last forever. Dan thanked the throng of people for coming to honor Champ and support the family. That done, Dan quickly folded the damp paper and retreated from the altar. As he passed the front bench, his mother extended her arm and called, "Chip." He pretended not to hear and returned to his seat.

There was a slight commotion as Mrs. Kerr abruptly stood and tried to make her way towards the center aisle. Mr. Kerr and Pup restrained her. Dan heard her say, "I have to find Champ. I want to ask Chip where he is." Dan heard Mimi sob.

The ceremony over, the military pallbearers took their places and escorted the casket down the center aisle. As they did so, the organist played a stirring rendition of "God Bless America." Soon the voices of the congregation drowned out that of the soloist. Unfamiliar emotions roiled in Dan as he and his family left to take Champ to his resting place.

Once in the blessedly cool limousine, he and his family sat in amazed silence at what they had just seen and heard. The procession to the cemetery didn't last long enough for the family attempting to stay cool in the limos. Before they knew it, the doors were opened and Dan and the rest of his family were escorted to chairs under a green canopy that boldly proclaimed Callahan on the front. The same priest who had officiated at the funeral now stood at the grave, book in hand. Most of the family had to stand due to sheer numbers. Dan and Rosalina stood just beyond the shade of the canopy.

The service was brief. Dan wondered if it was over when he heard the sweet plaintive bugle playing Taps. The traditional farewell to fallen soldiers dating back to the Civil War stirred a deep emotion in Dan. Tears stung his eyes and his chest heaved in sobs. Rosalina tightened her grip on his arm and he felt a hand gently massage his back.

"AAAYYY."

He didn't need to turn around; he knew his lifelong friend and neighbor was there for him. The last notes of Taps faded into the languid heat of the afternoon, only to be replaced by an echo from a bugler at a more remote part of the cemetery. The sweet sadness of the melody affected the entire family. Even Mr. Kerr dropped his stoic demeanor and sobbed quietly.

The pallbearers then raised the flag from the coffin and folded it with strict military precision. The last soldier moved with careful deliberation and presented the tri-cornered flag to Mrs. Kerr, who gazed uncomprehendingly at her stricken family. Despite her bewilderment, she took the flag and pressed it to her heart.

Suddenly everything was over: ten years of waiting, wondering, hoping, praying, despairing had come to an abrupt end. As he turned from his brother's grave, Dan heard a shrill keening split the air. He looked in the direction of the sound and saw a cardinal majestically perched in a nearby elm. Champ was home.

When Dan entered the VFW hall for the post funeral reception, the first person he saw was Aunt Julia in full regalia seated next to her devoted caregiver, Ramona. Dan smiled as he wondered if Biddy would make good on her threat to tell off the old bitch. Maybe after several glasses of wine, Biddy might have the courage. Dan grabbed a beer and greeted his favorite aunt, who looked like a southern belle cruising on the Mississippi. She wore an enormous white sun hat with a yellow dress that looked like it was made of crepe paper. He was tempted to tell her that the dress was a little loud for the occasion, but he didn't dare.

"Chippy," Aunt Julia prattled. "Have you met Romana? She thought it was too hot for me to go to the church and the cemetery, so we came straight here. Ramona is very good to me." Aunt Julia waved and smiled at everyone as she talked. Dan wondered how many highballs she had already had while she waited for the family to arrive.

The hall filled rapidly, and Dan invited John Murphy and Mike Dello Russo to join him and his family. Mike seemed ill at ease, but John was in rare form and kept everyone laughing with his boyhood tales when he was the most feared kid in town. Yet, John reminded his audience, there was one kid in town that John could never intimidate: Pup Kerr who, with his quick reflexes and athletic build, actually scared John. To which Dan added, "I was not so lucky. I was terrified of John."

The mayor, with the full approval of the City Council, paid for the post funeral reception. His Honor wandered from table to table, greeted people and shook hands. When he arrived at Dan's table, Dan asked the mayor if he had met Aunt Julia.

"Oh, yes," said the weary mayor. "She told me every mistake I've made since my inauguration. Your aunt doesn't mince words."

As he strode to the buffet table, Dan felt a new spring in his step and a lightness in his whole being. He felt like a kid again. People kept approaching and wanted to shake his hand. He was tempted to say that he was not the mayor, but instead he greeted all and sundry with an alacrity that he had not felt in a long time.

Dan glanced in Aunt Julia's direction and was delighted to see so many people offering their hands to her. Caustic though she could be, Aunt Julia was the last of her generation, a character in every sense of the word.

All the Kerr siblings had fanned out to host at different tables. Not surprisingly, Cissy was the hostess where Aunt Julia sat. Cissy's two sons, Mike and Matt, sat frozen in their chairs as Aunt Julia evidently was lecturing them about something. Dan decided to rescue his nephews, who looked absolutely terrified.

"Hey boys, make sure you listen carefully to Aunt Julia's advice. I always did."

Dan's words roused Matt from an apparent stupor. "Uncle Chip?"

"What, Matt?"

"Did I know Uncle Champ?"

"No, Matt. You weren't born when Champ went missing. He was a great athlete."

"Were you a great athlete, Uncle Chip?"

"I'm afraid not. When I was a kid, I wanted to be a writer. I didn't have any time to play sports."

Aunt Julia somehow heard this last remark and screamed at Dan, "Chippy, I thought you were going to write a book. Did you ever do it?"

"No, Aunt Julia," answered Dan, taking the skeletal, gnarled hand in his own. "I decided it was more important to eat and pay my rent than to write a book."

"You could write one now. You could make a lot of money, so your wife doesn't have to work for that baboon who calls himself the mayor. He's a disgrace. I didn't vote for him. He should be removed from office. I told him so when he tried to make nice with me and shake my hand. The very idea." Aunt Julia screeched these last remarks, and several people cast amused glances in her direction. "He's a snake, I tell you." Dan tried to make a light comment in response, but it fell flat. Aunt Julia continued to rant until Pup distracted and placated her with a highball.

Eventually, people began to filter out of the hall. All the food had been eaten, much to Dan's dismay, since he wanted to take some home. Presently, he wandered to his parents' table where they sat with the Salinas and Aunt Sue. Mr. and Mrs. Kerr both looked gaunt and exhausted. After the formal reception, the family reconvened at their parents' home. Dan didn't know why this was necessary, since they had been together for the entire day. Everyone was cordial, and after another round of drinks, Pup yelled for quiet. He ceremoniously raised a toast to Champ and then announced in all seriousness, "I'm running for mayor and I'm asking all of you for your votes."

"Does Aunt Julia know?" asked a slightly tipsy Cissy. "You better get her permission first."

"Don't expect my paper to endorse you," yelled an almost tipsy Dan. "I'm staying out of this fight."

"Here's to Mayor Kerr," bawled a very drunk Stanley. "He'll give us all city jobs."

After the get together was over and night fell, Dan told Rosalina that he was going for a drive. She gave him an odd look but said nothing. Dan drove to the cemetery. Champ's grave was now covered by a blanket of flowers of every conceivable color. Dan moved some of the blooms aside and placed Champ's baseball glove with a dirty and scuffed ball in the pocket amidst the flowers. He whispered, "To the best center fielder ever."

When he returned to his car, Dan unthinkingly turned on the radio. He cranked it up and Queen blared across the expanse of the cemetery, "We are the champions. We are the champions. We are the champions. We will, we will rock you."

Dan smiled and sang along. "That's for you, Champ."

ACKNOWLEDGMENTS

No manuscript becomes a book without the help of many people. I wish to thank Eileen Charbonneau for her discerning eye and meticulous editing; Elizabeth Beliveau for her artistic vision in designing the cover; the members of the writing group: Lee Baldarelli, Janice Hitzhusen, Jim Pease, Pam Reponen, Cindy Shenette, Rebecca Southwick, and our leader, Eileen O'Finlan. Thanks to all of you for your advice and encouragement and good company. And finally, to Jessica Meltzer who made the dream come true.

Printed in the USA
CPSIA information can be obtained
at www.ICGtesting.com
JSHW020343180923
48380JS00004B/176